P9-DMV-220

Secrets *of* My Heart

DISCARD

Kingston Public Library
6 Green Street
Kingston, MA 02364

Books by Tracie Peterson

*with Kimberley Woodhouse
**with Karen Witemeyer, Regina Jennings, and Jen Turano
For a complete list of Tracie's books, visit her website www.traciepeterson.com

Secrets *of* My Heart

WILLAMETTE BRIDES · 1

TRACIE
PETERSON

BETHANYHOUSE
a division of Baker Publishing Group
Minneapolis, Minnesota

© 2020 by Peterson Ink, Inc.

Published by Bethany House Publishers
11400 Hampshire Avenue South
Bloomington, Minnesota 55438
www.bethanyhouse.com

Bethany House Publishers is a division of
Baker Publishing Group, Grand Rapids, Michigan

Printed in the United States of America

All rights reserved. No part of this publication may be reproduced, stored in a retrieval system, or transmitted in any form or by any means—for example, electronic, photocopy, recording—without the prior written permission of the publisher. The only exception is brief quotations in printed reviews.

Library of Congress Cataloging-in-Publication Data

Names: Peterson, Tracie, author.
Title: Secrets of my heart / Tracie Peterson.
Description: Minneapolis, Minnesota : Bethany House, a division of Baker
    Publishing Group, [2020] | Series: Willamette brides ; book 1
Identifiers: LCCN 2019040907 | ISBN 9780764232251 (trade paperback) | ISBN
    9780764232268 (cloth) | ISBN 9781493422746 (ebook) | ISBN 9780764232275
    (large print)
Subjects: GSAFD: Christian fiction. | Love stories.
Classification: LCC PS3566.E7717 S43 2020 | DDC 813/.54—dc23
LC record available at https://lccn.loc.gov/2019040907

Scripture quotations are from the King James Version of the Bible.

This is a work of fiction. Names, characters, incidents, and dialogues are products of the author's imagination and are not to be construed as real. Any resemblance to actual events or persons, living or dead, is entirely coincidental.

Cover design by LOOK Design Studio
Cover photography by Aimee Christenson

20 21 22 23 24 25 26   7 6 5 4 3 2 1

To my sister Karen

You are such an amazing woman,
and I am so blessed to call you sister and friend.
You've been an inspiration to me.

CHAPTER 1

PORTLAND, OREGON
MARCH 1879

O h, my poor dear Mrs. Pritchard," the older woman declared as soon as Nancy opened the front door. "Poor grieving wife. But no! No longer a wife, but a widow." She *tsk*ed and pushed into the house without giving Nancy a chance to offer an invitation.

"I heard about your precious Albert's death while I was visiting my daughter in California." The stocky woman placed the basket she'd been carrying by the door. "I was completely overcome with grief for you and cut my visit short. I knew you would need the wise counsel of your closest friends."

Nancy would have rolled her eyes if she wasn't being stared at as though she might burst into tears at any moment.

"I can see it's still such a shock. Come, we must sit, and I will have the entire story."

"Mrs. Mortenson, I'm afraid you have caught me at a bad time."

"Oh, pshaw. There are no good times when you are in a state of grief, but fear not, I am in no way offended." Mrs.

7

Mortenson took a seat on the large mauve sofa without being asked. "Now, come sit with me, child. I know very well how these things can be." She carefully arranged her wool gown and shawl. "Although I have not been a widow myself, I have had many close friends who are. I believe I am well acquainted with this grief."

Nancy stared at her guest for a moment, noting the fixed look of expectation on the older woman's face. Agnes Mortenson was well known in Nancy's circle of acquaintances as the person from whom to get news—if one couldn't afford a newspaper. Mrs. Mortenson was sixty-seven years old, but while her snowy head suggested possibilities of wisdom and sage advice, nothing could be further from the truth. She was insatiable when it came to sticking her nose into the business of others and sharing said details with anyone who gave her the time of day. Worse still, she was known to embellish those details. Nancy had dreaded her return to town and the stories she might spread about Albert's death.

Knowing there was little else to be done, Nancy sank into the wooden rocker by the fireplace across from the older woman.

"I heard your husband was found floating facedown in the river near the ferry landing," Mrs. Mortenson began.

Nancy had envisioned the scene at least a thousand times. "Yes."

Mrs. Mortenson leaned forward. "And that he had fallen into the river farther upstream."

"Possibly." Nancy wasn't at all certain why she needed such detail.

The old woman leaned even closer. "But . . . there are those who fear he was . . . *pushed* into the river. Murdered." She let the word linger in the air.

Nancy hurried to suppress that rumor. "I hardly think so. Albert had no enemies of which I'm aware."

Mrs. Mortenson shook her head and *tsk*ed once again. "I've yet to know a man who wasn't wished dead by someone. Even dear Mr. Mortenson is constantly at threat. He does, after all, own a very productive ironworks. He's in constant danger."

Nancy nodded, knowing it would do little good to suggest otherwise. She hoped the old woman would get her fill of information and particulars and move on quickly rather than keep Nancy imprisoned for the entirety of the afternoon.

"It is possible, of course, that he fell," Mrs. Mortenson mused. "I've often said the docks and boat decks are much too slippery. There's so much activity amongst the ships that a man could be knocked into the water and never noticed until it was too late." Without drawing a breath, she changed the subject. "Do you suppose you will sell this house? It's such a lovely place." She gazed around the room. "Just lovely. I've always admired the way you furnished it."

Nancy was momentarily taken aback. "I, uh, have no plan to sell."

Mrs. Mortenson nodded. "It's just as well. A widow should never make rash plans unless she is forced to." She leaned forward again. "You *aren't* forced to, are you? You must be honest with me. Did Albert leave you settled comfortably?"

"No. I mean, yes. Well, that is, I don't really know the details of my husband's estate."

"Late husband," Mrs. Mortenson interjected.

"Yes, my late husband. I know he wasn't one to carry debt, so the house and store are free and clear."

Mrs. Mortenson bobbed her head up and down like a daisy waving in the breeze. "That is good, because you don't want to be known for debt. I would imagine the store he owned could provide a steady income, but you would have to hire someone to run it for you. Mr. Mortenson might be able to suggest someone. I'll ask him when I see him tonight."

Nancy didn't tell her not to bother. The old woman wouldn't have listened anyway. Nancy had known many a gossip in Oregon City but had hoped to avoid them in a larger town. In Portland it was easier to blend into the background and be overlooked— at least she had hoped to be overlooked. Unfortunately, she was still expected to attend church, and the women of that holy institution were notorious for gossip. It was funny—when Nancy had been at home, her mother had instilled in her the absolute assurance that gossip was a sin no less looked down upon by God than murder. But the worshipers here didn't see it that way. Even the pastor knew better than to preach sermons on gossip.

"And of course there are other ways to manage such a large house."

Mrs. Mortenson was still droning on about how she thought Nancy should arrange her life. It seemed everyone thought Nancy an easy mark when it came to such matters. Perhaps it was because she kept to herself and remained quiet when others openly spoke their opinions. It was possible that people believed Nancy to be completely void of opinion, although nothing could be further from the truth.

The problem was that everyone wanted to tell Nancy what was best for her, but Nancy wasn't sure they were right. Mainly because she didn't know what she wanted out of life.

"You look so pale, my dear. Are you ill?" Mrs. Mortenson's face took on a look of surprise. "You aren't with child, are you? Oh my goodness, all these years of wanting a baby, only to find yourself with child and the father gone. Oh, the tragedy of it."

She put a gloved hand to her throat. "Yet many a poor woman has found herself in such a position with only the wee one to remind her of what she once had."

"I'm not with child, Mrs. Mortenson. Please don't spread that rumor about."

The old woman gasped. "I am the soul of discretion, my dear. I would never tell such delicate news in a public forum. Such things should only be discussed in private, as we are here. But if you are certain that you are not with child, then perhaps you have taken on a fever. Mourning can bring that about, you know. I suggest you take yourself to bed with some strong chamomile tea and a hot water bottle. Perhaps your mother or sister could come tend to you. I would do so myself, but I did just return. I haven't even had time to share news of our daughter with Mr. Mortenson. She is so very busy, don't you know."

"I'm sure she is."

"Oh goodness, yes. With four boys under the age of twelve, it hasn't been easy. She finds not one moment of time for herself."

And all I have is time for myself, Nancy thought.

"She is fortunate enough to have a good maid and cook. Say, where is your housekeeper? Is this her day off? Honestly, I think domestic help expect far too much these days. I remember when a housekeeper might have a few hours in the afternoon to herself, but entire days? What will they think of next?"

"I let my housekeeper and cook go," Nancy said. "I never wanted them in the first place. I enjoy doing my own cooking and cleaning. It gives me a sense of purpose." She wished there was a way to hurry this visit along, but she had to be polite. "I have hot water on the stove. I could make you a cup of tea, if you like. I have some cookies too. Mrs. Taylor brought them to me yesterday."

"Dear Mary. She's a saint if ever there was one. She is positively without thought for herself and always striving to help the poor. I would do more myself, but Mr. Mortenson has so many clients who must be entertained. He could hardly bear to be without me these last three weeks."

"I'm sure." Nancy could well imagine him enjoying his quiet evenings. "But I'm happy to offer you refreshments."

"No, my dear. I must be on my way soon. I have been shopping this morning, as you might have guessed from my basket." She motioned toward the foyer. "A few personal items that I would not send my maid for."

Nancy fervently hoped that this would prompt her guest to reclaim her basket and be on her way. Unfortunately, it didn't.

"Will your mother and sister be coming to stay with you?" Mrs. Mortenson asked.

"No. I would rather they remain at home. Mother does a great deal of healing work, and my sister is but fourteen and tends to be flighty."

"Girls today are often that way. When I was a girl, fourteen meant adulthood. We were already considering a young man for our future husband. We were much more serious, but we had to be. The times called for it, don't you know." Mrs. Mortenson gave a knowing nod and pursed her lips.

Nancy had no idea what the old woman was thinking, but she looked ready to launch into another diatribe, and Nancy had little patience for it.

"I believe you're right, Mrs. Mortenson. I'm afraid I've not been myself since Albert's passing. I would like to lie down for a while."

Mrs. Mortenson looked confused for a moment but then nodded. "Of course, my dear. I have a great knack for sensing these things." Her expression suggested it was a great burden to bear. "I'll come again to call in a day or two, depending on what Mr. Mortenson requires of me. We might well be hosting dinner parties this week. I simply have no idea." She got to her feet, and Nancy rose as well. "He often finds it necessary to host his clients and then leaves me to settle the arrangements."

"I am grateful for your concern, but I'm sure with some rest and time, I'll be fine." Nancy made her voice sound as pathetic as she dared. She wanted Mrs. Mortenson to leave her alone but not be so worried that she spread it around town that Nancy was at death's door.

"I'll see if I can't locate some of that strong Chinese tea they use for illness. We had some when Mr. Mortenson took sick last winter. It did a world of wonder for him, and I'm certain it will restore your constitution as well." Mrs. Mortenson paused and tapped her brow with a gloved index finger. "I count thoughts like that as words from the Lord Himself—otherwise I would have no reason to think of Chinese tea." She smiled and reached out to pat Nancy's arm. "Be brave, my girl. This is a hardship that women often must bear. Be strong."

"I will. I promise." Nancy moved ever closer to the front door. "Thank you so much for coming to see me." She reached down and retrieved Mrs. Mortenson's basket.

The old woman immediately laid claim to it and smiled. "I knew it wouldn't do to wait until later. You would expect me to be here for you."

Nancy opened the door and stepped back. "I appreciate your efforts, but please do not put yourself out again on my behalf. You have so many responsibilities, and I would feel terrible should I cause you to be remiss in your duties."

Mrs. Mortenson paused and looked at Nancy as if she were

some sort of angelic being. "You are truly amazing, my dear. Truly selfless and of such a pure nature." She shook her head. "I know God will surely not call you to be widowed long. In fact, if I had more time, we might discuss that very thing. The West is not held to the same standards as the East. We have far too few women to let the young and beautiful go single for long. We will have to find you another husband, and soon."

Before she could launch into a further discussion about finding Nancy a husband, Nancy began to close the door. "Thank you so much."

She turned the lock as quietly as possible. She could risk the hurried dismissal of the old woman—her new state of widowhood would excuse the brash move—but the lock would suggest a barrier that might very well offend. Nancy knew the penalty for offending Mrs. Mortenson would not be expulsion from her company but rather more attention in order to sort through the problem.

A sigh escaped, and Nancy suddenly felt very tired. It had only been a few weeks since Albert's death, but already the steady parade of concerned friends and family had wearied her of ever seeing another person.

The grandfather clock chimed three o'clock. It was only midafternoon. What was she to do with the rest of the day? Perhaps a nap truly was in order. At least if she were asleep, she would have a good excuse for missing out on potential visitors.

She walked from the foyer into the sitting room and retrieved the book she had been reading before Mrs. Mortenson descended. The book had been a gift for her twenty-sixth birthday the week before. It had come through the post from Aunt Hope and Uncle Lance—mailed prior to the news of Albert's death. When family and friends had arrived for the funeral, her aunt had explained that it would be coming. Aunt Hope had confessed that she had not read the story herself but had heard from others that it was a romantic study of human nature.

Nancy turned the book in her hand. *The Europeans*. So far she wasn't all that impressed, though she did own that the author, Henry James, had an occasional turn of phrase that she enjoyed.

She made her way to her new bedroom with the book. Until Albert's death, the bedrooms were contained to the second story of the house. But after his body had been found and his coffin set up in the front room prior to burial, Nancy had felt better remaining on the first floor. She had taken what had once been a reading room next to Albert's office and turned it into a bedroom. When her brother Gabe had come to town, she had imposed upon him to transfer her bed, chest, and wardrobe from upstairs to make the move permanent.

As she made her way past Albert's closed office door, Nancy couldn't help but think of her deceased husband. He was a man of business and kept his focus on anything and everything that might benefit his investments. He was good at what he did and always seemed able to second-guess the value of property and stocks in such a way as to make money for himself. He was admired locally for his abilities as a businessman. Pity he couldn't have been as good a husband.

It wasn't that he didn't provide for Nancy. In fact, he provided in abundance. Nancy knew he prided himself on having a stellar reputation in business and the community. He wanted his neighbors and fellow Portlanders to know that he was able to bestow upon his wife any gift he saw fitting. Nancy, therefore, had a large, impressive home on the edge of the neighborhood that housed the elite and wealthy. The two-story, five-bedroom house was filled with beautiful things, which included an impeccable wardrobe of gowns that came directly from Paris. She and Albert had used fine china, silver, and crystal when dining and relied upon servants to see to their every need.

This had won the approval of the wealthy and allowed Albert and Nancy a glimpse into their exclusive world from time to time. Nancy had tried to find pleasure in that, but the standoffish attitudes of the elite left her feeling more alone than she already did in her amply furnished but empty house.

Empty because she had no children—and now no husband.

Even before his death, Albert was something of a distant and aloof companion. Her days after his death were so similar to the days before them that Nancy didn't have the heart to tell her friends she was more relieved than grieved. Of course, that only served to add to her guilt.

She crawled into bed fully dressed and laid the book at her side. Lying on her back, she stared up at the ceiling, wondering if she was heartless for feeling so indifferent. Eight years married to a man, and she knew so little about him. He seldom spoke of his childhood or past, and when Nancy pried, he was quick to change the subject. Perhaps he was without any kin or pleasant recollections. Maybe, as he so often said, there was nothing to tell. The most she had gotten out of him was that he had been abandoned to the streets after the death of his mother and had raised himself. There were no fond childhood memories or stories to share, and that was that.

And yet Albert Pritchard had made something out of nothing.

Nancy shook her head. She wanted to feel sadness at his passing, but there was nothing in her heart that could even contrive it. They had shared very little besides this house.

On their wedding night eight years ago, Albert had arranged

their lives in an orderly fashion. He had consummated the marriage and then announced that they would have separate bedrooms—explaining that he was often restless at night and might disturb her sleep. He visited her room on a fairly regular basis, but not because of any great passion or romance. He wanted a large family, as did Nancy, and knew what was required to get one. Only babies never came. Nancy didn't conceive even once and couldn't help but wonder what was wrong with them that they didn't have at least one child in eight years. She'd even gone to her mother for advice, but nothing had worked.

If Albert blamed her, she couldn't say. He never said a word on the matter. Nancy hugged her arms to her slim body. She remembered hushed conversations with women at church as to whether she might do something to encourage conception, and of course there were the numerous prayers on her account by those same women. If she hadn't already dismissed God's interest in her life, she might have prayed too. But God didn't care. He hadn't cared about her in years.

A loud knock on her front door caused Nancy to get out of bed. She had planned to ignore anyone who came calling, but the insistent manner in which this knock sounded left her convinced that the visitors would remain until she came to greet them.

When she opened the door and found her mother and father standing on the other side, Nancy knew she'd made the right decision.

"Oh, Nancy. We've been so worried about you." Her mother embraced her tightly. "You're skin and bones. Are you even trying to eat?"

"Mother, I'm quite well." Nancy pulled back and looked at

her father. "I certainly didn't expect to see you so soon after the funeral."

"That was weeks ago," her mother protested, stepping back. "Your aunt Mercy said she was worried about you, and it just confirmed my own feelings. Your father had to come to Portland on business, and I decided to come with him so that I could see you."

"I promise I'm fine." Nancy glanced past her mother and saw two small traveling bags. At least they weren't planning a lengthy stay. "Why don't we get inside out of the dampness?"

"A good idea," her mother replied.

"You two go ahead, and I'll get the bags," her father said.

Nancy nodded and stepped back to allow her mother into the house. She knew they would expect to stay at least one night. Hopefully no more. She really didn't want to listen to their pleas for her to return to the farm outside of Oregon City.

Her mother pulled off her heavy wool shawl. "You need a fire. There's nothing but embers here. Do you mind if I build one?"

"No, go ahead." Nancy sighed and plopped onto the sofa.

"It's getting late. Do you have plans for supper?" her mother asked as she went to work bringing the fire to life once again.

"No. I have a few odds and ends folks have brought me, so I wasn't of a mind to cook."

"We'll arrange for something," her father declared as he came into the room. "I left the bags by the stairs. I presume you want us to use the same guest room?"

"Yes." Nancy tucked her feet up under her.

"Are the horse and buggy still in the carriage house?"

"Yes, Father. Albert paid someone to come see to the poor animal. He comes still, but I've half a mind to sell the horse. I never use him."

"Having the ability to travel other than on foot is a good thing," her mother murmured.

"Everyone walks everywhere in the city," Nancy countered. "Albert was the only one who used the buggy on a regular basis, and usually that was for business or when we were asked to one of his business affairs. Otherwise, we always had things delivered to the house."

"Well, it's not like you don't know how to hitch a wagon." Her mother turned from the now-flickering flames. "You used to love to ride. Is the horse saddle broke as well?"

"Yes, he is, but one needs to have somewhere to go. I'm in mourning, and being out in public is frowned upon."

"That's why I think you should move home. We can easily help you close this house or even rent it out," Mother said, her expression serious. "As for the store, I'm sure your uncle Lance can look into the situation and arrange all the legal needs."

"Thank you, Mother, but I can manage it." Nancy hoped her tone would settle the matter.

"Now, let's not get into harsh words," her father interrupted. "I'm hungry, and I'd like to have some supper. Why don't I hitch up the buggy, and your mother and I can find one of those restaurants we passed on the way here. Grace, why don't you gather some dishes together, and we'll see about ordering something to bring back to the house."

Nancy knew he was trying his best to keep the peace. She nodded. "There are lanterns by the stove. You might need one since the day is rather glum and growing darker by the minute."

Her father nodded and gave her mother a smile. "Come on, Grace. We'll be back before you know it, and you can figure out how to fix the problems of the world then."

Her mother hesitated, then gave a nod. "We won't be long."

CHAPTER 2

Nancy woke the next morning to the aroma of coffee and bacon. For a moment she couldn't remember where she was. As sleep cleared, she remembered the quiet supper she'd shared with her parents the night before. None of them had said anything of much significance. Mother had filled Nancy in on what was happening in Oregon City, while her father had added tidbits of national news, as if she wasn't able to read for herself had she been interested.

No doubt her mother was the source of the coffee and bacon. Nancy had retired early the evening before, feigning a headache. Her mother had offered herbal remedies, and because Nancy didn't want to fight about it, she had taken them. Now, however, she would have to rise and face her parents, and she knew what would follow. They would once again bring up the wisdom of Nancy moving home. Never mind that she had been a married woman living in the city for eight years. They would treat her like a child who had strayed and needed to be brought back into the fold.

She pushed back the covers and shivered at the morning chill. Prompted by the cold, Nancy grabbed the same black dress she'd worn the day before. She struggled with the back buttons but finally managed to get them secured before going to her dressing table. She sat down and stared into the mirror as she began to brush her light brown hair. The woman who looked back at her seemed tired and older than her years. Her green eyes seemed dull and lifeless. With Albert's death, she felt she had somehow lost her identity. As Mrs. Mortenson had said, she was no longer a wife but a widow. Nancy knew how to be the first, but not the latter.

She braided her hair, then pinned it into a knot at the nape of her neck. She thought of what she would say to her parents and how she would once again defend her decision to remain in Portland. She had always been headstrong and capable of standing her ground, but she was so tired. Weariness seemed her constant companion these days. Those who had come to pay their condolences had noted it and said it was part of mourning, but Nancy had so long mourned her marriage and lack of love that she doubted their conclusion. No, this weariness seemed born of despair—hopelessness that she would never fill the hole in her heart. A desperation that things would never change.

From childhood she and her girlfriends had dreamed of finding their one true love—of falling in love and living happily ever after in a home of their own. Nancy gazed deep into the mirror. Why hadn't it come true for her?

She touched the corner of her eye where a hint of lines was starting to form. She was only twenty-six. Was that so very old? Was it possible that while married to the wrong man, she had somehow forfeited her youth? Her dreams?

A sigh escaped her. Surely it wasn't too late. Couldn't true love be found in one's later years just as it could in one's youth?

Nancy put aside her thoughts and slipped into her black

walking shoes. If her parents insisted on remaining in Portland for a few days, she might go for a long walk. There were parks and woodlands nearby where she could disappear. It might actually do her good to leave the house. After all, she had been stuck inside since word came of Albert's death. And prior to that, a lengthy winter had made the outdoors wet and unappealing.

Taking up her shawl, thoughts of a walk still lingering, Nancy contemplated just remaining in her room. She didn't have the energy to go for a walk or deal with her parents. She sighed again and pulled the shawl around her.

"If I don't go to them, they will come to me," she muttered.

She left her room and made her way toward the kitchen, where the sound of laughter could be heard.

"Alex, you are a troublemaker," Nancy heard her mother declare. "Stay out of those biscuits until we sit down to breakfast."

"I can't help it. I'm hungry, and your biscuits are the best to be had." There was a rustling sound and then her mother's gasp.

"Unhand me. Nancy might come in."

"Let her come. It's not like she's never seen her father kiss her mother."

There was a muffled reply, but Nancy couldn't understand the words. She leaned against the wall and pondered the love her father and mother held for each other. It was a love she had hoped to have in her own marriage. Sadly, it had never come.

Nancy remembered the joy her parents had in each other while she was growing up. Oh, they had their share of fights, but they always made up, and their love seemed only to deepen. Aunt Hope and Uncle Lance appeared to have the same kind of relationship, and although she rarely saw Aunt Mercy and

Uncle Adam, she had been told theirs, too, was a love of great depth and happiness.

So why can't I find the same?

"Now that you've been thoroughly kissed," she heard her father say, "I will take my coffee and biscuit and sit at the table. Surely the rumblings we heard earlier indicate our daughter will soon join us."

"I hope so. I feel so bad for her, Alex. She's clearly miserable."

"Well, of course she is. She's lost her husband."

"I think it's more than that," Mother replied. "I think she's completely displaced. I don't think she even knows what's missing."

"And you do?"

Nancy edged closer, in case her mother had some wisdom to offer.

"Well, we both know she's shut God out of her life for a great many years. She needs to right herself with Him, and then the rest will follow suit."

"True," her father replied. "Wiser words were never spoken, wife."

Nancy frowned. The last thing she wanted to do was have a discussion about her thoughts on God. It was time to put a stop to that here and now. She straightened and pushed back her shoulders. She would prove to them that she was just fine, and then hopefully they would leave her be.

She marched into the kitchen with a look of surprise on her face. "Well, I must say I'm not used to having anyone else in my kitchen since I let the cook go." She forced a smile. "But my, doesn't it smell delicious."

Her mother looked at her doubtfully, but her father was delighted to see her.

"You certainly seem to be in better spirits this morning," he declared.

"My headache is gone. The rest did me well. Mother, thank you for such a thoughtful gift. Shall I take over?"

"No. Why don't you have a seat, and I'll bring the food to the table." Her mother's expression was still wary.

Nancy smiled at her and nodded. "Very well. I shall let you wait on me." She went to the table and kissed her father's cheek before taking her seat. She reached for her napkin and snapped it open. "So, will you two go shopping before you head home?"

"Probably," her father replied. "I have to tend to business with the sawmill."

"I imagine it was hard getting away from the farm. Isn't it about time for the ewes to lamb?" Nancy poured herself a cup of coffee and smiled. "This smells so good." She added a healthy amount of cream to her cup, then picked up her spoon. She stirred while watching her mother bring a plate of biscuits to the table.

"We've plenty of time before the lambing, and besides, Hope oversees all of that. Your little sister has taken an interest in it as well."

"Seems like something Meg might enjoy." Nancy wondered how long she could keep up this farce. Already she was tired of the pretense.

Her mother set a bowl of sausage gravy on the table. No doubt she had sent Father out to purchase the ingredients, for Nancy knew that her larder was all but empty. The thought of eating her mother's biscuits and gravy made her stomach rumble. She had learned to cook at her mother's side and could make the dish for herself any time she chose, but it wasn't the same as having her mother cook especially for her.

"Come on, Grace. I think Nancy's as hungry as I am," her father said, laughing.

"Well, it's no wonder if she is. She hardly ate a bite last night, and her cupboards were so bare that I'm convinced she hasn't eaten much since Albert . . ." She let the words fade and threw Nancy an apologetic smile. "Let's pray," she said, taking her seat.

Nancy bowed her head as her father offered a blessing. As soon as he finished, she reached for a biscuit. She would prove to her mother that she was eating just fine, even if the looseness of her gown was apparent.

"Did you sleep well?" Nancy asked as she broke the biscuit into several pieces before covering it in her mother's thick gravy.

"Well enough. You know how hard it is for your mother to rest soundly away from home."

"I do." Nancy moved the food around her plate. Looking up, she found her mother watching her intently, so she stuck a big spoonful in her mouth. To her surprise, it tasted better than anything had in weeks. She swallowed and found her stomach happy to accept the offering. She nodded. "It's wonderful."

This seemed to satisfy her mother momentarily, not that Nancy cared by that point. The fact that her stomach wasn't aching in rejection of the food was enough to keep her eating.

"She's right. This is wonderful. Some of your very best," Father said between bites.

"It's just biscuits and gravy," her mother countered. "You've both had it a million times."

Nancy finished hers and reached for another biscuit.

"See there, Mother," her father declared. "And you were worried."

Nancy met her mother's gaze. It was clear the concern remained. Her mother had always had the ability to see beyond her children's façades. Did every mother possess that talent, or was it just Grace Armistead?

Desperate to move the conversation along, Nancy made the mistake of blurting out the first thing that came to mind. "Mrs. Mortenson came to visit yesterday. She thinks I should remarry right away. She said the West doesn't have enough women to go around, and I shouldn't wait a full year before seeking another husband."

When her mother nearly choked on her coffee, Nancy knew she'd chosen the wrong topic.

"I don't think you have to rush into anything," her father replied as her mother worked to clear her throat.

"Indeed not. Nancy, you have no reason to hurry into another marriage. That's why your father and I are here. We want you to come home with us and rest for a while. You needn't remarry unless you want to."

"But I do. Want to, that is." Nancy shrugged. "I have this wonderful house with all its lovely rooms, and someday I'd like to fill them with children."

"But you just lost Albert." Mother shook her head. "No one expects you to worry about such things just yet."

"And it's precisely because of this big house and the store that we would like you to come home. We can ease your burdens for a time so that you can think through exactly what you want to do," her father interjected. "We can hire someone to manage the store for you."

"Or get an agent to sell both the store and the house."

"No!" Nancy knew her reply was more forceful than she'd intended, but she wasn't going to let her parents make her decisions. Calming her tone, she continued. "I don't wish to sell them. Perhaps in time I'll sell the store, but not the house. I love this house, and I intend to live out my days here. For now, I believe I'll open it as a boardinghouse . . . for women. Even you can find no argument against that, Mother."

Grace Armistead dabbed her napkin to her lips. "Nancy, I'm not trying to argue with you. I simply care about your well-being."

"And I appreciate that." Nancy picked up her coffee. "But I don't need you dictating to me how I should live my life. I've been on my own for years, and I am capable of continuing in that state."

"You haven't been on your own. You've had Albert." Her mother looked at her as if daring her to dispute the comment.

Nancy nodded. "Yes, I had Albert, and he encouraged me to think for myself and to be a strong, capable woman." She gave a brief smile, then sipped her coffee.

"I think all your mother is saying is that the city is full of corruption, and some people will try to get the best of you since there is no one here to watch out for your best interests."

"Perhaps Gabe could come and stay awhile with you," her mother suggested.

Nancy frowned. "I thought he was running the family's saw-mill in Oregon City."

"Yes, but I know he could manage some time away. If he was here to show others that you aren't alone, then perhaps no one would try to take unfair advantage of you."

"No one is trying to take advantage of me, Mother, unless it's you." Nancy immediately regretted her words but didn't apologize. "Now, please stop worrying." She set the cup down rather hard on the saucer. She knew her outburst would only cause more concern. "See there," she quickly added, "I'm stronger than either of you think."

"We know you're strong, Nancy." Her father reached over and patted her hand. "Maybe the real reason we're here is that we need to know that you're all right. We love you."

"I know, Papa." Nancy hadn't used that tender name since she married Albert. Perhaps it would calm his worries. "I don't wish for either of you to worry, but my life is here now."

A silence fell over the table for several long moments. Nancy collected her irritation and stuffed it deep inside. She didn't want to argue with her parents, and at least they weren't throwing God in her face.

But then, as if her thoughts could summon their comments and judgment, Nancy's mother spoke.

"You do know that you can never outrun God, don't you?"

Nancy raised her gaze to her mother's green eyes. "I have no desire to run a footrace with the Almighty." She barely held her annoyance in check.

"You know what I mean, Nancy. What you need—what I know you long for—is that union with God, but for whatever reason, you have turned away from Him."

It was impossible to keep up the pretense with such topics on the table. Nancy pushed back her plate. "I believe it was God who deserted me, Mother. Now, I would rather we ended this conversation. You and Father should get back to your business. I'm sure you're needed at the farm. Take your time finishing breakfast, and I will happily clean up later." She got to her feet.

"Nancy." Her father barely whispered her name, but he knew the effect it would have. In all her years of growing up, he'd had but to lower his voice to a hush to elicit her full attention.

She turned and looked at him. His black hair showed signs

of gray, but his dark eyes were full of life—and love. She knew they both loved her, but her anger wouldn't allow her to admit her need for that love.

"Child, you must let go of your bitterness. I don't know why you feel as you do, but I know your heavenly Father loves you with a love that runs even deeper than my own. And"—he gave her a hint of a smile—"even though it's hard for me to fathom that, I must concede it's true. Your mother and I just want you to know that love is there for you . . . to offer protection, consolation, and hope."

"It offers everything but acceptance," Nancy murmured. She hated upsetting them and hated herself for causing them pain, but she couldn't hold back her words.

"But that isn't true, Nancy. We are willing to accept that you want a life different from what we might have chosen for you," her mother said. "We only wish to give you time to think through what you truly want."

"I suppose I want what everyone else wants," Nancy said, feeling the fight go out of her. "I want love and a family of my own. And I want the right to choose the man I marry and figure it all out for myself. I want you both to understand and trust me to do this. I will find the life I want to live and the man I will love—or at least endure—without anyone else interfering. That way there is no one to blame but myself if it doesn't work out."

"But love is about so much more than endurance, Nancy." Her mother's words were soft but pricked like needles.

"And you can hardly expect anything good to happen when you go into a situation expecting it not to work out," her father added.

Nancy heaved a sigh. "I didn't expect either of you to understand, which is why I didn't come back to the farm or invite you here. Maybe it would be for the best if you both returned home and left me to figure this out for myself. Now, if you'll excuse me."

She left them sitting at the table, looking wounded by the words she'd hurled at them. Why was she so mean-spirited? So disrespectful? She loved them dearly, but for the life of her she couldn't bring herself to let them comfort her.

No wonder God had ceased to love her. She was a terrible person.

CHAPTER 3

Days later, Nancy still regretted her unkind words. Her parents were good people. All of her family were good people. There wasn't one of them who wouldn't come to her rescue if she so much as wiggled her finger. So why was she so determined to push them out of her life?

She worked on cleaning the upstairs bedrooms and contemplated her misery. Her mother and aunts had come west on a wagon train back in 1847. Nancy often imagined what a grand adventure it must have been. Her mother had married a man she didn't love, purely for convenience's sake. He had died on the trail, freeing her to choose another husband. Nancy and her mother had that in common, but Nancy still couldn't bring herself to seek her mother's counsel.

At the end of their wagon train journey, the Flanagan sisters—Grace, Hope, and Mercy—had found themselves wintering at the mission set up by Marcus Whitman near what was now an incorporated town called Walla Walla in Washington Territory. That November a Cayuse attack on the mission left most of the men dead, and the women and children were taken hostage for a month.

Nancy had heard the stories from her mother of how her aunts, Mercy and Hope, were among those hostages. Her mother had been away from the mission, helping a sick friend, and Nancy's father, who had worked as a trapper and occasional guide in the area, had to all but tie Grace up to keep her from storming the mission to reclaim her sisters.

While that had been more than thirty years ago, the massacre at Little Bighorn had occurred just three years earlier, which kept negativity and fear toward the native peoples at a record high.

Nancy supposed that was partly the reason her mother wanted her to come home. She was worried about her daughter being hurt, and Nancy understood that. There were so many unspoken secrets about what had happened at the mission, but Nancy knew it wasn't good. Enough people had talked about the ordeal down through the years. She could remember one of her girlfriends explaining in detail how the Indians had killed the men at the mission, along with Mrs. Whitman, then forced the women to become wives to the warriors. It was hard to imagine such torture and lack of humanity.

"But it's not like we're going to have an Indian raid on Portland," she said, pulling the sheet off a bed.

The four upstairs bedrooms had been closed up since Albert's death. One of Nancy's relatives had thoughtfully covered all of the furniture after the funeral. Now it was just a simple matter of removing the sheets and taking inventory. She wanted to put an advertisement in the paper as soon as possible and take in as many boarders as she could. She planned to offer rooms to rent for single occupancy or double. Perhaps she would even consider three to a room if a trio showed up wishing to live together. The room rental would be one price, and other amenities would be added from there. That way if there was more than one person to a room, they would have the discount of sharing the rent, but each person would still have to pay individually for meals and anything else they requested.

Nancy found it pleasant to consider a future with boarders. She enjoyed cleaning and cooking. There was a great satisfaction for her in keeping house, and boarders would make her feel useful.

She went to the window and gazed outside. It wasn't raining, so she opened the window to air out the room. There was a damp chill to the air, but it invigorated rather than discouraged her. Moving to the next bedroom, she again pulled off the dust sheets and opened the window. This time the figure of a man coming up the walkway caught her attention. It was Gerome Berkshire.

"Oh bother." She wiped her hands on her apron and made her way downstairs, knowing he wouldn't just go away.

Gerome Berkshire was a dashingly handsome man in his thirties. He had been a good friend to Nancy's husband, but he was also clearly interested in Nancy. He hadn't even had the decency to hide that fact when Albert was alive, and now that he was gone, Gerome was on her doorstep almost constantly.

Nancy opened the door before he could even knock, which left him standing awkwardly with his hand raised. "Good morning, Mr. Berkshire."

"Mrs. Pritchard." He gave a bow, tipping his hat at the same time, and then faced her with a grin. "Nancy, you look amazingly well. You must be doing as I suggested and getting more rest."

"Yes, I'm doing quite well despite my loss." She glanced past him. "It's good to see such a bright and clear morning."

"I thought so too." He ran the back of his thumb along his dark mustache. "I thought perhaps you would take a walk with me. Just a short one in a private corner of the park. I doubt there would be very many people there at this hour of the day."

"You forget, Mr. Berkshire, that my husband hasn't even been gone a full month. I am in mourning and, as such, would not want to disgrace Albert's good name."

"Of course. It was thoughtless of me to suggest it. Might I come in instead and have a cup of coffee with you?"

She shrugged. "I suppose so, although I'm sure there are those who would advise me against it, since I am alone." She opened the door wider and stepped back. "But I've never been one to overly support social boundaries and rules."

Gerome entered the house, taking off his hat. "This is such a lovely place."

"Yes, I think so." Nancy took his hat and placed it on an oak receiving table before heading for the kitchen. She knew he would follow. "I hope you don't mind if we just sit in the kitchen."

"Of course not, my dear."

She grimaced at his term of affection. Making her way to the stove, she tapped the coffeepot with her hand and felt that it was still warm. Nevertheless, she stoked the fire in the stove and let the pot sit on the burner for a few minutes while she retrieved cups and saucers, sugar and cream.

"You're lucky," she said. "My parents were just here a few days ago, and they saw me amply stocked with supplies."

"You have only to say the word to me should you need anything at all," he replied.

Nancy motioned him to the table. "Have a seat, and I'll bring the coffee. Would you care for some cake? Mrs. Taylor brought me some yesterday."

"I believe the coffee will suffice. Frankly, I've come more on business than pleasure."

"I see." Nancy retrieved the coffee and a couple of spoons before coming to the table. She placed the spoons beside each cup. "I hope the coffee is hot enough for you."

"I'm sure it will be just fine."

She poured them each a cup, then returned the pot to the stove.

Gerome waited to sit until he had assisted Nancy into her chair. "I am glad to see you faring so well. It makes what I've come to say a little easier."

She looked at him, her wariness returning. "Please speak your mind."

"I'm concerned as to your plans for the future."

Nancy frowned. "Why is everyone so worried about my future?"

He gave her a tolerant smile. "Well, isn't that apparent? We care about you. When situations like this arise, it is the place of your friends and family to lend aid where they can and to ease your burden."

"But I don't feel burdened." If her reply surprised him, Gerome said nothing, and his expression didn't change. "I'm fully capable of dealing with the responsibilities left to me."

"Please forgive me for daring to differ with you, but I don't think that's exactly true. Have you hired a lawyer to go over your husband's will?"

Nancy hadn't even considered whether or not Albert had a will. Had her friends and family left her alone for even a few hours, she might have had time to think about it. Now she had to admit she didn't know if Albert had a will, much less a lawyer.

"No. I haven't. I've been mourning my husband's demise. I didn't figure it was something I had to settle right away."

"Oh, but you must be on top of the matter, lest unscrupulous sorts take advantage of you." He cleared his throat. "As you know, I am qualified to practice law in Oregon. I would be happy to handle the matter for you. Albert often sought me for legal advice."

"I'm sure he did, but I can manage this myself and in my own time." She sipped her coffee. "I have an uncle and cousin who are lawyers."

Gerome wasn't to be silenced. "The management of the store alone needs your immediate attention. It's been closed since your husband's death. You're losing revenue every day, and you cannot get that back. Not only that, but there are bound to be shipments due for delivery. How about I hire someone to manage the store for you?"

Nancy's husband had managed the hardware store on his own for nearly nine years. She had suggested on more than one occasion that he hire a boy to help out. Someone who could manage things when Albert was ill or out of town. But he hadn't wanted anyone else knowing his business. He was private like that. It was one of the reasons he was a stickler for paying cash for everything. He didn't want to owe any man, and he wanted what he owned to be free and clear of any obligations.

"I know you think otherwise, Gerome, but I am fully capable of managing things for myself. I have an education that allows me to manage mathematical transactions and understand business correspondence. However, if I need help, I promise I will seek it out. For now, I simply see no need."

He gave her a look of grave concern, then seemed to forget

all about it and smiled. "Have you been keeping up with the local news?"

"Not exactly. Is there something of interest I should know about?" she asked, grateful for the change of topic.

"There was an article in the newspaper about the school for the black children. I'm not the only one who thinks such things are uncalled for. This state has laws on the books that forbid black people to live in Oregon, yet those laws go mostly unenforced. But with those laws in place, how can we allow schools that accommodate children of color? Worse still is the idea of integrating them into schools with white children. It's complete hypocrisy. I know Albert felt as I do."

"Yes, Albert was strongly opposed to any person of color being allowed to become a citizen of Oregon." She had never felt the same way herself, but she'd spent many evenings listening to Albert air his feelings on the subject.

"Thankfully sound minds have prevailed, and we've never ratified the Fourteenth and Fifteenth Amendments."

"I was under the impression we had. I recall that the Fourteenth was ratified."

"Yes, but it was also rescinded by our state. Those of us who knew the trouble it would cause thankfully spoke up. The Fifteenth might well have been passed in this country as a whole, but Oregon has not ratified it, nor will we. The people in our nation's capital who believe they can impose their will on Oregon will have a rude awakening. Oregon will never yield. There is a reason we made it illegal for blacks to live in this state. You have to look no further than the shantytowns and criminal activity where there are high concentrations of blacks and other ethnic groups. We will not give them the vote or consider them citizens."

"Perhaps if those people received proper help, things would be different."

"They cannot change, my dear. They were like children when they were slaves and children out of control now that they are free. The freedom has ruined them, and they've quickly become criminal in their intent."

"Surely at one time, in their own countries, they were more than capable of managing their lives."

"If that were the truth, they never would have been captured and sold into slavery."

"But they were taken hostage, some by their own people. I learned that just after the war when Mother and I were in California." She looked at him with a raised brow. She had often argued with Albert on this topic and wasn't about to be bested by the likes of Gerome Berkshire. "It was by no fault of their own that they ended up here in America as property. One man had even been the chief of his tribe."

"Did you not consider that he might be lying? How easy it would be to say you were a chief, a man of importance, yet how was he allowed to be taken? Where were his people? His guards?"

Nancy was ready for this question. "His entire village was taken in the night by other natives and sold to white traders."

He paused and gave her a smile. "You make a wonderful cup of coffee, Nancy. Furthermore, you are correct that those poor black men and women were forced into chains and sold into slavery. That's why I think they should be sent back to whatever origin they came from."

Nancy had heard this argument as well. "Would you want someone telling you that you had to go back to your place of origin rather than remain here in America? If I remember correctly, didn't you once mention to Albert that your grandparents came here from Albania?"

"True enough, my dear, but my parents and I were born here. We're as American as anyone else."

"So you only want to send back the black people who were born in Africa? Most of those who live here were born here. Will you allow them to be citizens? After all, they were born here, so by your own argument, they are Americans."

"I believe each state should be allowed to decide that for themselves, and Oregon says no."

Nancy shook her head. "But wasn't that in part what we fought a war over? States' rights versus federal government? I thought the war concluded that all states would be united as one."

"Yes, but there are still strong states' rights, and I believe this should be one of them. As I said, sound minds rescinded the Fourteenth Amendment and will never ratify the Fifteenth."

Nancy got up and retrieved the coffeepot. These were the kind of arguments she didn't mind. She had enjoyed such debates with Albert and before that with her brothers, uncle, and father on other topics. Women weren't thought to be interested in such matters, but Nancy found it all rather fascinating.

"And yet a state refusing to ratify an amendment does not make it null and void." She held up the coffeepot. "More?"

Gerome shook his head. "I can't tarry. I have an oration to give at two. In fact, I will be speaking about some of these very things. You should accompany me."

"I'm in mourning, Gerome. Remember?" She returned the pot to the stove without pouring herself another cup. "But I appreciate the invitation and your concern for my well-being. I assure you I will send word if there is something I need you to handle for me. Until then, however, I am fully capable of managing my affairs." She walked with him to the door and picked up his hat from the receiving table. "Thank you for checking up on me, but I am truly fine."

She extended the hat and he took it, allowing his fingers to touch hers. His dark-eyed gaze searched her face. "I hope you know that I care deeply for you. I have always, well, been envious of Albert's position in your life. Perhaps in time . . ."

She opened the door. "Good day, Mr. Berkshire."

He hesitated, then gave her a curt nod. "Good day, Mrs. Pritchard."

Gerome reached the end of the sidewalk and paused to stare back at the large two-story—three-story, if one counted the attic—Gothic Revival house. He could remember when Albert Pritchard had announced he was building it for his soon-to-be wife. Gerome had suggested a less imposing style, but Albert had informed him that Nancy herself had picked out the house, with its wrapping porch and turret. She had seen the architecture in *Godey's Lady's Book* during their courtship and mentioned she'd very much like such a house one day. Albert had greatly enjoyed surprising his young bride with the gift.

And why not? She had been thrilled when told it was to be their home. Gerome could still see the way her face had lit up—the way she had thrown herself into Albert's arms and showered him with kisses. One day he hoped Nancy might offer him the same reward. Of course, he would have to find some other audacious gift with which to impress her, and that would cost money. Money he didn't have to spare. Yet.

He walked to where his man waited with his enclosed carriage. "Grayson, take me to the Lakewood home."

"Very good, sir." Grayson tipped his hat, then helped Gerome into the carriage.

Gerome settled back against the leather seat. He wasn't pleased with the way his conversation with Nancy had turned out, but then, he hadn't known what to expect. Nancy and Albert Pritchard had always been an odd pair. They seemed quite happy with each other in many ways, but there always seemed to be an impenetrable wall around them. They refused to reveal too much of their personal life to friends and family, and that had always irritated Gerome. He and Albert had been friends for a long time, but Albert had shocked him when he'd announced that he was taking a wife.

The carriage slowed and came to a stop in front of Samuel Lakewood's impressive three-story home built in the Second Empire fashion. The brick house displayed the mansard roof and imposing tower that were characteristic of that architectural style. Lakewood was said to own an identical home on the East Coast and had built this home to match just before the War Between the States broke out. Heavily invested in a large shipping firm he'd inherited from his father and grandfather, Samuel had called the war "Lincoln's folly" and moved his entire family west until the fighting had ceased. While in Portland, however, he had made a fortune and decided to stay on after the war.

Gerome stepped from the carriage and marveled at the impressive grounds that bespoke wealth, with flower beds and statues amidst paved walkways.

"Boss, I was beginning to wonder if you were coming," Newt Hanson declared, appearing from one of the small groves.

Gerome tolerated the comment and shrugged. "I had business with Mrs. Pritchard."

Hanson grinned. "That kind of business wouldn't be too hard to endure."

Gerome frowned. "She is a lady of esteem and a new widow to boot. You'd best mind your tongue."

"Sorry, boss." Hanson had the decency to look contrite.

"Well, don't let me catch you speaking that way again. I plan to one day make her my wife, and I won't tolerate any such talk." Gerome didn't give him time to respond. "I'm glad you're here. I have some business I need you to take care of."

Hanson nodded. "I'm your man."

That brought a smile to Gerome's face. "I know you are. Bought and paid for."

CHAPTER 4

Nearly a month to the day of her husband's body being
discovered, Nancy opened Albert's office in order to
tackle the job of finding his will. Many people believed the first of April to be a day for pranks and tomfoolery,
but Nancy felt it the perfect day to deal with the reality that
she was a widow and had no idea where she stood regarding
her finances and future.

Albert had been meticulous in his organization and housekeeping. He never wanted Nancy in his office and thus kept it
tidy by his own hand. Maybe that was why she hesitated to
enter and stood in silent contemplation in the doorway.

She gazed at the dark room for several moments before
squaring her shoulders. She was an intruder here, just as she
had been in almost every area of Albert Pritchard's life. He
had kept himself so private that at times she feared he must
be running from a terrible past. Other times she just accepted
that he was a man of few words.

She hesitated to move forward, as if she could feel Albert's
recriminations.

"This is ridiculous. It's my office now."

She marched across the room to raise the shades first. A fine layer of dust wafted into the air as the shades rolled up. Nancy pushed back the lace curtains to look out on her lawn. Soon she would have to hire a boy to tend the yard and cut the grass. Albert had always managed such matters, and she had no idea where he found workers. She supposed she could speak with Mrs. Taylor about it. The older woman lived only a few houses away.

Letting go of the curtain panel, Nancy turned to face the office. A large mahogany desk sat in the middle of the room, perfectly positioned atop a beautiful Oriental rug of blues and golds. To the right of the desk was a wall of bookshelves, and behind a portion of those books was a lockbox in which Albert kept important papers. She knew this only because she'd walked in on him once putting it back. Surprisingly enough, rather than reprimand her, Albert had simply nodded and told her that the box contained important papers. They never spoke of it again.

On the opposite end of the room, a marble-framed fireplace stood with two large leather chairs positioned at either side. Albert had often held meetings here with one or more gentlemen. Even so, for all the men who had come and gone in this room, Nancy was the only female who had crossed the threshold. And she could count the number of times she had done so on one hand. Albert preferred she not make a nuisance of herself when he was working, and she refrained from challenging his authority. Although she had often wondered why he felt the need for such secrecy.

She made her way to the desk. The surface was clear except for a pen and inkwell and a stack of blotting paper. The drawers to the desk were locked, but Nancy had already guessed they would be and had brought the key from Albert's bedroom.

She opened the drawers and began to sort through the various neat stacks. She came across a small black journal and opened it. Here she found a list of household expenses and names and addresses for various vendors and repairmen, including the man he used for yard work. Flipping through the pages, she found a variety of people listed, as well as a single page that noted her birthday, their anniversary, and various things she had at times mentioned interest in. She could see from the list that Albert used these thoughts when purchasing gifts for her. She shook her head at his meticulous order.

Poor Albert. He hadn't had a spontaneous thought of his own. Everything was carefully considered and plotted out.

She put the book aside and continued to search for any sign of a will or letter to explain his final wishes. She was on the final drawer when she found an envelope with her name clearly printed on the outside. Beneath that was written:

To be read upon my death.

Nancy pulled the envelope from the drawer and stared at it for several minutes. For some reason, seeing this letter, holding it now, made her sadder than she'd been upon hearing of Albert's demise. Being in his office, going through his personal things—it just made everything so final.

She tore open the envelope and pulled out the letter. Unfolding it, she drew a deep breath. The letter was brief and without any formality or sentiment.

Nancy,

If you are reading this, then I am dead. I have left all my worldly goods to you, as my will clarifies. You will find my will in the lockbox behind the books. The key is beneath the lampstand.

Albert

Nothing about his love or their years together. Nothing about his hopes for her well-being. Nothing.

She went to the lampstand. Albert had purchased the brass lamp when they'd first married. It was a replica of a ship's lantern and one of the few things he had purchased for himself out of sentiment. He had told her that he spent many years in his youth working on the Columbia and Willamette Rivers. His life on the water made for some of the best years of his life. How ironic that it should be the river that took his life as well.

She lifted the heavy lamp and found a key in the hollow beneath. Carefully replacing the lamp, Nancy couldn't help but feel a sense of anxiety. Until today, she hadn't really considered Albert's will, but now she felt an urgency to know what it said.

The lockbox sat behind a row of books. The way they were positioned and the sizes of the books made that row look no different than the rest of the shelves, but the box was there nevertheless. Nancy pulled it out and slipped the key into the lock. It easily opened, and inside Nancy found several papers. The will was on top, and the other papers proved to be deeds for the house and store and a bill of sale for the horse.

She ignored the rest and took the will to the window, where she could read it more easily. The handwriting was definitely Albert's. She scanned the pages. As he'd said, Albert had left her everything. He'd listed everything of particular value, leaving out details as to the full contents of the house and store. It had been witnessed by two men, neither of whose names Nancy recognized. She considered what was to be done next. Gerome had mentioned a lawyer. She knew several, including her uncle Lance Kenner, but he was in Oregon City, and using him would mean a trip home—which she had no desire to make.

She supposed she could just send him a letter, but she figured enough time had already passed.

John Lincoln and his wife, Eliza, attended Nancy's church. She had often heard that John was a well-respected lawyer. She would go and see him. No doubt he could manage the will and estate. She glanced at the clock. With any luck at all, she could go to John's office and be back before late afternoon. She wasn't sure where his office was, exactly, but she also needed to go to the bank and figured they would surely be able to assist her. Now it was just a matter of deciding how she'd get there.

An hour later, Nancy was dressed and ready to go. She had chosen her heavily veiled hat to avoid having to greet people on the street. They would see by her attire that she was in deep mourning and, out of respect, most would leave her be. The rest she would deal with on an individual basis.

When the boy came to exercise the horse and feed and water him, Nancy asked if he might instead drive her to town. "I've business that shouldn't take more than an hour or two. I will pay you double what you normally earn for your work here."

"Sure, I can do that, missus," the young man replied. He tipped his hat. "I'll have ol' Racer hitched in a quick minute."

The boy was as good as his word. Nancy was soon settled into the small buggy with the young man at her side.

"I'm sorry, I don't remember your name," she murmured.

"David. Folks just call me David." He slapped the lines, and Racer started down the street. "Where we goin' today, ma'am?"

"The Ladd & Tilton Bank. I need to get some cash in order to pay you. I know very little about the arrangement you had with my husband."

David smiled. "He paid me ten dollars a month, ma'am. He kept entries on when he paid me in a little red book in his desk.

He paid at the end of the month, so I didn't get the money for last month."

Nancy nodded. She had seen that book. "Very well. I will see to your pay for March. I don't know yet if I'm going to keep the horse and buggy, but I do want to continue to employ your services for the time being. In fact, could you check in with me each day after you care for the horse?"

"I'd be happy to, ma'am."

She studied the slim boy. "How old are you, David?"

"Sixteen, ma'am."

"And you work full-time instead of going to school?"

"Ain't no reason for me to go to school, ma'am. I know what I need to know."

"Oh? What is that?"

"Horses." He smiled at her. "Horses is what I'll make a livin' at, so I have no need for books."

"I see." She nodded. "And what about your family?"

"Same for them. Horses is what we know. My pa, and my ma too. I reckon my brothers will be the same, though they're a bit younger than me."

"I have two brothers," Nancy murmured. "There were three, but one died. I have a younger sister, as well." She wasn't sure why she felt the need to tell him this.

"There were ten of us children at one time," he said, keeping his gaze on the road. "Four were called to Jesus, like your brother."

"How sad. That must have been difficult for you."

He nodded. "It was especially hard for my ma. Pa said nobody ever mourns the loss of a child as much as the mother."

Nancy said nothing. Losing her little brother had been more devastating than any other experience in her life. Her pain was

TRACIE PETERSON

certainly no less than her mother's. Even now, fifteen years later, the loss still cut her to the quick, and the memory was more than she could bear.

David seemed to understand her need for silence and said nothing as he drove through the busy morning traffic. Nancy barely paid attention to the world around her as her anxiety increased. She should have just sent David to the bank and lawyer's in her stead. She was almost ready to tell him to take her home when he announced they had reached the bank.

He jumped down after securing the carriage and helped Nancy to the ground. "I'll be right here if you need me."

She gave him a nod and swallowed the lump in her throat. "Thank you. I shouldn't be long."

She made her way inside the large bank, ignoring the people milling around her. Her purpose was singular. She would receive cash from her account and inquire about the location of John Lincoln's law office.

"Good morning, madam. How may I assist you?" a smartly dressed teller asked. His smile faded a bit at the sight of her mourning clothes.

She pushed the bank draft she'd brought from Albert's office toward him. "I'd like to cash this."

"Of course." He took the draft and looked it over.

"I'm also in need of the address for John Lincoln. He's a lawyer, and I know his office is near the bank."

"I'm uncertain of the address, madam, but I'm sure we can ascertain that for you if you'll just wait here."

The teller left his area, and Nancy watched as he made his way to a man seated behind a desk at the far end of the room. The man glanced across the sea of people to where she stood, making her feel awkwardly on display. She hadn't realized that she would feel uncomfortable coming to town, but she did. In fact, she found herself fighting the urge to run from the building.

What's wrong with me? It's not like I've never come to the bank before. She had often come downtown on her own. Why should she feel so out of place now just because Albert was dead?

Thankfully, the teller returned before her anxiety rose high enough to make her flee. "I have that address for you, madam, as well as the cash from your transaction." He handed her a slip of paper.

Nancy studied the address while he completed her transaction. She put the cash in her drawstring purse and thanked him for his help before making her way from the bank.

David stood beside the buggy, waiting. He offered Nancy his arm as she climbed into the small, two-person carriage and settled in. She felt the tightness in her chest ease as David joined her.

"Where to now, ma'am?"

She handed him the address.

He glanced at the paper and nodded. "It's just around the corner. I'll have you there in a quick minute." He slapped the lines lightly and eased the horse into the busy traffic.

John Lincoln kept an office on the ground floor of a large brick edifice that looked to be entirely devoted to legal services. Nancy once again felt intimidated as she made her way inside. She quickly found the office door with gold stenciling proclaiming *John Lincoln, Attorney at Law*.

A skinny young man looked up from his work, then quickly rose to stand at attention. "Good morning. How may I help you?" He pushed up his eyeglasses and fumbled to button his coat.

"I don't have an appointment, but I would like to see Mr.

Lincoln. Would you tell him Mrs. Pritchard would like to discuss her late husband's affairs?"

"Yes, ma'am. Won't you have a chair?"

She nodded and slipped into a round-backed wooden chair by the door. The young man turned down a short hall. At the end, he knocked on a closed wooden door before letting himself inside the room. Nancy heard the murmured exchange but couldn't make out any of the words. She felt suddenly exhausted and found herself longing for home.

I feel like an old woman—tired and worn from the cares of life. I'm only twenty-six, and I feel as if I have one foot in the grave.

The bespectacled young man soon returned and offered her a smile. "Mr. Lincoln will see you now. Please come this way."

Nancy rose and followed him to John's office. She felt a sense of relief at the familiar face greeting her.

"Mrs. Pritchard, welcome," John Lincoln said, coming around his desk. "May I tell you how sorry I am for your loss." He took her gloved hand and led her to a leather chair.

"Thank you, Mr. Lincoln." Nancy sat once again and pushed back her veil.

He frowned as he considered her. "You look rather pale. Would you care for some water?"

"No." Nancy shook her head. "I'm afraid this is my first time out of the house since the funeral, and I'm feeling . . . well, rather out of place."

The older man gave her a sympathetic smile. "Well, let me see what I can do to help. Cyrus tells me that you've come to discuss your husband's affairs."

Nancy nodded and reached into her purse. She pulled out the short will and handed it to Mr. Lincoln. "I was informed by a

friend—actually, one of my husband's former associates—that
I should be dealing with the will and my husband's business.
I'm hoping I might solicit you to manage this task for me."

Lincoln took the will and smiled again. "I'm honored that
you deem me worthy."

Nancy began to relax a bit. "I feel I know you and your sweet
wife well enough to be comfortable in your management of the
matter." She paused, wondering if he'd think it strange if she
confessed how little she knew about her husband's dealings.
"I'm afraid . . . well, that is to say, I wasn't overly involved in
my husband's business and know very little about what might
need attention."

"You needn't apologize. Few wives are involved in such matters." He took his seat and studied the will. "It seems very
simply stated. Did your husband have any family?"

"No. He was orphaned at a young age and always told me
there was no one else."

"Then we shouldn't anticipate any challenge to your husband's wishes." He put down the paper. "Now, what do you
know of the hardware store your husband ran?"

"Albert's store is near the river. He catered primarily to the
men in that area—particularly riverboat crews and their needs.
He was quite private about his business. I plan to go to the store
soon so that I can collect the papers from the safe."

"That's a good idea. It would be wise to consolidate everything in one place, and that way I can look over the papers and
arrange to pay off any unmet loans or inventories."

"Albert always insisted on cash-only transactions. I can't
imagine there were any loans. He abhorred borrowing money."

"A wise man, to be sure." John Lincoln leaned back in his
chair. "I admire a man who refrained from debt."

"Yes, well, that was Albert's way."

Silence fell over the room while John studied her. "May I call you Nancy?" he asked. "I feel we have known each other for such a long time, and you are rather like family."

"Of course," she replied, trying not to appear surprised. It seemed strange that this man should say such a thing. They saw each other regularly at church, and Nancy had once attended a dinner at the Lincoln house, but they were certainly not close.

"Nancy, many people will try to take advantage of you. There are at least a hundred confidence men slithering about the city, trying to rob the unsuspecting and entangle the inno-cent. I would like to ask that you do nothing, make no decision and sign no papers without first consulting me. I do not ask this because I believe you incapable of managing your affairs, but these tricksters are quite devious and often seem validated and completely trustworthy. I know a man—a good friend, in fact who was recently taken in by such deception and lost over twenty thousand dollars."

"Twenty thousand?" Nancy didn't even attempt to hide her surprise.

John nodded. "And the duped man was Harvard educated. So, please, come to me first. Even if it is a family member's suggestion or that of a close friend. People are easily mis-taken."

Nancy could hear the sincerity in his voice. He wasn't just trying to take charge of her affairs. He genuinely cared. "I will seek your counsel first, and in doing so would like to ask your advice about something."

"Of course." He smiled, seeming relieved. "Please go on."

"I will probably be of a mind to sell the store. I haven't de-cided for certain, but it seems reasonable. I know nothing about the business and have little desire to learn. However, my house is quite large, and I would enjoy turning it into a boardinghouse for women. I believe, as I mentioned, that both are free of any legal entanglements."

"I believe a boardinghouse would be a good way for you to support yourself, Nancy. And the location of your home would bring in a better type of client. Let me go over your husband's affairs, and we should be able to know for certain within a week or so if there are any problems."

"Thank you." She sighed.

With their meeting concluded, Nancy figured there was no time like the present to pick up her husband's papers and ledgers from the store. She directed David toward the docks. Her husband's hardware store was located only a few blocks from the river, which made it convenient for the ship and dockworkers to get what they needed for repairs.

"I'd like you to come in with me," Nancy told David as they came to a stop in front of the store. The building was brick with a wood awning that desperately wanted a coat of paint. Albert had been waiting for a dry spell in order to see that particular job done by his own hand. He seldom if ever hired someone to do something he felt comfortable tackling himself.

David followed her into the building. "Would you like me to light some lanterns?"

"Please." Nancy glanced around the large store. She'd only been here a handful of times. There was nothing sold here that would interest a lady, and most of the materials were things she doubted many men would recognize.

Once David had ample lighting for them, Nancy made her way to the back room where she knew Albert kept a small office. She glanced around the room, trying desperately to sense something familiar—something of Albert—but instead she was met with cold indifference. The room was meticulously ordered, as was her late husband's way, but there was nothing personal to the place. It could have been anyone's office in any stranger's place of business.

"Is there anything you'd like me to do?" David asked.

Nancy thought for a moment. "See if you can't find a small wooden crate so we can take home all the papers and contents of the desk."

"Sure, Mrs. Pritchard." He left one of the lanterns on the desk and took the other to go on his search.

Nancy took a ring of keys from her purse. She made her way to the safe and tried first one key and then another until she managed to unlock the door. It was difficult to see inside, so she retrieved the lantern and shone it into the safe.

There were several ledgers, stacks of invoices and bills of sale, a moneybox, and additional papers that weren't readily identifiable. She opened one of the ledgers but couldn't make sense of it. It appeared to be in some sort of abbreviated short-hand or code. She picked up one of the other books and found the same style of entries.

"I found this. Do you suppose it's big enough?" David announced, returning with a large crate.

She set down the ledger. "I think it should suffice. It will depend on what's in the desk. Come empty out the contents of the safe and put them in the crate while I open the desk."

"Yes, ma'am." David bent quickly to the task while Nancy fumbled with the keys again to figure out the desk lock.

Once the desk was open, it was easy to see that Albert had kept anything of value in the safe. The drawers of the desk were all empty save for several catalogues her husband had probably used to place orders. Nancy didn't bother to relock the desk or the safe.

"Do you suppose there is anything else the lawyer might need?" she asked aloud, not really anticipating an answer.

"He'll want an inventory of everything in the store."

She looked at David in surprise. "Yes, I suppose he will. Perhaps one of the ledgers will contain that information. If not, we may have to get someone in here to take an account. Although I don't know who might recognize the goods carried here."

"Your lawyer could probably locate someone," David offered. "Even if he doesn't know someone, he might be able to put the word out."

"Of course. I'm sure you're right." Nancy made a mental note to write John a letter to request such a person.

They made their way back out to the buggy. David waited while Nancy locked the store door. He placed the crate on the buggy floor, then helped Nancy up. Once she was settled, he claimed his seat and propped his feet on the sides of the crate.

"I'm sorry there isn't more room," Nancy said, frowning. "I could hold the crate on my lap."

"No, it's just fine, ma'am. No sense in you having to bear the weight." He picked up the reins. "Are we bound for home now?"

"Yes, please." The day was starting to grow overcast as thick clouds moved in from the coast. "Hopefully we'll beat the rain."

David drove them back to the house, commenting from time to time on one thing or another, as if to keep Nancy entertained. He told her about a new theater that was soon to open for plays and musical gatherings. How he knew about such things, she didn't ask. As they neared her neighborhood, Nancy contemplated what she would do with the rest of her day. It was nearly noon, and to her surprise, she was hungry.

"I can fix us some lunch, if you're hungry," she offered.

David shook his head. "I have to get on with my other jobs. I usually just bring an apple and some cheese. I left it in the carriage house, so it'll be there waitin' for me when we get back."

Nancy smiled and nodded. "Why don't you just go to the carriage house rather than dropping me off out front? I'm sure it's going to start raining any minute, and I'd like to keep those papers dry."

When they reached the house, David did as she suggested. Nancy hurried through the garden path to the back door and unlocked the house. David followed with the crate of goods, and Nancy directed him to put it on the table in the front foyer.

As he turned to go, Nancy stopped him. "I want you to have this for your extra trouble." She handed him a five-dollar note. "I know I'll be needing you at other times to drive me. In time I should be able to manage for myself, but for now . . ." She let the words fade into silence.

"I'm happy to help you, Mrs. Pritchard." David took the bill and grinned. "And my ma will be grateful for this. I'll see to the horse and buggy now. Good day to you." He tipped his hat and made a dash for the carriage house just as a loud knocking sounded from the front door.

Nancy closed the back door and took off her hat and veil as she made her way to the front of the house. She put her things aside on the receiving table, then opened the door to reveal a man she didn't know.

"May I help you?"

He smiled. "I'm Mr. Hanson—a customer of your husband's."

"I'm sorry, but my husband is dead."

"Yeah, I heard about that." The large, beefy man rubbed his

bearded face. Then, as if he'd just realized she was a lady, he pulled off his cap. "Fact is, your husband took an order for me and I paid in full, so now I need to know where my shipment is."

"I'm sorry. I'm just now attending to some of those things. I can have my lawyer look into it. What is it that you ordered from my husband?"

"Whiskey and rifles. Quite a lot of both. I paid him in full. Your books ought to show that."

"I'm afraid you have the wrong person, Mr. Hanson. My husband didn't deal in whiskey or firearms."

The man smiled. "Well, it's clear he didn't tell you about it, but the facts are what they are. He dealt in them, all right. I bought from him more than once, and I want my goods."

Nancy shook her head, not knowing what else to say or do. He was intimidating in size, and if he chose to cause her trouble, she doubted there was anything she could do about it.

"I suppose I shall have to figure out where your things are, Mr. Hanson. Can you give me a day or two?"

He grinned. "Sure. I like the idea of coming back to pay you another visit."

She did her best to appear unmoved by his comment and leer. "Very well, then. Might I suggest you come again on Friday? Say, at two. I'm sure that will be enough time for my lawyer to figure this out for you." With any luck at all, she'd have Mr. Lincoln present to deal with Mr. Hanson when he returned.

She didn't realize how frightened she was until after Hanson had gone. Closing the door behind her, Nancy quickly locked it and then leaned back against it to ponder what had just happened. Albert had never told her anything about guns and whiskey. He dealt in machinery pieces and tools. What in the world was this about?

CHAPTER 5

A re you sure she won't mind that you've brought me along?" Seth Carpenter looked at his new employer with a grin. "I mean, it's not like we aren't old friends, but I don't want to cause problems for you."

"I think Nancy will be delighted to see you again," John Lincoln replied before lifting the knocker. He sounded it several times, then turned back to Seth. "I'm sure at a time like this that old friends from home must serve a comforting purpose."

Seth wasn't convinced Nancy would see it that way. After all, he'd been her brother Gabe's best friend—not hers. He thought back to the last time he'd even seen Nancy. She couldn't have been more than sixteen or seventeen. In her earlier years, she had been a pest to Gabe and Seth. Typical of little sisters, she was constantly interfering in their affairs and threatening to tattle on them when she didn't like what she saw. In the latter years, however, Nancy had seldom had much to do with her brothers or their friends, and short of seeing her at church, Seth had found she was usually absent during his visits.

The door opened, and Nancy Armistead Pritchard gave John a smile. "Mr. Lincoln, I'm glad you could make it today."

"I'm sorry for the delay. I had hoped we could meet sooner, but so many things conspired against us." He paused and turned to Seth. "I believe you know Mr. Carpenter."

Nancy turned to face Seth and paused with a curious look on her face. "Seth? Seth Carpenter?"

"One and the same." Seth tried not to show his surprise at her stunning beauty. Her green eyes were startling in their intensity. Had they always been so bright? How was it that he didn't remember her having green eyes? "It's good to see you again, Nancy—Mrs. Pritchard."

"No, please call me Nancy. I wouldn't know how to accept anything else from you." She backed away. "Please come in, gentlemen." She took their hats and paused to put them on the table beside a crate of papers and books. "As you can see, I've been gathering my husband's business papers."

"Very good," John replied. "We'll be certain to take those back with us."

She led the way to a very nicely furnished sitting room. The fire in the hearth was more than welcome on the chilly day.

"I never figured to see you again, Seth. What brings you around today?" she asked.

"He's working with me now," John answered before Seth could say another word. "I advertised to take on a partner, and Seth responded. It's a comfort to me to know that you are acquainted with each other."

"The Carpenters are longtime friends of the family," Nancy answered, giving Seth a quick glance. "My older brother Gabe and Seth were the best of friends. I, on the other hand, was better acquainted with Seth's sister Clementine."

"Speaking of which," Seth interjected, "she is moving to Portland to teach at the school just a few blocks from here. John tells me you're opening your home to boarders, and I'd love to secure a place for her here and now."

Nancy smiled for the first time. "That would be delightful. I would love to renew my friendship with your sister. I shall save a room for her. The very best one, in fact."

Seth's smile broadened. "That would be wonderful. I know she'll be pleased." He was pleased too. It would also give him a good reason to stop by on a regular basis to visit.

"As you know," John said, his voice taking on a professional tone, "I wanted to stop by and talk to you about your husband's affairs. So far I have ascertained that, just as you thought, the deeds on the business and the house are free and clear. Furthermore, there doesn't seem to be any challenge or problem with the terms of the will. I will, of course, continue to search out his associates and look carefully for owed debts and so forth. You pointed out the crate of papers on the table. Is that everything?"

Nancy shrugged. "I'm not sure, but I believe it is. I've not really gone through what's there. I . . . well, I didn't feel up to it."

"That's not a problem, I assure you. If we need anything more, we'll let you know."

"I thought perhaps you might want an inventory of the store, but I can't say whether one is included." She looked so weary and tired. Seth wondered at the toll her circumstances had taken.

"It's easy enough to hire someone to take an inventory," John said, nodding to Seth. "Would you be so good as to note that for me?"

Seth pulled a small notebook from his pocket as well as a pencil. "Happy to."

"There is another matter that I'm uncertain how to manage," she continued.

"And what would that be?" John asked.

"A man came to the house. He said his name was Hanson. He said that he had purchased a large supply of goods from my husband and had come to collect them. I told him to come back on Friday, but I'd much rather you handled this matter."

"We can certainly arrange for that," John declared, nodding again at Seth. "Note that as well."

"The problem is this," Nancy said, shaking her head. "Mr. Hanson said he purchased whiskey and rifles from my husband, but I never knew Albert to deal in either commodity. I looked through some of his bookkeeping, but it appears to be in code, so I have no idea if the sale took place or not. If it did, I have no idea where he might have kept such things. I saw nothing of the kind in the store. I even sent the young man who tends my horse back to the store to look. He found nothing."

John considered the matter for a moment. "Perhaps your husband had a warehouse elsewhere. He might have stored a great many goods there. Perhaps whiskey and firearms were a new line he was taking up."

"Perhaps, but if there was a warehouse, I am completely unaware of it. I can't even imagine how to go about finding out if it existed."

"We can manage that with advertisements in the paper. We'll do the same for clearing your husband's name of all debts, should there be any. It's a fairly simple matter, so you needn't worry yourself over it. Seth." John nodded at him, and Seth made another note.

A knock at the door interrupted their discussion, and when Nancy stood, John and Seth did likewise.

"I can't imagine who that is. I have no other appointments."
Nancy left them and soon returned with a gentleman.

Seth had no reason to immediately dislike the man, but there
was something that just put him on edge. The fellow was tall
and dark-eyed with a thick but neatly trimmed black mustache.
His dark eyes seemed to take in everything at once, yet his gaze
quickly settled on Seth and John.

"John Lincoln. I'm surprised to find you here."

"Gerome Berkshire. It has been a long time," John replied.
"This is my new associate, Seth Carpenter. Seth is an old family
friend of Mrs. Pritchard's."

"Ah, so that explains your presence." Berkshire seemed relieved.

"Well, it does in part," Seth couldn't help but add. "We are
also here on business."

"Business? What business do you have with a lawyer, Nancy
dear?"

Seth didn't like the stranger's familiarity. However, before he
could speak a word of protest, Nancy answered him.

"John is handling Albert's affairs. As you will recall, you
were pressing me to tend to them. That crate you saw on the
front table is full of Albert's business papers."

"Is it now?" Berkshire's voice took on a strange tone. "I
know what I told you, my dear, but I didn't intend for you to
pay someone else for what I would do for free. You hardly need
part with your precious savings in order to set things in order. I
can easily manage all of this for you. After all, as a dear friend,
Albert often sought my counsel."

"Yes, but as a dear friend, perhaps it is better that you refrain."
Seth gave Berkshire a fixed look. "After all, you are mourning the
loss of that friend, and as such, it could affect your judgment."

"Nothing affects my judgment," Berkshire countered with a fierce scowl.

"Even so, I have to agree with my associate," John interjected. "Personal relationships can often muddy the waters in such circumstances. I'm happy to handle the matter for Mrs. Pritchard. Since you were a close friend to her husband, perhaps you could stop by my office to discuss your business affairs." He looked to Nancy and smiled. "I am averse to discussing further business in the company of others. Perhaps we could arrange to meet next week—in my office."

"Yes, that would be fine," Nancy replied, smoothing the black fabric of her skirt as she sat down. "In the meantime, I just want to make sure it is all right to move ahead with my plans for the house."

Berkshire's scowl deepened. "What plans are those?"

Nancy gave a light shrug. "I intend to open my home as a boardinghouse. For ladies only. It will be a perfect way for me to garner income."

"Surely you needn't worry about income. I know Albert was well situated."

"But it's important that I have money continuing to come in. Money that I earn myself. I don't want to be dependent upon anyone else."

"But that is why I've encouraged you to let me hire a man to run the store. Surely even you can't disagree with the sense of that, Mr. Lincoln." Berkshire completely ignored Seth and continued. "I know a good man who was well acquainted with the store and the type of goods sold. We could easily put him into the position and see the store up and running again."

"I believe I'm going to sell the store," Nancy declared.

Seth watched Berkshire's irritation grow by the second.

There was clearly something about the arrangement that didn't set well with him at all.

"I must advise you, my dear, to do nothing rash. Albert wouldn't want you throwing away a good business simply because your lawyer was pushing you to do so."

"I've done nothing of the sort, Mr. Berkshire, I assure you." John's tone revealed his offense at such a suggestion.

"No, in fact, it was my idea." Nancy easily dismissed Berkshire's concerns. "Now that we have that settled, would you care for some refreshment? I have coffee and tea, as well as some cake."

Seth hoped John wouldn't leave Nancy alone with Berkshire. To encourage their stay, he piped up. "I could use a cup of coffee."

Nancy was quickly on her feet. "It will only take a minute. Please excuse me."

"I'll help you," Seth said, jumping up before anyone could protest. He moved toward Nancy and pressed his hand to the small of her back, guiding her from the room. "I wouldn't want you to carry a heavy tray."

He nudged her toward the kitchen and could see by the look on Berkshire's face that he was unhappy with this turn of events. With any luck, the man would be gone by the time they returned.

"I hope you don't mind my imposition," Seth said, dropping his hand as soon as they entered the kitchen. "I don't like the way that man acts in regard to you. He seems to feel he has some sort of right to you."

Nancy smiled. "Unlike you, of course."

Seth chuckled. "Well, we are old and dear friends."

She nodded. "The oldest and dearest."

"Well, I haven't time for coffee," Gerome told John Lincoln. "Please give Nancy my regrets."

He got to his feet. He had come to deliver some IOUs he had created to Nancy. His desperate need for funds left him with little choice but to finagle money out of her. But he couldn't do that in the presence of her lawyer.

"Of course." Lincoln got to his feet and extended his hand. "It was good to see you again."

Gerome shook his hand and nodded. "You as well."

Gerome made his way to the foyer and retrieved his hat. He saw the crate of papers and books and wondered if what he was looking for might also be among them. There was no time to go through the collection, however. Perhaps he could arrange for one of his men to break into John Lincoln's office.

Then another thought came to mind. He pulled the IOUs from his pocket. He'd thought this a rather clever scheme. He had created what looked like hasty, spur-of-the moment agreements, as though Albert had needed a last-minute loan. Gerome had purposefully left his name and all signatures off the paper while making it clear the loan had been on Albert's part. He'd copied the information twice on the same page, then torn it in half as he'd often seen his poorer cohorts do when lending one another money. He had planned to present them to Nancy and explain that Albert was occasionally short of cash for particular purchases. He knew Albert never borrowed money, but he had been prepared to explain that this was a common practice between the two of them, always taken care of within a few days or weeks. Just a little help between friends. Only this time Albert had died before he could repay the notes.

Lincoln and Carpenter's presence made giving Nancy the notes impossible. They might be suspicious. However, if they found the IOUs in the paperwork Nancy provided, they could scarcely say anything about it.

As quickly as he could, Gerome lifted several of the loose papers on top and planted the IOUs underneath. No one would be the wiser now, and he could appear with his half of the notes and explain the lack of signatures and names was due to the informality and hurried situation in each case. Lincoln was a smart man and might find the notes suspect, but Gerome wasn't overly worried. Let the fool think what he would. Gerome would appeal to Nancy's kind heart, and the money would be his soon enough.

"I still can't believe my good fortune in getting to room in your boardinghouse," Clementine Carpenter said as she and Nancy shared their first evening together. She had the same reddish-brown hair as her brother and hadn't changed much in appearance over the years, being still petite and graceful. "When Seth told me about you opening your home to guests, I was overjoyed."

"As was I." Nancy poured them both a cup of tea. Clementine was her first boarder, but Nancy hoped others would soon follow. She had placed an ad in the newspaper just that morning. "Would you care for cream or sugar?"

"Just a little cream, please."

Nancy added the cream and handed Clementine the cup and saucer. "It seems like a lifetime since I last saw you." She settled back with her cup of tea. "Are you enjoying being a teacher?"

"To be sure. It's all I ever wanted to be."

Nancy chuckled. "Except for a short time when you wanted to be a tightrope walker in the circus."

Clementine's eyes widened. "I remember that. We had both seen the circus performers, and I thought it would be ever so daring to walk on a tightrope."

"Do you remember how we strung a rope in the hayloft and tried walking on it?"

"Such a disaster. I'm glad we had plenty of hay to break our falls." Clementine shook her head.

Nancy generally avoided talking about the past but found this a rather pleasant exception. They continued reminiscing about their childhoods, laughing over their antics as young girls. Soon the teapot was cold and empty, and Nancy felt lighter than she had in weeks. "Have you been back to the farm lately?" she asked.

"Oh yes. I make sure to see the folks several times a year. How about you?"

Nancy shook her head and looked away. "No. I haven't been back there since I left."

"Truly?" Clementine's tone betrayed her surprise. "You haven't seen your family at all in that time?"

"They've come to see me here." Nancy shrugged and nodded toward the teapot. "Should I make more tea?"

Clementine shook her head. "No, I need to finish unpacking. But I hope we can make a habit of this and pick up where we left off. Minus the tightrope walking." She grinned and placed her cup and saucer on the tray.

Nancy forced a smile. The joy of their earlier discussion faded, and she could feel the heaviness in her heart settle upon her. "If you need anything, just let me know."

As the weeks went by, Nancy was more than pleased with her business endeavor. The boardinghouse had turned out to be a great idea, and all of her upstairs rooms were quickly rented to an eclectic group of ladies.

Clementine was proving to be just as even-tempered and delightful as she had been as a child. Nancy enjoyed their evenings together. After their first night of getting reacquainted, they had moved on from the past and now spent their time together discussing the future. Clementine was always one to look forward, thankfully.

Clementine was also enthusiastic about several causes, especially education for all children—rich or poor, white or black. She also held strong opinions about women being given the right to vote. It was, she contended, absolutely necessary for women to have the same legal rights as their male counterparts. Nancy found it invigorating to listen to Clementine speak on these issues, but some of her other boarders were less accepting.

The next woman to take a room was an elderly and very private soul, Mrs. Virginia Weaver. Mrs. Weaver was a former Southerner whose husband had passed away five years earlier. She was genteel and frail, and rapidly losing what little he'd left to her financially. In order to better stretch her money, the widow had sold their small house and furniture and had taken a room with Nancy.

However, though her money was extremely tight, Mrs. Weaver paid Nancy extra to take her meals in her room. It wasn't a problem, but it did seem odd that a woman who was meticulously counting pennies and had asked for a discount on the rent if she was willing to forgo Nancy's housekeeping should then turn around and pay extra to eat alone in her room. And Mrs. Weaver could eat. For all her frailty and small frame, she had a voracious appetite.

Two sisters, Bedelia and Cornelia Clifton, took the third room. Very religious and pious spinsters in their forties, the sisters desired a quiet existence where they could live modestly and see to each other's needs. Bedelia was the elder and clearly in charge. She ordered Cornelia around, making her wear a shawl even when it wasn't cold and restricting her from a second helping of cake. The humor in that was that Nancy had caught Bedelia more than once in the kitchen, seeking a second piece herself. They reminded Nancy of a couple of contented hens clucking about their business until Cornelia stepped out of the pecking order.

The final guest had come just a few days earlier by way of Clementine. Mimi Bryant was a widow in her fifties who had recently taken up teaching again at the same school as Clementine. Her husband had been the school's director, and upon his death the previous January, Mimi had little choice but to give up their home and return to work. Her husband had been a poor financial master, leaving nothing to his wife save debt. Having taught school prior to marrying, Mimi simply returned to what she knew best and managed a classroom of first graders at the same private institution where Clementine taught.

It was surprisingly pleasant to have the house full of people. Back in March, when family had gathered for the funeral, Nancy had thought it unbearable to have so many people around. But her boarders were different. Where family had insisted on tending to Nancy and her needs, the boarders looked to Nancy for their well-being. Nancy provided a home, meals, laundry, and cleaning services. It might take a while for them to get used to one another, but Nancy felt confident that her boardinghouse would be a blessing to all.

From the start, she had established a daily routine. She told each woman she would serve breakfast promptly at six each morning, lunch at noon, and supper at six in the evening.

Almost immediately Mimi and Clementine pointed out that once the school term started, they wouldn't be able to leave the school until a little after noon. Nancy told them they could join in late. Bedelia and Cornelia accepted the schedule but did stress that Sundays would have to be altered, as their services would not let out until nearly one. Mimi pointed out that often she was invited elsewhere to share a meal after church. Nancy did her best to accommodate everyone even though she felt control of the situation slipping away. She had never anticipated that her boarders might protest her plans.

After some debate, they all agreed that Sunday luncheon would be the responsibility of each woman. Nancy would make sure there was a variety of foods readily available, even going so far as to keep a stew or casserole warming on the back of the stove. Otherwise, the women were free to either eat or not eat according to their desires.

Now, with everyone about their own business, Nancy tidied the kitchen and pondered what she would serve for lunch. She had a large ham that she could slice up and serve with canned green beans. She'd baked fresh bread just that morning, but given the surprising amount of food these women ate, she would have to bake again that afternoon.

Even so, the thought brought a smile to her face. She had purpose now. There were people depending on her, and her work kept her far too busy to worry about the strange ledgers she'd found in Albert's safe or if there was a warehouse somewhere holding extra inventory. Thankfully, John Lincoln and Seth were seeing to those things. Furthermore, Mr. Hanson hadn't returned, although Nancy had been prepared to send him to John Lincoln if he had. It seemed life was settling into some semblance of order.

At the sound of someone knocking on the front door, Nancy wiped her hands on her apron, then took it off and placed it over the back of the kitchen chair. She glanced at the grand-father clock as she passed on her way to the front door. It was ten minutes after eleven. Who would be calling at this hour? Perhaps Seth and Mr. Lincoln had come to discuss business.

Opening the door, she was disappointed to find Gerome Berkshire on her porch. Nevertheless, she forced a smile. "Mr. Berkshire."

"Mrs. Pritchard. It's such a nice day that I thought I would stop by and see how you're doing." He pulled off his hat and gave a little bow.

Nancy didn't move away from the door. "I'm quite well. Thank you. I have a full house of boarders now, all very nice ladies."

"I'm glad to hear that. I suppose it keeps you very busy."

"It does." She wondered what he really wanted. "What can I do for you?"

"Might I come in? There are some things I'd like to discuss. It has to do with business arrangements I made with Albert. I've put it off as long as I felt I could."

Nancy smiled. "You needn't have. John Lincoln is managing everything, along with Seth Carpenter. I'm sure you could set up an appointment with them and manage whatever problems you have."

He frowned. "I would rather work with you, Nancy. My arrangements with Albert were more handshake agreements than paper transactions. Lawyers tend to want to deal only in those things that can be proven."

"And your dealings with Albert would have no proof?"

"I doubt it. As I said, we agreed with a handshake and occasionally very informal notes. But you know me well enough. You know you can trust me to be forthright with the terms. I would never try to deceive you."

"Of course not, but the fact of the matter is that if it has to do with business, then Mr. Lincoln probably knows more about it than I do."

The expression on Gerome's face made his frustration clear, but Nancy couldn't do anything about it. Not only that, but she had no interest to try. She wanted nothing more than to resolve Albert's affairs and be done with them.

"Now, if you'll excuse me, I have to get back to my duties." She started to close the door, but Gerome put a hand out to stop her.

"Nancy, you do know that I care very much about you. I've been doing my best to refrain from making you uncomfortable, but I've always cared deeply for you. I want to help you in any way possible."

She held his gaze for a moment, then gave a curt nod. "Thank you. I'm touched by your concern. Good day."

With that, Nancy returned to the kitchen, knowing that Gerome was probably still standing on her porch, staring at the closed door. She knew he hoped to stir her feelings for him to a deeper friendship that might lead to courtship.

"That will never happen," she murmured, shaking her head. She would remarry one day, of that she was certain, but it wouldn't be to Mr. Gerome Berkshire. Of that she was even more certain.

CHAPTER 6

"Good morning, ladies," Nancy declared, placing a platter of hot cakes on the table. "I trust you slept well."

Bedelia Clifton took her seat. "Cornelia and I passed the night quite well, although we suffered minor indigestion earlier in the evening. I fear the chicken and dumplings you served were too rich for our constitution."

"I am sorry to hear that," Nancy said with a smile. After several weeks with the women in residence, she could always count on something being too rich or sweet for the Clifton sisters. Nevertheless, she also recalled that Bedelia had taken seconds.

"I suffered no such problem," Clementine said as she took her place opposite Bedelia. "I thought them wonderful. I could have eaten them again for breakfast."

Nancy might have chuckled but for Bedelia's gasp of disapproval. "One should never eat chicken before the noon hour."

"You eat eggs, and those come from chickens and might have even grown to be chickens but for our intervention." Clementine unfolded her napkin. "I think folks have created a lot of silly rules that have little to do with reality."

"Wisdom is often lost on youth," Bedelia replied. The mousy Cornelia nodded in support.

Mimi entered the room. "Sorry for my tardiness. I couldn't find my buttonhook."

"That is why I have a specific place for every article I own," Bedelia said, looking to her sister. Cornelia nodded again and opened her mouth as if she might comment, but Bedelia continued. "Everything is in its place. That way, one always knows where any particular item may be found."

"Wise counsel, to be sure." Nancy took her seat. To placate the Clifton sisters, she had agreed to a collective grace being spoken at the table. "Shall we pray? I believe it's Clementine's turn."

They all bowed their heads, and Clementine offered a brief prayer of thanks. *Amens* were murmured, and then the women began passing platters and bowls, syrup and butter. It was several moments of controlled chaos.

"Did Mrs. Weaver get her tray?" Clementine asked Nancy. "If not, I could run it upstairs for you."

"No, I took it to her first thing. She should be content."

"It is quite strange that she never joins us for meals," Cornelia finally spoke.

Nancy handed Bedelia a platter of sausages. "She is a very private person, and there's nothing wrong with that. These new surroundings and so many people living under one roof are probably difficult for her after living alone."

"She's from the South, you know," Bedelia stated, as if that explained everything.

"Yes," Mimi replied. "Is that important?"

Bedelia pinched the bridge of her nose. "I would not have mentioned it if it weren't. The Southern rebels lost the war. She no doubt still bears the shame and humiliation of that even these long years later. And frankly, I'm of a mind that they should. It was an evil war." She lowered her voice. "Not only that, but I believe it left Mrs. Weaver a bit tetched. She talks to herself and . . ." Bedelia paused for effect, then lowered her voice even more. "She sings."

"There's nothing wrong with singing," Clementine countered. "I like a good melody myself. Perhaps you have heard me singing and thought it to be her. After all, your room is between ours."

"No, it was her." Again, Cornelia bobbed her head.

"Well, singing certainly doesn't imply insanity." Nancy decided a change of subject was needed. "Say, did you see in the paper that there's to be a creditor's sale at the store of Mrs. Ach? Black and colored grenadines will be twelve and a half cents a yard, and French lawn in a variety of colors will be twenty cents a yard. There is a small sewing room just beyond the staircase. You are all welcome to use it anytime you like."

Clementine nodded. "I nearly forgot to tell you that I went past Marshall & Co. and they are offering ten pounds of sugar for a dollar and five pounds of coffee for the same."

Nancy nodded. "That's good to know. I'll see what else they might have on sale. I'll leave David a note to come see me when he's done caring for the horse so he can drive me into town."

"I could come with you," Clementine added. "I could certainly benefit if you're going to look at the fabrics. And it sounds like a pleasant way to spend a Saturday."

"The buggy is hardly big enough." Nancy thought for a moment. "Perhaps I could drive, and we could go together and not take David. I suppose that might work."

The rest of the meal passed much the same, with light

conversation about the week to come. Once they concluded, Nancy went upstairs and knocked on Mrs. Weaver's door.

"It's me, Mrs. Weaver. I've come for your tray."

She heard the old woman shuffle across the floor and draw back the bolt on the door. It was humorous to Nancy that the old lady insisted on keeping the bolt set even during the day.

Mrs. Weaver opened the door a few inches to make certain it was really Nancy. "I will try to start bringing it down myself," she said, pulling the door back farther.

"There's no need for that, Mrs. Weaver. You pay for the service, and there's no reason I cannot accommodate you."

The tray sat on a table just inside the room. Nancy entered and picked it up with a quick glance around the room. "Are you certain you wouldn't like me to do your cleaning? I hate to think of you tiring yourself out."

"No. No. I'm perfectly capable." The old woman wore a lacy cap that hadn't been popular since the war. "I don't wish to be a burden."

"You aren't a burden but a boarder. I simply want you to have the best. You always stay shut up here in your room, and you are more than entitled to use the house and enjoy the amenities we offer. Like the bathroom. It's completely modern with running water."

Nancy didn't wish to embarrass Mrs. Weaver, but her insistence that she have a chamber pot rather than use the shared facilities only added additional duties to the poor woman's day.

"I don't mind staying in my room," Mrs. Weaver said in a hushed voice. "I prefer to live my final days in solitude and quiet."

Nancy smiled. "Very well, then. So long as you have what you need. I will continue, however, to hope that you might one day join us for our meals and evening chats. The other ladies are quite interested to know you." She headed for the door, tray in hand. "Please let me know if there's anything else you need."

Mrs. Weaver said nothing more, and once Nancy was outside the room, she heard the bolt slide back into place. The poor woman was clearly insecure about her surroundings. Nancy shook her head and started for the first floor. Hopefully in time Mrs. Weaver would learn that she could trust Nancy and the others.

The church ladies' sewing circle met at Nancy's on the first Thursday in June. She had forgotten all about agreeing to host the group until Mrs. Taylor had mentioned it at church the previous Sunday. Nancy had considered canceling but decided against it. Perhaps it would be good for her boarders to meet her church ladies. All of the women were God-fearing, even if they didn't attend the same churches, and would surely enjoy one another's company. And if not, the boarders were always able to seek solace in their rooms.

"Nancy, these shortbread cookies are delicious. Would you share the recipe?" Mrs. Taylor asked.

Mrs. Taylor was one of the best cooks in the church, and Nancy had no doubt that she could make equally tasty shortbread. She smiled. "It's a simple recipe that my mother taught me. Just three ingredients. Two cups of flour, one cup of butter, and half a cup of sugar."

"Well, they are marvelous. I must try it for myself," the older woman said, taking her third cookie.

"They are delicious, Nancy. I've always enjoyed your baking," one of the other ladies declared.

"Her meals here are nicely done," Bedelia Clifton said, surprising Nancy with her praise as she came into the dining room where they were gathered. "One always fears when boarding that the food might suffer, but in our situation, we are quite blessed."

"Oh, I am not surprised by that," Mrs. Taylor said, smiling at Nancy. "I've sampled Nancy's cooking for years at church potluck suppers."

"Miss Clifton and her sister sometimes offer to help me prepare our meals," Nancy said, thinking it only right that she return the compliment. "I am blessed with good boarders."

Bedelia smiled and gave a nod. "One must always be willing to help where needed. The Lord expects no less of us. Which is why I've come to see if I might lend a hand in the sewing. I'm quite good with a needle. Cornelia is as well, but she's under the weather. A summer cold, don't you know."

"Oh, that is too bad," one of the church ladies declared.

"I, for one, would be happy to have you join us, Miss Clifton," Mrs. Taylor said. "We are making blankets and quilts for the poor. Today we are hemming edges. Do join us. You may borrow a needle from me."

Bedelia pulled a needle case from her pocket. "I have my own, but thank you." She took the chair by Mrs. Taylor and opened the case. "I find it valuable to always have a needle and thread readily available."

"Indeed," one of the other women replied.

They sewed around the table for nearly an hour, sharing conversation about the city and what was happening to assist the poor. Nancy learned that several churches in the area were working together to fund a poorhouse. They wanted to build something for those who had no shelter during the winter months.

Nancy thought of her more-than-ample house. There were still rooms she hardly used. Perhaps she could turn them into bedrooms as well. After all, she'd had no trouble filling the upstairs rooms, and in each situation the women were operating on very limited funds. But for the grace of God they might also be among those in need of the poorhouse. Women really were up against all odds when they had no family to care for them. Especially the elderly women, who could rarely earn a living.

The door knocker sounded, and Nancy excused herself to see who it was. To her surprise, Mrs. Mortenson bounded in without waiting for Nancy to greet her.

"Oh, my dear, you look so pale," the old woman said, her lips tightening into a straight line. "I've been quite worried, and when I heard at church that you were hosting the sewing circle today, I was gravely concerned. Do you think it wise for your health?"

"I'm feeling perfectly fine, Mrs. Mortenson. Won't you come in and join us in the dining room?"

"For a short time, but alas, I cannot sew. My eyes, don't you know. They're weak, and the doctor has demanded I rest from tedious chores."

"Of course."

"Agnes, we didn't expect you today," Mrs. Taylor said, rising to greet her friend as she came into the room. "So glad you could come."

"Well, I won't be able to sew, as I was telling Nancy, poor girl. The doctor has simply forbidden it. My eyes are too weak."

"Never mind that," Mrs. Taylor said. "Join us anyway. We were just discussing the new poorhouse."

Mrs. Mortenson looked around and noted the only empty chair. "I see this must have been Nancy's place."

Nancy quickly brought another chair into the room. "Here you are. No need to worry."

Agnes Mortenson placed her ample frame upon the wooden chair and touched her hand to her feathered hat as if it had come loose. "You are all doing some lovely work. I'm certain the poor will appreciate your efforts. Goodness, but there seems to be so many more of them than there used to be. Mr. Mortenson said there were four older men sleeping near the docks by his manufacturing company. He took them wool blankets several months back, and they were most grateful."

"My husband said a dozen or so men were rounded up and run out of the park just two days ago," one of the women added.

Mrs. Mortenson shook her head and lowered her voice. "Some are criminal types. One can never be sure, but often you can tell by the eyes and the forehead."

Seeing the cookie platter had nearly emptied, Nancy excused herself to refill it and bring more tea while the women discussed the plight of the poor. She hadn't been in the kitchen long, however, when she heard the focus of the conversation turn to Nancy herself.

"The poor child is much too young to stay a widow. The Bible makes that clear. She needs a husband," Mrs. Mortenson said in an authoritative tone. "It's not good for her to be alone."

"She isn't alone," Bedelia Clifton chimed in. Nancy had to smile at the thought of Mrs. Mortenson receiving her come-uppance from the younger spinster. "She has all of us here at the house."

"Yes, yes, but you will come and go. You are but boarders paying for your room. Nancy needs someone who will remain— someone to love her and give her children. Although"—Mrs.

Mortenson lowered her voice—"it remains to be seen if Nancy can bear children."

Nancy frowned and filled the teapot with hot water. She didn't like that these women were discussing her condition.

"The Lord gives children as a gift and will give to whom He desires. Many a woman is childless for the greater glory of the Lord," Bedelia remarked with as great an authority as Mrs. Mortenson. "We can see that in the Good Book as well."

Mrs. Taylor came into the kitchen as Nancy was pouring water into the teapot. She had only to glance at Nancy to see her discomfort. "Pay them no mind, child."

"I try not to, but I must admit I question my circumstances as much as they do. I feel such an emptiness in my life. I've long wanted to be a mother. I see others with their arms full—their homes full of children—and wonder why I might not have had just one. One child to satisfy my longing."

Mrs. Taylor smiled and put her hand on Nancy's arm. "Perhaps a child is not the answer."

Nancy frowned. "Then what is?"

"You once told me yours was a loveless marriage," Mrs. Taylor said, lowering her voice. "Perhaps such love would have gone a long way to filling your empty places. However, I tend to believe that the true void comes from your anger with the Lord."

Nancy quickly turned away to replace the waterpot on the stove. "My mother would agree with you." She had little desire to discuss this topic, but Mrs. Taylor was too dear a friend, and an older one at that. Nancy would do nothing to insult or demean her by arguing with her.

"He is always there for you, child."

Nancy met the older woman's gaze. Her skin was wrinkled and lined from years of care, but her eyes were sharp. "Do you truly suppose He would be there for me when I've avoided Him most of my life?"

If her question shocked the old woman, Mrs. Taylor showed no sign of it. "I was once that way myself. I had little time or interest in God, but He changed my heart."

This topic rubbed on the open wound that was Nancy's heart. "My mother always says that God is there for me—that He understands me and why I make the decisions I make." She paused, remembering their last visit. "Which brings me to something equally discomforting. I'm afraid I wasn't very kind to Mother or Father when they were here last. I haven't even bothered to write and apologize."

"Perhaps you should."

Nancy focused on putting cookies on the platter. "I should, but I can't seem to bring myself to do it. What if they won't forgive me this time?"

"Do you honestly believe your mother could refuse to forgive you? I've met her and spoken to her at church. She loves you. Just as God loves you. Neither would refuse forgiveness, Nancy. You should just write to your parents and explain your heart."

"Maybe I would, if I could figure out my heart." Nancy straightened as she placed the last cookie on the tray. "There. We'd best get these to the ladies, although they seem happy enough." She could hear their laughter through the closed kitchen door.

"Oh, I nearly forgot why I came to find you. One of your boarders returned just now with her brother."

Nancy knew that could be none other than Seth Carpenter. The laughter rose in volume, and Nancy smiled. "Sounds like they're enjoying his company." She picked up the pot of tea. "I hope I have enough cups on the sideboard."

Mrs. Taylor grabbed the platter of cookies and followed Nancy into the dining room, where Seth was regaling the ladies with some tale about his childhood adventures.

"Oh, here she is." Mrs. Mortenson chuckled and elbowed the lady next to her. "I think our plan is perfect."

Nancy felt a shiver go up her spine. "What plan? What's going on?" She put the pot on the buffet and waited for someone to speak.

"Clementine mentioned that I knew you," Seth said, smiling, "and the ladies wanted to know how we are all acquainted."

"I see. Well, we are neighboring friends from long ago."

"Which makes Seth quite perfect for our plan," Mrs. Mortenson began. "You see, we are of a mind that you must remarry, and soon. The Bible says it's not good for man to be alone."

"Paul also says that widows would do well to remain single," Nancy countered.

Mrs. Mortenson looked momentarily flummoxed, but Bedelia Clifton was not. "Indeed, it is good to remain single. You can better focus on your work for the Lord if you haven't a man to concern yourself with."

Clementine looked at Nancy with an apologetic smile. "The situation is this. The ladies were discussing the possibility of you and Seth getting to know each other better. That's when Seth mentioned that he knew you quite well, and because of that, Mrs. Mortenson thought it only right that you two should . . . well, consider—"

"An outing," Seth interjected. "I told them I would be more than happy to escort you to dinner and a play tomorrow evening."

Nancy didn't know what to say. She looked at the expectant expressions of her friends and then again at Seth's smiling face.

"Tell him you will, please," Clementine begged. "That way I won't have to go in your stead."

Seth moved toward Nancy. "No, don't feel you have to go. I just wanted you to know that I would be happy to take you."

Nancy could see the sincerity in his eyes. "I . . . well . . . it's only been a few months since Albert died." She looked at the women around her table. "What will people say?"

"That you're young and deserving of love," Mrs. Mortenson declared. "Besides, who cares what they will say? The only people who matter are right here with you today, and we're encouraging you to go."

"Well, some are," Bedelia said with a huff.

"I promise to bring you right home if you don't enjoy being out," Seth said, his voice soft.

Nancy felt her resolve slip away. "Very well, then. I will go with you."

CHAPTER 7

Nancy couldn't believe how easy it was to be with Seth. Over dinner, they talked about the old days in Oregon City and the dreams they had for their futures.

"The town hasn't changed that much," Seth said just before finishing off his steak.

"I doubt Oregon City will ever change. It's a quaint town that seems to be lost in time." Nancy hadn't thought of it with fondness in some time. "I sometimes miss the slower pace."

"Me too. After living in Washington, Oregon City is as silent as the grave."

"Hardly," Nancy said, laughing. "My family and their saw-mills see to that."

Seth asked after her aunts and uncles and then shared some of what had been happening in his family. Eventually the talk came around to Albert.

"I was surprised when I heard you'd married a stranger," Seth said.

"Yes, well, I suppose you were no more surprised than everyone else." She shrugged. "But I had my reasons, although now I'm not exactly sure what they were. I know that must sound terrible, but I think I married more to get away from my family and Oregon City than because of love."

She was surprised by the things she admitted but did her best not to show it. Seth made her feel safe, and sharing the past was not nearly so intimidating with him.

"I think people often marry for reasons other than love." His comment held no condemnation. "In fact, I think love is probably rarer than you think."

"I can believe that." Nancy considered her own choice. "I thought Albert very interesting. He told me things but never seemed to be trying to impress me. He was who he was and never tried to impress anyone. I liked that about him."

Seth chuckled. "I always figure, why try to impress people? Folks are either going to like you or they aren't. If I'm not myself, they'll find out soon enough, and if they only liked the impression I gave, then they're going to be disappointed."

"Exactly." Nancy smiled. Seth seemed to understand her, and that gave her a great sense of acceptance.

By the time they reached the theater, she felt more at ease than she had in years. Albert had hated plays and musicals, so they rarely went. He didn't mind, however, that Nancy had gone on occasion with friends, but for her it wasn't as much fun. There was no one to talk to later about the story or the characters. With Seth it was completely the opposite.

"Did you enjoy the play?" he asked, helping her with her shawl as they made their way outside. "I thought the character of Mrs. Wigglesworth was hysterical. I'm afraid that if I met the actress on the street, I'd probably burst out laughing."

Nancy giggled. "I'd keep imagining her saying, 'I do believe I have the vapors!'"

Seth roared with laughter. "Exactly."

"I had heard such good things about this little comedy, but since Albert died, I didn't figure I could make it to the play."

"That's when you need something like this the most," Seth argued. "Laughter and good friends."

"Yet tradition hides us away. People who experience a death are supposed to die themselves, in a way."

"That makes little sense. When a person loses someone, that is the time they should be surrounded by loved ones. Friends and family can make all the difference in seeing a person through bad times. Like tonight. I believe you needed a diversion."

Nancy knew he was right. "Thank you. You have certainly been a good friend, and I enjoyed this evening out very much."

"I like being your friend, Nancy. There's something comforting about having a past with someone and knowing their history. It makes me feel safe to be myself."

Nancy felt her cheeks flush and looked away. "I suppose I should admit that I was apprehensive for the very reasons you think beneficial. You know too much about me."

He leaned in closer. "And I pledge to guard all of your secrets to the grave."

She could hear the teasing in his tone, but at the same time there was a depth of sincerity she hadn't expected. Nancy hadn't felt entirely comfortable coming out that evening, because even if she and Albert's marriage had lacked love, she was still in mourning. Mourning for her youth. Mourning for her dreams.

Of course, the people standing around them at the theatre didn't know her or her circumstances, and because she'd chosen to wear dark green instead of black, there was no reason they should. Still, she knew and was uncomfortable at just how much fun she'd had with Seth Carpenter, and of how well he seemed to anticipate her every need.

"Say, would you like to walk instead of catching a cab?" he asked. "It's a pleasant evening, and the streetlights will show us the way."

"I would be fine with that." She glanced around at the many people fighting to get a carriage. "Besides, I think it would be some time before we were able to secure a ride."

"I agree." He took her arm, and they began the long walk back to the boardinghouse.

For several blocks they said nothing. Nancy wondered what Seth was thinking. The evening had been forced on him, and she suddenly felt guilty for that even though she'd had nothing to do with it.

"I want to apologize for the way you were backed into a corner regarding this evening," she said.

"Whatever are you talking about?" He looked at her and shook his head. "I was hardly forced to invite a beautiful woman to spend the evening with me."

She felt her face grow hot. "I know the church ladies were rather ruthless in their attack. I heard a good portion of it."

"They were just enthusiastic. They love you, Nancy, and didn't want to see you wasting away in mourning. I feel the same way. You're much too young to give up on life."

"I'm not giving up on it. I'm just taking time to figure out what I want."

"And have you figured that out?" His tone was light, suggesting he was teasing.

"To some degree. I've been working to figure it out a little each day."

"What have you come up with so far?" They stopped at the

street corner until the way was clear, and then Seth held fast to her arm and pulled her along. "Come on, pick up the pace or we'll be run down by that oncoming freight wagon."

Nancy craned her head around Seth's tall frame to see what he was talking about. The wagon was bearing down on them fast. "Goodness, you'd think they'd be more mindful of people."

"They don't have to. They're bigger," he said, laughing as they reached the other side. "Now, back to my question. What have you come up with so far?"

"Regarding what?" Nancy hadn't really forgotten what they were talking about but had hoped Seth would.

"What you want in life."

"Oh. Well, I suppose I want what most everyone else wants. I want a good life, a home, and a family."

"What else?"

She frowned and settled her gaze on a line of distant houses. "I don't know. Not for sure. I'm still thinking it through."

"Tell me about Albert Pritchard."

This surprised her. "I'm not sure I can. In his death I have learned how little I knew him in life."

"How did you meet?"

"The first time was when he did some business at the sawmill in Oregon City. I happened to be there with Mother. He caught my attention."

"How? Was he witty? A great conversationalist?"

She smiled. "He was handsome, and I was just a girl."

"And was it love at first sight for you both?"

She saw no reason to lie to Seth. "No. It wasn't love at all. I mean, I think at first I had a girlish infatuation. I saw the potential for him to take me away from Oregon City and my folks."

"And you wanted that?"

She nodded. "More than I wanted anything else."

"But why, Nancy? Your family is a great bunch of folks, as I recall."

She shrugged. "I suppose it depends on which side of the gate you stand. My folks are good people—my aunts, uncles, and cousins, they're all good. I guess I just wanted something more."

"And Albert gave you that?"

"To be honest?" She slowed her step and looked at Seth in the dimming light. "No. Albert didn't turn out to be the man I thought he was."

"And you were married for eight years?"

"Yes. Eight long, lonely years." She bit her lip. She hadn't meant to say that aloud.

"I'm so sorry, Nancy. I had no idea."

"Most people didn't know, and frankly I don't know why I'm telling you except that you're an old friend and easy to talk to."

"I hope you know you can always talk to me about anything."

His voice was soft and so sincere. Nancy felt touched by his kind spirit. "Thank you."

"It's not like it takes much effort."

Nancy laughed. "My family would say otherwise."

"Families often do. Now, please continue. Did Albert own the store when you married? Was he already established in Portland?"

"Yes. He had been running the store for about a year before we wed. Before that, he worked on the river. He was good at saving his money and at making a profit. In fact, when he first proposed, he told me we would have to wait three years to marry until he had a decent profit set aside. Then one day, barely six months later, he told me that the store had been wildly successful and we could marry right away. I was just eighteen and knew my parents wouldn't approve, so I ran away to marry him here in Portland."

"I remember Gabe telling me that in a letter. I was back east at school, and I remember your marriage upset him."

"I'm sure. It was quite the gossip for a long time." She grew uncomfortable and changed the subject. "What about Albert's papers and ledgers? Have you managed to figure it all out?"

"I've been working on it. There are some peculiarities, to be sure."

"Like the coded ledger entries? I looked through them when I was collecting them. I had no idea what most of the notations meant, but they seemed particularly strange."

"Indeed. I'm working on it, along with the nameless IOUs."

"I didn't notice those. I suppose I was in a hurry to collect things and be off."

"Well, they caught my attention because John said your husband didn't believe in having debts."

Nancy nodded. "That's true. If he couldn't pay cash for something, he didn't buy it. He saved his money faithfully and always told me to do the same with any extra that came my way."

"Yet he borrowed money from someone, at least according to those IOUs."

"I can't see that being the case. Are you sure they aren't IOUs from someone who has borrowed from Albert?"

Seth slowed his step. "No. That much is clear. These are pledges for Albert to repay. The only thing in question is to whom the money is owed."

They had reached the boardinghouse, and Nancy could just make out someone on the porch. "It would appear I have a guest." As they drew near, she stiffened. "That's Mr. Hanson.

He's the one I mentioned coming to see me months ago. He says Albert owes him weapons and whiskey."

"I'll speak to him about it," Seth said, slipping his hand in hers. "Don't be afraid."

"It just makes me uncomfortable. I know so little about what Albert did in his business. I feel bad if this man paid out a great deal of money and has nothing to show for it."

"I assure you, John and I will see him fairly dealt with."

They approached the porch steps, and Nancy pulled away from Seth's hold.

Hanson got to his feet. "Evenin', Mrs. Pritchard. Do you remember me?"

"Yes, I was just explaining who you are to Mr. Carpenter. He's one of my lawyers."

Seth extended his hand. "Mr. Hanson."

They shook hands, sizing each other up. Hanson spoke first. "I meant to return sooner, but business kept me away. I've come to find out about my whiskey and guns."

Nancy looked to Seth. "I know nothing about them, Mr. Hanson. However, Mr. Lincoln and Mr. Carpenter have been handling my husband's estate."

"We would be happy to speak with you in our offices," Seth declared, taking a step back to stand with Nancy.

"Why can't you just speak to me here and now?" Hanson asked. "I want my goods."

"I understand that, but there's something you must understand. There are no holdings of whiskey or guns at the store. No record of a sale or even an order of such items with your name on it."

"We dealt in a handshake," Hanson said gruffly. "It's always been good enough in the past."

"Were you used to purchasing firearms and whiskey from Mr. Pritchard?"

"Yes. We'd been doing it for years."

"To what purpose?" Seth asked. "Were you setting up a militia?"

Hanson wasn't to be intimidated. "I travel and resell to folks who aren't close to a city."

Seth nodded. "Do you by any chance know if Mr. Pritchard had a separate warehouse somewhere?"

"I figured he did, but I don't know where."

"And neither do we, unfortunately. If there are whiskey and weapons to be had, then they must be stored in another location, since there was no sign of them at the store. And so far no one seems to have any idea where that might be. It almost appears as though Mr. Pritchard was trying to conceal his connection to that inventory."

"It doesn't change the fact that I want my goods. Understand?"

Hanson was at least double Seth's weight, and Nancy feared what might happen if he decided to strike a blow.

"I completely understand." Seth smiled and reached inside his coat pocket.

Hanson stepped back and looked defensive. When Seth drew out a business card, Hanson remained stiff, and his eyes narrowed.

"This is my card," Seth said. "The address to our office is just under my name. Come see me tomorrow around ten, and we'll do what we can to accommodate you. I'm sure we can figure out something—perhaps a refund, if you can help us with any kind of proof of your order."

Hanson took the card. "A refund, eh?"

"Of course. If Mr. Pritchard took your money and didn't supply the goods you ordered, then you are entitled to a refund."

The screen door opened, and Clementine smiled at them from just inside the house. "I thought I heard you out here. Seth, can you come to the kitchen and help me with the stove? The oven door is loose."

"Sure thing. I'll be right there." He looked at Mr. Hanson. "I'll see you tomorrow." Seth headed toward the door.

Nancy followed quickly behind him, but not quickly enough. Hanson reached out and grabbed her arm. She wanted to call out to Seth, who was already deep in conversation with Clementine, but Hanson gave her no chance.

"Listen to me, lady. I don't want a refund. I want to know where those guns are. The whiskey too. I'm tired of waiting, and you'd best get to finding my stuff."

"But with a refund you could easily purchase replacements. I fail to understand why you must have them from my husband's stock."

"Look for a map. He should have had one—maybe several. He's probably got the goods hidden near the river somewhere."

"But why? It's perfectly legal to sell whiskey and firearms."

"Not to the Indians, it ain't." Hanson tightened his hold. "Understand?"

"No." Nancy shook her head. "Why would any decent man sell either one to the Indians? It's only been three years since Little Bighorn and the death of all those soldiers. Why would you want Indians to have whiskey or guns?"

Hanson laughed and pushed her back toward the door. "That's something you should have asked your husband. What I want is for you to find his hiding place and do it quickly.

There's bound to be something written down somewhere. You just need to find it. Oh, and leave the lawyers out of it. They don't need to know."

"I won't be pushed around, Mr. Hanson. I am taking this matter to the authorities first thing in the morning."

He shook his head and gave her a leering smile. "I don't think so, Mrs. Pritchard. If you go to them, I'll make sure they have all the evidence they need to put the blame solely on you and your husband."

"Me? I had nothing to do with it."

"Maybe not, but I can sound pretty convincing. It wouldn't be all that hard to tie you and him to the whiskey and guns."

Nancy could hardly breathe. "I don't know anything about any of this. You couldn't offer evidence against me because there isn't any."

"Well, it's easy enough to make up. I guess you'd better figure it out, and quick." He turned and sauntered down the porch steps as if nothing were amiss. "We had a good thing going, your husband and I, and I don't intend to start over. You find those caches and get in touch."

Nancy shook so hard she had trouble gripping the doorknob. How dare he treat her in such a manner, and with Seth just steps away. Apparently Hanson wasn't afraid of anyone or anything, and that was enough to make him a definite threat.

But while that was troubling, Nancy could hardly fathom the information he'd just shared. Albert had been selling whiskey and guns to the Indians. Why? He hated people of color— maybe Indians most of all. Why would he sell them anything, much less weapons?

CHAPTER 8

Seth pored over the ledgers and paperwork that Nancy had furnished from her husband's offices. The collection of ledgers she'd found in his safe were written in a type of code, but after a few hours of playing with the letters and numbers, Seth was able to figure it out. This was an accounting of rifles and liquor bought and sold. There was no information related to whom Pritchard had sold the goods, but it was at least proof of their existence. Given there were five books, Seth believed there were probably five separate caches of goods. Perhaps not big warehouses as they had previously thought, but instead maybe nothing bigger than a hidden shack or even someone's attic. Maybe Pritchard's attic. Seth would have to ask Nancy if she'd been up there to look around.

He leaned back in his leather chair and frowned as he considered the time. Ten thirty. He hadn't really expected Hanson to show up, but there had been that lingering hope that he might. Seth didn't know much about Hanson, but he intended to. He wanted to know the company the man kept and what he did for a living. It was clear he was involved in supplying the Indians with illegal arms and drink, and that Pritchard had supplied him. There was no doubt others were involved. Hanson was a nobody, and there were still those strange IOUs that lacked the name of the lender. They totaled a considerable amount, so no doubt someone would be seeking payback. Hanson didn't have that kind of money, so there had to be another person, if not several, who were moneyed and capable of financing this plot, and that was why Seth was here.

Months ago, Seth had been approached by the government back east to help them with an ongoing problem. The Oregon Indians were for the most part peaceful, but from time to time there were problems and uprisings. Not even two years earlier, when the Nez Perce were to have been moved from the Wallowa Valley in northeastern Oregon, it turned into an all-out war between the Indians and whites. Chief Joseph had surrendered his people eventually, but that didn't end the hostilities. There would forever be a battle between the white man and his Indian neighbor. These days, most of the skirmishes were minor and generally the result of too much alcohol, but the government wanted it to end. They wanted to quell any further concerns once and for all. The country was rapidly moving toward a new century, and there was no room for such attitudes in the modern world.

Seth rubbed the bridge of his nose where the spark of a headache was brewing. But for a handful of troublemakers, they could have peace. Most Indians had been rounded up and put on reservations, but that wasn't enough for those white men who found coexistence impossible. It wasn't enough to force the Indians off their own land and onto small reservations—often nowhere near their original homeland. These men wanted to see an end to the Indian race altogether. They had no desire to live in peace.

Their protests had been loud and clear. The men who sought the demise of the Indians pointed to Little Bighorn and the

Red River battles. They argued that the Indians refused to be civilized and would forever fight against the white man. And people listened. People were easily frightened when bombarded with detailed descriptions of battles and mutilations. Entire lectures were given back east about women and children being killed in their sleep by the heathen savage.

Hate-filled men loved to stir up hate. Worse still, some of those men saw nothing wrong with pushing things to a conclusion that suited their needs, especially if a profit could be had. They would pretend to be a friend to the Indian, all while supplying them with whiskey and beer. Once they had a firm influence over the men of the tribe, these false friends would start talking about injustice and how the Indians should rise up to force the whites to yield their land. Then guns came into the picture. It was a natural progression. Once the Indians were armed and started making demands, it brought down the army to quell them, and the next thing they knew, they were being relocated to an even smaller reservation in an even more remote location. Seth had heard more than one of the white men responsible declare that it was like taking candy from babies and resulted in reservation land returning to proper white ownership.

When the removal of the Indians had first started, they were to have been given all the land west of the Mississippi, but little by little that land was whittled down. What had once been large, spacious reservations with plenty of resources were now reduced to insignificant acreage with poor soil and very little game. The Indians were supposed to assimilate and imitate the white man in their clothes and speech. They were no longer to be Nez Perce, Modoc, Cayuse, or Tillamook. Instead they were told to cut their hair in the white man's fashion, speak the white man's language, and forget their cultural heritage.

"You look rather distressed."

Seth opened his eyes to find John Lincoln standing in the open doorway of his office. "I'm troubled."

"Hanson ever show up?"

"No. I didn't figure he would." Seth stood. "Still, it's enough to know he's involved. It's more than I had a week ago. Not only that, but now I have no doubt that Nancy was in no way involved with her husband's affairs."

"I was sure she wasn't," John said, smiling. "I've known her from church all these years, and I've never heard her speak against the Indians or any other people."

Seth nodded. "Still, I had to learn it for myself. A lot of folks pretend to feel one way but really feel another. When Hanson said what he did, however, I heard the fear in her voice. I know she's confused by all of this."

"Are you going to tell her about your investigation?" John asked, his eyebrows raising just a bit. "Tell her you overheard what Hanson said to her that night?"

"I can't. Not yet." Seth shook his head. "I can't risk it."

Nancy looked at the trunks and crates she had stacked in the corner of her bedroom. They were all that was left of Albert, save the store. She was determined to figure out what he had been up to. He had lived a life she knew nothing about—perhaps had even died because of it. She remembered Mrs. Mortenson mentioning the possibility of murder. If Albert had been involved in selling guns to the Indians, perhaps someone *had* murdered him. How terrible that would be.

"Poor man," she whispered to the room.

This thought made her feel even guiltier. How could a person live with someone for eight years and not know them any better than she did Albert? How could her husband have been involved in the illegal sale of arms and liquor to the Indians? Many times she'd shared articles from the newspaper on the problems created by the Indians getting ahold of liquor, and he knew Uncle Adam and Aunt Mercy worked on a reservation to help the Indians. She had often commented on their work and the letters they had sent. He'd even met them once when they came to Portland.

Nancy had been afraid when the Nez Perce War broke out. Afraid for her aunt and uncle, as well as for herself. What if the other tribes decided the Nez Perce had the right idea and rose up in rebellion? Could they hope to escape unharmed?

Albert had thought her fears unmerited. He'd reminded her of the army posts and the large number of soldiers who would fight on their behalf. He had also declared he would fight to the death to protect her and their property.

A shiver went up her spine. She knew Albert had hated the Indians. He hated anyone who wasn't white. He'd applauded the efforts of those communities who gathered up the Chinese, blacks, Mexicans, and any other people of color and ran them out of town. Like Gerome, he felt America belonged solely to white people and that if the others wanted to remain, they would do so as subservient slaves.

How could she not have known he was so bigoted and ugly when she married him? But she had seen Albert only as a way to depart her home, where painful memories of her brother's death and the restrictive, religious nature of her parents sent her looking for an escape. Sadly, that escape hadn't brought any real peace of mind or happiness.

She sighed and brought one of the trunks to her bed. She

opened it and sifted through the contents. It was mostly clothing. She would donate it to the church's collection for the poor.
A smile came to her lips. Perhaps a poor black or Indian man
would benefit.

She went through the next trunk and found more clothes
as well as a few articles of a personal nature: Albert's shaving
mug and brush, his razor and hairbrush. She held the brush
and touched the strands of sandy-colored hair.

"Oh, Albert. What did you do?"

She'd never really considered him to be a bad man. The truth
was, most white men felt as he did toward people of color.
White men were convinced they were superior in every way.
Better educated. Better prepared for life. And given they had
done little to help the newly freed slaves or the Indians trapped
on reservations, perhaps they were. Still, that wasn't the fault
of those who'd been ignored and pushed aside.

Aunt Mercy had once told Nancy how eager the Indian children were to learn to read English, but not at the price of forgetting their own language. They longed to know more about
the white man's ways, but in the hopes of helping their people,
not for the purpose of forgetting their ancestry.

Another truth Nancy had learned was that not all Indians
wanted war. Aunt Mercy and Uncle Adam had spoken numerous times about the desires of the Indian people. Most just
wanted to be allowed to roam as they once had or to return to
the land of their birth. They didn't want war with the white
settlers. In fact, they wanted nothing to do with white people.
Albert had done nothing more than shrug when Nancy had
shared this information. He refused to discuss it, choosing instead to disregard such thoughts and the people involved.

Nancy sorted through the rest of Albert's things, finally

coming to a crate of books she'd taken from his nightstand. He had loved to read before going to bed. She looked over the titles. Most were histories, save one. She hadn't realized this one was different until she opened it and began leafing through the pages.

It was a journal with a royal blue cover, filled with drawings of the river and its different trouble spots. Albert had meticulously drawn out the shoreline and any obstacles, and numbers noted the water's depth and the current's speed. At the top of each sketch was listed the latitude and longitude and the river's name. Most of the drawings were of the Willamette or Columbia and dated years before she'd even met Albert.

She came to the end of the drawings and found blank pages for the last quarter of the book. She was ready to set it aside when she saw that at the very end there was another set of drawings. These were similar to the others, depicting shorelines and obstacles, but they contained no longitude or latitude. No date or river name.

Nancy felt the hair on her arms rise. Was this what Hanson had been talking about? Were these maps to Albert's secret store of weapons? She turned the page and found another drawing and then another. There were a half dozen in total. She studied them for some time. Each showed specific details regarding the river and the landscape. One even noted a rocky ravine and a waterfall. There were also several numbers marked on the shoreline, but she had no idea what they meant.

The second drawing held her attention the longest. There was something familiar about it. She turned it first one way and then another. It reminded her of the river's shoreline in an area where she and Albert used to picnic in the early days of their marriage. The outings had always been spontaneous.

Albert would suggest out of the blue that they go for a picnic. He would tell her to pack a lunch and then spirit her away using the buggy. They would drive along the river for several miles to the south. She was almost certain she could find it again.

Nancy had always been encouraged by those outings. She felt certain with each occasion that Albert was changing for the better—that he was learning to enjoy her company. But each time, as she began to set up their picnic, Albert would excuse himself, telling Nancy to stay while he explored to make sure the area was safe. She had offered to go with him, but he had laughed it off, telling her he wouldn't be long. Perhaps he was scouting out a place for his secret cache. Perhaps he already had the cache and was checking on his supplies.

She looked at Albert's things now deposited in piles around her room. David would be there to see to the horse soon, and she'd ask him to load it all up and take it to the pastor's house. Maybe she could also ask him to take her for a drive.

Nancy shook her head. She couldn't tell anyone about this just yet. She needed to know what Albert had been involved in, but she didn't want to help Hanson get the guns and cause problems on the reservation. He might be watching her even now.

She thought of Seth. She could tell him what she'd found—what Hanson had threatened. Seth knew her. He wouldn't believe that she'd taken part in the illegal sales.

Or would he?

She hugged the river journal to her chest. "What should I do?" She glanced heavenward. If she prayed for guidance, would God even answer? He hadn't answered before, all those years ago. He hadn't been there when her little brother had died.

Her heart hardened. No, she wouldn't pray. She wouldn't be disappointed again by a God who didn't care.

CHAPTER 9

"S ister and I will return promptly at four," Bedelia Clifton announced. She buttoned a lightweight coat over her spindly frame. "We will be sorting clothes for the poor at the Methodist church until then if you need us."

"Very good. I hope you have a grand time of it." Nancy finished clearing the luncheon dishes from the table, stacking them on the tray she'd just retrieved from Mrs. Weaver's room.

"Oh, we will," Bedelia assured her. "We always sing hymns of praise and take turns reading Scripture. It's a blessing to the soul."

Nancy nodded. "I'll be doing laundry today—delicates—so if you have anything you'd like me to take care of, please see that it's in the basket."

"Oh dear, no. Sister and I are quite capable of handling our private articles." Bedelia shook her head. "I've always been uncomfortable doing it any other way."

Nancy stacked the last of the silverware on the tray. "That's fine. Everyone has their preference."

"Sister, I cannot find the mate to my yellow glove. I have

one." Cornelia Clifton held it up as proof. "But the other has simply disappeared."

"You are always losing your things. How many times have I told you that if you pin each pair of gloves together, this wouldn't happen? It's such a simple means of management and perfect for when it's time to launder them. Goodness, how will you ever manage without me? Come, let us go to our room and search out the missing glove."

Nancy smiled as Bedelia led her sister back upstairs. They were such a funny pair. Bedelia believed herself to have the answer for everything, and Cornelia quite willingly allowed her sister to order her about and begrudge her a simple mistake. Nancy couldn't imagine her younger sister, Meg, allowing such treatment.

She took the tray of dishes to the sink and began washing up. It wasn't long until she heard Bedelia berating Cornelia as they made their way downstairs once again.

"You only have one pair of yellow gloves, sister. Remember this. Gloves do not materialize out of thin air, and if you need to buy another pair, we will have to plan for that. Our budget is quite firm. When we return home, we will simply have to search again."

"Perhaps I won't need yellow gloves in the future," Cornelia replied in a hesitant voice.

"Not need yellow gloves?" Bedelia gave a huff. "That will indeed be the day."

Nancy almost laughed out loud. She didn't own a pair of yellow gloves, nor had she ever needed them.

She dried her hands on her apron and headed back to the dining room to see the ladies off. She smiled at poor Cornelia, who had changed her entire ensemble to match the pale blue gloves she now wore.

"I will see you ladies at four," Nancy said.

As they reached the front door, Seth Carpenter was just coming up the walk. Nancy quickly raised a hand to her hair, hoping she didn't look too bad.

"Mr. Carpenter," Bedelia said as she stepped through the doorway. "I'm afraid Mrs. Pritchard is not receiving. Sister and I are just heading out, and she will be very much alone."

Seth smiled and tipped his hat. "Ladies." He looked past Bedelia to Nancy. "Are you going to town?"

"Not me. They are," Nancy replied. "I plan to work here."

"Wonderful. Then I can discuss some business with you."

"That would hardly be appropriate without someone else here," Bedelia replied, looking down her pointed nose.

"Mrs. Weaver is here. She is chaperone enough." Nancy was eager to dismiss the meddlesome sisters. She wanted to talk to Seth and learn what he had to discuss.

"It's not appropriate for a young widow to entertain a man in the house alone. Mrs. Weaver will not even venture from her room, and Mr. Carpenter's sister and Mrs. Bryant have gone shopping. A young widow such as yourself cannot receive a man in such circumstances." Bedelia looked at Nancy as if daring her to say otherwise. She had the tone of a disapproving mother, and Nancy had little patience for her.

"I am a grown woman—a widow and a homeowner, Miss Clifton. I believe I know how to care for myself. Not only that, but this man is my lawyer."

"It isn't a matter of knowing how to care for yourself, nor his occupation. This is about your reputation and modesty. To have a man in the house without the company of others suggests a far too intimate situation. Added to that is his obvious interest in you and the fact that you have gone out together as a potential courting couple."

"We are hardly courting," Nancy protested and looked to Seth for support. "He's here as my lawyer. I have to manage my late husband's affairs."

Her frustration was mounting by the minute. How dare this homely spinster challenge her integrity?

"A godly woman would guard her reputation at all costs," Bedelia said in her authoritative manner. "A Christian woman would know the value of such things."

"So now you're telling me I'm not a Christian?"

Bedelia merely looked at Nancy as if waiting for her to get the joke.

Nancy was in no mood. "Perhaps I need less judgmental tenants."

"Ladies, I believe I have a solution. Nancy, you and I can sit on the porch in plain view of the world. I won't keep you long, and that way your reputation will be in no way compromised." Seth smiled at Bedelia. "Would that be acceptable, Miss Clifton?"

Bedelia considered the matter for a moment. "I suppose it would suffice." She looked at Nancy. "It is not my place to judge the heart, but the appearance of evil must be managed for the sake of all who live here." She raised her chin a little higher and turned to Cornelia. "Let's go, sister. We're already late due to your gloves."

The two women made their way down the steps and headed downtown. Nancy wanted to throw something at them. How dare they treat her like a wanton woman! All simply because she saw nothing wrong with inviting her lawyer into the house. And that was all it was. After all, she'd grown up with Seth being around all the time. What was the harm now?

"I'm sorry about that." She moved to the open door. "Come on in."

Seth shook his head. "Let's just stay out here. I offered the solution, and it's not an uncomfortable day. Besides, you have a lovely porch." He went to the rocker and plopped down.

"I won't be dictated to by those religious harpies. I've done nothing wrong." Nancy stormed over to the wicker settee. "I'm a woman of honorable reputation." The more she reiterated that fact, however, the guiltier she felt.

"I agree. Just think of it this way. You saved poor Miss Clifton from spending the afternoon thinking of what sinful things we might have done had we gone inside the house." He smiled. "Honestly, Nancy, don't let it bother you. Perhaps her faith and self-control aren't as strong as yours."

"I'm just tired of people having something to say about what I do or don't do. People are always judging me."

"What do you mean by that?"

Nancy sat down, feeling a weariness seep through her body. "Since I was a child I've felt falsely judged. I had the best of intentions but was often told otherwise. My teachers, for example, believed me to be divisive if I suggested there might be another solution to a problem. Math, for instance. I was quite good at math, but there were times when I found other ways to solve a problem. They were unwilling to hear me out and told me I was a troublemaker."

Seth couldn't seem to refrain from smiling, which only heightened Nancy's frustration.

"What's wrong with using a different solution for the same problem?" she asked. "I find different solutions all the time. I believe it's more important to save time and effort. What's wrong with that?"

"Well, in the case of math, it can completely alter the answer. For example, if you should add or subtract when multiplication is called for, you will end up with a wrong answer. Say you are looking for the square footage of a room and decide to add the length and width instead of multiply?"

"Yes, well, that's not the way I did things." She folded her arms across her chest. "Forget mathematics. People like Miss Clifton misjudge me where religious matters are concerned. I thought Christians were supposed to love one another and treat others as better than themselves. Instead I've been misjudged and condemned most of my life. And all because I dare to question God or the religious people who run His churches."

Seth nodded. "There are some very judgmental people in the world. No doubt about that."

"And now that woman has the audacity to question whether I'm even a Christian."

His expression softened. "Now, to be fair, she didn't really say that."

"Well, maybe I'm not." Nancy let out an exasperated sigh. "I've tried to live by the rules and failed miserably. I grew up in a Christian family and presumed that made me a Christian as well. Especially since I believed the same things they did. One God, three parts—although it's terribly hard to understand the whole Father-Son-Holy Ghost concept." She cocked her head to one side. "My father did a good job with that one time using an apple as an example. He told me it was just one apple, but it had skin and seeds and fruit—all very distinctive parts. Yet still one apple." She shook her head. "I'm digressing. I simply mean that I know what the Bible says, and I try to live my life as a good woman. Then someone like Bedelia Clifton comes along and suggests otherwise, and it makes me angry."

"But being good doesn't make you a Christian, Nancy. Being

a Christian means you are 'of Christ.' You believe in Jesus and follow His ways—you accept Him as your Savior and pattern your life around His teachings."

"I've tried." Nancy thought back to the day her brother Douglas had died of the measles. "Do you remember that I had another brother?"

"Douglas." Seth smiled and nodded. "He was a sweet little boy, and I remember you two were always together. It was almost as if he were your baby."

"He was, in many ways. Mama was always so busy." Nancy smiled. "I was just seven when Doug was born. Gabe was ten, and James was four and always into mischief. Our poor mother had her hands full just in seeing to him."

"Speaking of James, I hear he is back east at seminary, becoming a minister."

Nancy rolled her eyes. "Yes, much to our parents' absolute delight. I suppose all that rambunctious nonsense he pulled as a child has given itself over to pious study and a desire to live a quiet and worshipful life."

Seth laughed. "That is often the case with children we think are headed to a bad end. I'm glad to see James found his way. Now, please continue. I didn't mean to interrupt."

She calmed and shrugged. An image of Douglas came to mind, his sweet cherub face framed with dark curls. "Doug was everything to me. Mama would nurse him and then hand him off to me to care for. He was born just before school was out for the summer, so we had all that time together. When fall came, I begged my mother to let me remain at home, but she said my education was too important. Every day when I came home from school, I would find the baby and take care of him. Being with him was all I wanted. By the next summer when he was one, I was completely devoted to him. I felt like he was my own."

"I remember that. Every time I saw you, Douglas was on your hip."

She grew sad, hating to remember the loss. "Everything changed for me after Douglas died."

"It was hard on Gabe too."

Nancy looked at him. "I didn't know that. Gabe never talked about it."

"He did with me. He cried a lot. It was such a sad situation. My whole family was devastated. You might recall that Clementine had the measles at the same time. Apparently, a lot of folks did."

"I didn't know that. I was so focused on Douglas." She remembered his ragged cough and fevered brow. "I felt so helpless. He was so sick. I prayed and prayed, and still he died."

"I'm so sorry, Nancy. I know it must have been devastating for you and your family."

"Father kept talking about how we'd see Douglas again one day and how death wasn't the end. He made the loss seem trivial, and for me it was anything but. I prayed so hard for Doug. I sat at his bedside, wiping him down with vinegar water, talking to him, holding him. I had the measles quite young so I was at no risk, but James hadn't, so he was kept away. He caught a milder case and thankfully recovered, but not Douglas. I blamed myself. I kept thinking I must have done something wrong. I prayed for him to recover, and when he didn't, I blamed God for not caring."

"I can understand that. It would be hard to understand why God would allow him to die."

"Not hard. Impossible. I had heard all my life that we had

only to pray and God would answer. No one told me that God's answer might be different from mine." Nancy gazed past Seth to the street and then to nothing at all. "For the longest time I would wake up in the night hearing Douglas cry. I would hear him call to me out in the sheep pasture. I would think of something I could make him and then remember he was gone. Nothing was ever right after that, and I only wanted to get away from the farm."

They sat in silence for several minutes, and then Nancy confessed, "Maybe I'm not a Christian."

"I am," Seth said. "I had a strange encounter with God. Like you, I grew up in a family who believed and thought that meant I was saved too. When I was back east at school, I found it easier and easier to forget about church and the Bible, however. I drifted into another world where intellectual discussions were more important than those about faith."

"What happened?" Nancy had never heard anything about Seth after he left the Oregon City area.

"Some friends and I spent the afternoon at the horse races. I gambled and enjoyed some alcoholic drinks with them, as well as flirted with women of questionable reputations. I saw nothing wrong with sowing my wild oats. When evening came, my friends and I continued to celebrate our gambling wins. By the time I returned to my apartment, I was well into my cups and quite useless. As I fell asleep, I remembered thinking how disappointed my mother would be if she knew how I spent my day. She and Father always made clear the sins of drunkenness and gambling. But, you see, religious matters seemed unimportant. Something to scare children into obedience or help elderly folks face death. I just didn't know what I believed anymore."

"Yes." Nancy nodded. "I know exactly what you mean."

If Seth heard her, he didn't acknowledge it and instead continued with his story. "Later that night, I was awakened. The building was on fire. I was on the fourth floor, and the smoke was awful. I tried to make my way outside, but the exits were ablaze. I went back into my room, closed the door, and tried to figure out what I could do. It was immediately sobering, and I feared death.

"I began to bargain with God. 'Just get me out of this, Lord, and I promise to do whatever you want.'" He smiled, but it didn't hold the joy that had been there earlier. "The heat and smoke intensified, and still I had no answers. There was the window, but a four-story drop didn't sound encouraging. I remembered a drainpipe I thought might be useful, but it wasn't directly under my window, so it was questionable whether I could reach it."

His expression grew grim. "I was in real trouble. I realized as the fire quickly consumed the building that I was probably going to die. I made my way through the choking smoke to the window. I managed to get it open and could see a commotion of people down below—spectators, firemen, police. I hollered, but no one seemed to hear me. I began to cry out to God, but not as a barter." He smiled. "I begged God to help me—to let me live—but I was also resigned that if I was to die, I would be on good terms with Him. I asked His forgiveness and mercy. I told Him I was sorry for the way I had betrayed Him and wasted time. I realized that I had taken for granted all the blessings He had given me."

"And what happened?" She smiled. "Obviously you're here."

He chuckled. "Yes. A fireman appeared at my window almost immediately. I don't remember much, because the smoke rendered me unconscious. When I came to, I was on the ground and woke just in time to see a portion of the building collapse."

"How awful. You must have been terrified."

"I was, but I was also strangely at peace. After the worst of it was over and the fire under control, I went to seek out my rescuer. Strangely enough, no one knew a man of the description I gave. Furthermore, they called me mad and said I couldn't possibly have been rescued from the fourth floor. They didn't have a ladder that reached that high."

Nancy's eyes narrowed. "What? How could that be?"

Seth smiled. "The fire chief told me that only the hand of God could have brought me out of that building. He said the fire was too hot for his men to get within fifty feet. All they could do was let it burn. Ten people died that night. It should have been eleven."

A shiver went up Nancy's spine. "Do you really believe God sent an angel to bring you out of that building?"

"I don't know any other way I escaped death. It completely changed my focus. I realized I didn't want to waste my life. I wanted to do whatever I could to right wrongs and help causes that would benefit mankind. I wanted to serve God—really serve Him."

"I suppose that's understandable. When you have an encounter like that—one that has no other rational explanation—then I could see crediting God." She thought again of Douglas. Of watching his life slip away—of her mother holding him as he breathed his last. "If only He had sent my brother an angel."

"But that's the thing, Nancy. He did."

She looked up at Seth, tears in her eyes. "Then He should have sent me one too."

"He gives His angels charge over us. Maybe in your grief you couldn't see yours. We can't know the mind of God and why one person lives and another dies. I felt guilty for a time that I had lived, and then I realized that God had let me live for a reason. He had a plan for me. It was completely up to me to fulfill that destiny. Just like it's up to you to move forward with yours."

"I wish I knew what my destiny was." Nancy thought of her current situation and of her husband's drawings. She wanted very much to trust Seth and tell him what she'd found, but something held her back. Something she couldn't quite name.

"In time, I think you'll know," he said. "Right now is a time of transition. You don't want to make rash decisions. Take your time and figure out what's important to you, Nancy."

She nodded. "I'm trying to do exactly that. Like opening the house to boarders. I like it. I like having the ladies here, despite Bedelia's harsh judgment."

"Clementine loves it here. She says you are a supreme hostess and an amazing cook."

Nancy smiled. "Your sister has always been generous with her praise. I remember how she was when we were young. She always had a compliment for everyone. She got the highest marks for congeniality at school."

Seth laughed. "I'm sure she did. I think that's why she likes teaching, and her students always adore her. She makes each of them feel good about themselves and takes time to find out something particular to their interests. It's the mark of a good teacher. She can hardly wait for the fall term to begin."

A marked wagon came to a stop in front of Nancy's house. "Oh, it would appear my groceries are being delivered," she said.

"I'll lend a hand." Seth got to his feet. "Although we must say nothing to poor Miss Clifton about two men being in the house with you."

Nancy smiled and waved to the deliveryman. Once he and

Seth had managed to get everything inside, she paid the delivery-man and sent him on his way. It was then that she noted the newspaper he'd left. The grocer did that from time to time, hoping to encourage Nancy to purchase a subscription. She imagined he got a commission from his brother-in-law at the newspaper's subscription office.

She fixed a tray of refreshments and brought them and the newspaper out to the porch. "I thought maybe you'd like something to drink or eat."

Seth jumped up and took the tray from her. "I will enjoy anything that allows me more time with you. After all, I truly did come with a purpose other than dissecting the past and our religious views." He placed the tray on the small wicker table. "Shall I pour the tea?"

Nancy shook her head. "I'll manage it. Sit. There's a newspaper, if you'd prefer that to discussion."

"I see there's something about the Middleton murders down south." Seth scanned the paper and set it aside. "Looks like they believe the wife helped lure the couple to their death."

"What if she didn't?" Nancy found it the perfect opening to ask questions about her own situation. "What if she knew nothing about what her husband had planned—what he was doing?"

"If she didn't, then she can't be charged with crimes, but of course they will weigh the evidence and not just go by what she says. It's easy to say you had no involvement."

His words struck at her as if he knew what she was thinking. Did he suspect that she had some part in Albert's schemes?

"In a society that treats women very poorly at times, I feel sorry for her trying to prove her innocence," she said.

"She's bound to have friends and family who will vouch for

her. And, as I said"—his words were soft and full of compassion—"the court will look for proof, not speculation. Women are trapped by their gender and restricted to situations where they have little defense. I believe there are honest and good lawyers and judges, however. And I believe, too, that men will often err in favor of the gentler sex rather than predetermine guilt by association. We know how overbearing and demanding men can be."

Nancy couldn't help but feel he was speaking directly to her. Dare she hope that she had a confidant and trusted friend in Seth Carpenter? He was, after all, a longtime friend of the family. Surely she could tell him the things she'd learned—at least in time.

CHAPTER 10

Summer had turned exceptionally pretty, with rains causing an abundance of flowers, particularly roses. When they'd first moved to this house, Nancy had planted several beds of roses, and seeing them in bloom made her happy. It was a colorful reminder of her hard work, but more than that, it reminded her of various friends and family, as most of the bushes had come from them.

Clipping spent blooms from the roses around her porch, Nancy thought of her mother. She looked at the small pink blooms of the plant and remembered it was one of Grace Armistead's favorites. She'd given Nancy a cutting to transplant shortly after her marriage to Albert.

"I hope this will remind you of me and how much I love you," Mother had said. *"Always remember you have a family who loves you, Nancy."*

A wave of guilt washed over her. She really needed to write to her parents and apologize for her terrible behavior during their visit. She'd received a letter from her mother a couple of weeks back and had been so overcome with guilt that she'd hardly done more than scan the lines. Now her guilt was coupled with the continued harshness she felt toward Bedelia. They'd said nothing more on the matter when the sisters returned home, but Nancy still held the older woman's ridiculous rules of comportment and judgmental attitude against her.

The funny thing was, in the past it wouldn't have eaten at Nancy the way it did now. She wouldn't have given the matter much thought. She would have simply eradicated Bedelia from her life and gone on with her own affairs. She supposed, however, that because Bedelia lived at the house and was always there to condemn her, Nancy found it impossible to forget her words.

"You look like you're enjoying yourself."

Nancy rose from where she'd been kneeling and greeted her visitor. "Mrs. Taylor. How wonderful to see you."

Mary Taylor smiled as she made her way up the sidewalk. She used her ornate cane more as an accessory than a necessity, and Nancy thought it made her look stately and refined. "It's a beautiful day."

"Yes, and since the boy just cut the grass yesterday, I thought I should do my part to refresh my roses." Nancy put the shears in her pocket and dusted her gloved hands. "Would you care to join me? I was about to have some refreshment."

"That sounds lovely."

"We can sit on the porch and enjoy the day."

"I must confess, it was my desire to do just that. I'm so glad you have time for me."

"I always have time for my friends." Nancy supposed that hadn't always been true, but of late it was. In the wake of losing Albert, she found her personal relationships in need of nurturing. It wasn't easy, however. She'd always believed that her life didn't need to be scrutinized by anyone for any reason. Not even for the sake of friendship. She had avoided people and the closeness of friends, always holding everyone at arm's length. Now she found she wanted more.

Nancy went inside and put the kettle on for tea. She washed up and changed from her gardening coat, then set a tray with all they would need for their impromptu tea party.

When the kettle began to whistle, Nancy pulled the pot from the stove and poured hot water into a china teapot. It was such a treat to have Mary stop by. Nancy had never known her grandmother, and Mary had come to fill that role.

"Here we are," Nancy said, exiting the house with the large tray. "I hope you've made yourself comfortable."

"Indeed. This is one of the most pleasant porches in town," Mary Taylor declared from the rocker. "I have a great fondness for it."

"I do too." Nancy placed the tray on the table. "I pity the woman who has no porch, for you can enjoy them rain or shine." She poured the tea and handed a cup and saucer to Mary. "So, tell me what brings you out today."

"I had a few errands to see to, and your house was on the way. I thought it only right that I come see how you are faring."

It was the perfect opening to discuss the matters that had been on Nancy's heart, but she hesitated. It was hardly good manners to just jump in with one's troubles. She wanted Mary's counsel, but it could wait.

"I'm doing well. And what of you and Mr. Taylor? Did you decide about painting the house?"

Mary chuckled. "That debate will continue another day. Mr. Taylor has gotten completely caught up in purchasing dairy cattle. I don't know why he suddenly has the urge to start a dairy farm, but it seems important to him."

"A dairy farm? Goodness, you won't move from Portland, will you?"

"No. This is a joint venture between Mr. Taylor and two other gentlemen, neither of whom desire to live on a farm but rather wish to have the investment for the future. I believe it to be sound, with our growing population, but his focus on this new project has brought everything else to a standstill."

Nancy nodded and extended a plate of oatmeal cookies. Mary took one and settled it on the edge of her saucer.

"I can tell there is something on your mind, Nancy. I suppose I could even go so far as to say that I felt God's urging to come see you because of it."

"God told you to come see me?"

"In a sense." Mary smiled. "Why don't you tell me how you are doing? What's really been on your mind?"

"I . . . well . . ." Nancy stopped and drew a deep breath. "I've been troubled by several things."

"Albert?"

"No. Not exactly. I suppose I should be the grieving widow, but I'm not. Does that shock you?"

Mary gave a chuckle. "No, my dear. I knew there was little love lost between the two of you."

"There was little of anything between us. I quickly realized that after his death. He was so seldom at home. I don't know why I didn't wonder about it before, but it was simply the way it was, and I didn't question it." Nancy shook her head. "No, this is more about my coming to terms with my poor attitude. The last time I saw my parents, I was hardly civil. Then a short time ago, one of my boarders was stern with me about guarding my reputation, and I was unkind. I don't know why it bothered me so much, but her implication was that because I didn't care about my reputation, perhaps I wasn't a Christian woman." She bit her lip, then decided to plow ahead. "And that got me to wondering if perhaps I wasn't."

Mary nodded. "We all must come to the place where we make our faith our own or reject it outright."

"Did you ever struggle with that?"

"Oh mercy, yes. I grew up in a family for whom church was nothing more than window dressing and a social statement. My family didn't care at all what the Bible had to say but went to church in order to be seen by the right people—in the right pews. My mother told me once that poor people found comfort in God, but the wealthy used Him for their advantage."

"Goodness. That is rather shocking. Use God?"

"Everyone does at one time or another. I've seen people use God like a mighty sledge to drive others into despair. I've seen them use God as a means of control—suggesting that God somehow made a personal arrangement with them to be in charge. But in my family, they used God merely as a symbol of how good they were—how we were rich and blessed because we were somehow dearer to Him. It was deplorable, to be sure."

"But I've only ever known you to be a godly woman of great faith. You have inspired me at times to see how very far I have strayed from the truth." Nancy lowered her head. "You've made me reconsider the Bible and how I have neglected God."

"You don't know the woman I used to be," Mary said, thoughtfully stirring her tea. "There was a time in my life when God meant no more to me than the social acceptance I mentioned."

"What happened to change that?"

"I nearly died."

Nancy's head snapped up. "A friend of mine, Seth Carpenter, shared a similar situation. He said he didn't want much to do with God because he was young and influenced otherwise. Then he nearly died one night in a fire. He prayed to God and was rescued, but not just any rescue. An impossible rescue. He was on the fourth floor, and a fireman came and took him out the window, but that was all he remembered. When he went to thank the man, he was nowhere to be found, and the other firemen said he didn't exist and that he couldn't have saved Seth from the fourth floor because they didn't have a ladder that reached that high. Seth believes an angel saved him—that God intervened. Do you?"

"I believe God intervenes all the time. I believe He did so for me. I was a young woman about to give birth. The doctor said the baby's head was stuck and that most likely he would have to cut the baby from my body. He felt that if he did this, I would die, but that if he didn't, we would both die."

"How terrible." Nancy's hand trembled, causing tea to slosh onto the saucer. She put the cup aside. "What happened?"

Mary chuckled again. "Well, obviously I'm here." She shook her head. "But only by God's grace. There I was, barely a girl of nineteen. Life had hardly begun, and I was looking forward to being a mother and raising a family. I wanted very much to live. The doctor explained everything to my husband and family, and even though money was no object, there was nothing money could do to save me. The doctor suggested a minister be sent for. I didn't know the man, he wasn't from our church, but when he arrived, he prayed with me. It was unlike any prayer I had heard from those lofty pulpits. It was a prayer of contrition on my behalf—a prayer of hope despite the darkness of the hour.

"When the doctor was ready to perform the surgery and deliver my child, there came an interruption. An injured man needed immediate attention. While the doctor went to tend the man, the minister continued to pray with me. He asked if I believed God could and should save me and my baby. I told him I felt confident that God could do anything but was less certain that He should. I told him I knew very little of the God that he spoke of, and the minister continued to share with me from the Bible. It was unlike anything I had ever experienced, Nancy. God was no longer a lofty deity—unreachable, unattainable. He was right there in the room with me. I felt the baby in me cease to struggle."

"He died?" Nancy blurted without thinking.

"No. But the pain and the feeling that I was being ripped apart ceased. I remember thinking this was death, and at that moment, having learned the truth of God, I was ready for whatever came my way. The minister led me in prayer, and I told God that I would put my trust in Him forever. That if I were to die in that moment, I knew I would awaken in His presence. Then I felt the urge to bear down. I pushed, and the doctor returned, ready to operate. He saw that I was bearing down and commanded me to stop, but I couldn't. He came to see what was happening and found that the baby was being born. My son lived, and so did I."

"And that changed your heart toward God."

"Child, it changed everything. My husband was changed and my parents too. That minister led them all to a right knowledge of God and salvation." Mary's eyes were damp with tears. "It forever opened my heart to who Jesus is and why I need Him so."

Nancy could hear the sincerity of her words. This wasn't just a story to her, this was Mary's life—a moment of spiritual awareness that had transformed the physical as well. Now Nancy had two stories of God's divine intervention to ponder.

"Then why could God not have saved my brother?" she asked.

Mary reached over and squeezed Nancy's hand. "He could have, Nancy. God could have saved him to live on this earth. But sometimes that's not the answer, and it hurts us when it seems God has rejected our prayers—our needs—because it feels like He has rejected us. But that isn't true."

"How can it not be? I was a little girl acting on the only truth I knew. I had been taught that God was loving and giving and that if I prayed for something, He would give it. I promised Him my best—my life, my love, my all—if only He would save Douglas."

"Child, we can't barter with God. He will do as He will do. Our faith is tested in times such as those—where we cannot understand, where the pain is so great that we can scarcely draw breath. I've never told you this, but I lost two little ones years after nearly dying giving birth to my first."

Nancy felt terrible for not even considering this possibility. "I'm so sorry. I didn't know."

"Of course you didn't." Mary dabbed the napkin to her eyes. "I lost two daughters when they were barely walking. One died from a terrible fever, and then two years later, the other died when she fell in the river and drowned."

Nancy's eyes filled with tears that spilled down her cheeks. "How could you keep trusting God after that?"

Mary gave only a hint of a nod. "How could I not? What alternative was left to me?"

Her words pierced Nancy's heart. She wanted so much to be rid of the terrible ache in her heart—the emptiness that she was becoming more certain was due to God's absence. Yet how could she trust Him?

"A choice must be made, Nancy," Mary said as if reading

Nancy's thoughts. "God will not impose Himself on you. He calls tenderly to you—He loves you and desires for you to love Him in return."

"But I'm afraid." There it was. Fear. Fear so huge, so encompassing, that Nancy felt it nearly cut off her air. "What if He wants nothing more to do with me? What if I hurt Him too much with my rejection? What if I pushed Him too far away from me?"

Mary put her cup and saucer aside and leaned forward. "You don't have that kind of power, Nancy. God is not subject to man's laws and thinking. He's there for you and wants you to come back to Him."

A sob broke from Nancy's throat. "But how? What do I do?"

"Let go of your misery and fear—give it to Him. Ask Him to receive your heart—to be your God. Trust Him."

Nancy fell forward, burying her face in the skirt of her gown. She cried as she hadn't cried since the night Douglas had died. She felt a hand on her back, comforting her, and knew Mary would stay with her no matter how long her tears fell.

But better still, Nancy knew God was there as well, and the certainty of that filled her with a wonder she had never known.

Could He forgive her?

CHAPTER 11

"G abe Armistead, as I live and breathe." Seth beheld the friend he'd not seen in at least five years. "You haven't changed a bit."

"Seth, it's good to see you again." Gabe extended his hand, but Seth pulled him in for a hug. The two men embraced, laughing.

"How did you know to find me here?"

"The folks." Gabe glanced over his shoulder. "This is where you work now, eh?"

"Indeed. I'm working with John Lincoln, a very respectable lawyer." Seth motioned to one of the two leather chairs in his office. "Have a seat. I want to hear what you've been doing all these years."

"Mostly running the family lumber mill in Oregon City. My uncle Edward and his sons have a separate mill there, and together we have a partnership in a mill here in Portland. Keeps us all very busy."

"I can imagine." Seth took the other chair. "Are you married?"

Gabe shook his head. "I almost got hitched a few years

ago, but she changed her mind, and God changed mine." He laughed. "It turned out to be the best of decisions, and we all remained friends. Otherwise there's been no one special, and I've been way too busy to go to all the trouble of getting to know someone. How about you?"

"Well, there was no one for the longest time. I had little interest in anything save the law. Now, however . . ." He let the words trail off as he considered what he might say to Nancy's brother regarding his interest in her.

"Now there is someone?"

Seth nodded. "I'd like there to be."

"What's she like?"

"Your sister Nancy."

Gabe looked confused. "She's like Nancy?"

"No. She is Nancy. I've been working with John on her legal matters, and I've developed feelings for her."

Gabe laughed out loud. "My folks would be delighted to hear that. They worry about that girl something fierce, and I know they would be happy to have someone like you watching over her and keeping her out of trouble."

"Well, that remains to be seen. The fact is, she's got a lot on her shoulders. That dead husband of hers left a world of troubles behind. We're still trying to sort it all out."

"I never liked the fellow. He was determined to keep Nancy from the family. I once tried to talk to him about coming around more often. I told him how important family was to us and how we were all real close, and we wanted him and Nancy to be close too. He told me to mind my own business and leave them to tend their own. He said he'd grown up without anybody and didn't need anyone now. I nearly punched him in the mouth."

Seth grinned. "I'm surprised you didn't."

"It took all my Christian charity." Gabe shook his head. "I can't say anyone is sorry that he's gone."

"I think that includes Nancy," Seth replied without thinking.

"I'm bettin' you're right. I never did see why she married him. He hardly gave her the time of day, but he did buy her a lot of stuff. Ma used to wonder at the amount of money he must have spent to build that monstrosity of a house."

"I can understand why. It's quite the place. My guess is no less than ten thousand dollars."

"Ten thousand dollars." Gabe shook his head. "I could do a lot with that kind of money."

"We all could." Seth checked his pocket watch. "Say, it's nearly noon. Why don't we make our way over to Nancy's and beg some lunch? She puts on quite the spread for her boarders."

"Ma said she'd taken in boarders. Seems like a good idea when you have a house that size."

Seth got to his feet. "She wanted to be able to support herself."

"She doesn't need to, you know. Pa has a trust with money for her. He has one for each of us."

Seth grabbed his coat. "I think Nancy likes feeling needed. She said something once about hating to feel useless. I think her houseful of ladies gives her purpose."

"Well, I know Ma would prefer her purpose be back on the farm." Gabe rose and shook his head. "They're hoping I can convince her to leave Portland."

"Do they realize that I'll be here, trying to convince her to stay?" Seth asked, throwing his friend a challenging look.

Gabe laughed. "My money is on you. I never did have the power of persuasion where Nancy was concerned."

Seth locked up the office and followed Gabe outside. It was one of the prettiest days he'd seen all summer. The sky was void of clouds, and everything seemed crisp and alive.

"You definitely picked the right day to come to Portland," he said.

"Are we walking?" Gabe asked.

"It's pretty enough but quite a distance. I'll get us a cab, and that way your reunion will come about much quicker." Seth whistled and waved at a carriage parked across the street. The driver quickly brought his horse around and pulled the carriage up in front of Seth and Gabe. Seth gave him the address, then settled into the small space with Gabe's broad shoulders taking up most of the room.

"You get much bigger and they're going to write songs about you," Seth said.

Gabe only rolled his eyes and shook his head. They chatted about the town as the carriage made its way west. Seth pointed out a new bank, several new stores, and a club where men could meet after hours.

"It's said you can get a good game of cards or an intense lecture on divinity all on the same night. You need only pay the hefty dues of ten dollars a month."

"Ten?" Gabe shook his head. "I have better places to put my money and can play cards and get lectured for free at home. Sometimes I swear my mother should take the pulpit. Especially if vinegar is involved. She absolutely believes there is nothing vinegar won't cure, clean, or fix."

Seth laughed heartily, remembering Grace Armistead's penchant for vinegar. They soon arrived at Nancy's and saw, even as they disembarked from the carriage, that she was entertaining a gentleman on her front porch.

"Looks like she's busy," Gabe muttered.

Seth paid the driver and turned to see who the man might be. He recognized Gerome Berkshire almost immediately. Further inspection showed his horse and buggy at the curb. "She'll be glad for our interruption. The man is a pest."

Gabe stiffened. "Does he cause Nancy problems?"

"Nothing she hasn't been able to handle. I'm not sure of his involvement with her dead husband, but I believe he fancies Nancy, and that matter I will see to myself."

Nancy and Gerome were on their feet as Seth and Gabe approached the porch. Nancy ran down the steps to greet her brother. "When did you come to town, Gabe?" She remained on the next to the last step to hug him.

"I figured it was due. I hadn't had time since the funeral, and I felt bad about that."

"I've hardly been easy on my company, as I'm sure Mother must have told you." She turned to Seth and smiled. "Thank you for bringing him by and for coming as well. Would you like to join us for lunch? We were just about to go inside."

"I must admit, lunch was on my mind." Seth drew off his hat, and Gabe did likewise.

She nodded. "Then come along, both of you. Seth, you know Mr. Berkshire. Gabe, this is Mr. Berkshire. He was an associate of my late husband's."

"Mr. Berkshire." Gabe's tone was guarded.

"Mr. Berkshire had business with Albert regarding a shipment of goods, Seth. I'm hoping you might help him figure out more on the matter. He is the second man to claim Albert owed him goods, so I'm hoping we can get to the bottom of it."

"Of course," Seth said. "Mr. Berkshire, why don't you give

me the particulars? Better still, could you come by my office this afternoon and perhaps bring your receipts?"

Gerome Berkshire looked less than pleased. "I might be able to arrange it."

Nancy took the gentlemen's hats and placed them on the foyer table before showing them to the dining room, where the Clifton sisters were just taking their places.

"Bedelia, Cornelia, I would like you to meet my brother Gabe." She turned to her brother. "Gabe, this is Miss Clifton and Miss Clifton."

He gave a brief nod. "Ladies."

Bedelia eyed him almost suspiciously. "Nancy's brother. You certainly are tall."

Gabe laughed. "Yes, ma'am. Our father is as well."

"He'll be short enough seated at the table," Nancy said, motioning for the men to take their places. "The gentlemen would like to join us for lunch today if you ladies don't mind."

"Well, it is your house," Bedelia declared, staring at each man before drawing her napkin onto her lap. "I hope we shan't have explicit discussions on tasteless subjects."

"Of course not," Nancy replied before anyone else could.

Gerome and Gabe took their places, but Seth felt compelled to follow Nancy into the kitchen. From the scowl on Gerome's face, he knew his decision didn't set well.

"Sorry for just showing up like this. I can at least make myself useful," Seth said, looking around the kitchen to see how best he might help.

"Not at all. I'm glad you're both here. If you'd be so kind as to carry this tureen, I'll get the biscuits."

"Smells good. What's on the menu?" Seth picked up the large

tureen only to realize it was plenty hot. He put it back down and grabbed a towel.

"Chicken and noodles in cream. My mother's recipe. And later, if you're still hungry, I made two berry pies."

"Sounds like heaven."

They made their way back to the dining room, where Bedelia was actually smiling at a story Gabe was telling. Seth wasn't sure how Gabe had managed to win the older woman over so quickly, but it was to everyone's benefit, and he wouldn't speak against it.

"Gabe, would you offer grace?" Nancy asked.

He nodded and bowed his head. "Father, we thank you for the food you've provided and the hands that have prepared it for us. I ask a special blessing on the lives of the ladies here, and the gentlemen too. Guard our hearts, Lord, and show us thy ways. Amen."

"Amen," Bedelia said in a hushed sort of reverence. Gabe was impressing her, to be sure.

Seth pulled the lid off the tureen and put it aside before offering the ladle to Bedelia. She helped herself and then dished up some for Cornelia. Seth put a good amount of food on his plate before passing the dish to Gabe. He could see that Berkshire watched him with hooded eyes. He reminded Seth of a snake just waiting to strike.

What had Berkshire come here to accomplish? Was he trying to court Nancy? It was obvious that he was interested—too interested. Nancy had mentioned he was rather possessive of her since he and Albert had been dear friends. Perhaps he thought Nancy was part of an inheritance Albert owed him. If so, Seth intended to set him straight.

But then reason took over, and Seth forced himself to calm.

Berkshire and Albert had been close business associates, and Seth couldn't allow his personal desires to ruin any potential leads he might find for his investigation.

Nancy used the very public moment of dining with her brother, Gerome, and Seth to apologize to Bedelia. Since asking God to help her live for Him, Nancy had known there were fences to mend. She had thought about it for a long time and felt convicted that for this particular woman, a more formal apology was needed. Bedelia liked to be the center of attention—especially when it proved her to be right about something.

"I hope you will excuse me for interrupting the conversation." Nancy looked around the table until she held everyone's attention. "Some time ago, I was rather rude to Miss Clifton. My heart was less than kind, and I regret having been so harsh with her."

Nancy paused and gave Bedelia a smile. "Miss Clifton, you made me pause to consider my heart and the difficulties I was struggling with in my spirit. I want to take this moment in the company of witnesses to apologize. You were right to insist on my convictions and my modesty, and for that I thank you and hope you will forgive me for my harsh tongue."

Bedelia's eyes were wide with surprise. She looked almost disbelieving. "I, well, of course I forgive you."

Nancy beamed a smile. "Thank you. You are very gracious. Now, I hope everyone will eat up and enjoy the meal. There's pie for dessert, so save room."

She focused on buttering her biscuit but knew that Bedelia was touched by what she'd done. Nancy felt good for humbling herself, even though it wasn't easy. She had to constantly fight against her nature to yield her heart to God. Mary had said it was often that way for strong-willed people. But she had also promised to pray for Nancy, and that had given Nancy strength to pursue what needed to be done.

Seeing Gabe reminded her that she had to resolve matters with her parents as well. Years of rebellion and anger had kept her from even considering the wounds she had caused them. And, of course, there was still so much she had to sort through regarding God. She had prayed for forgiveness and that He might show her how to bear up under the painful memories and loss. She had prayed, too, for God's help in truly yielding her heart and mind to His will rather than her own. However, she had been strong-willed and rebellious most of her life, and it didn't come naturally to stop being that way now. It was no doubt going to take God's intercession before Nancy could be even a smidge of the woman He wanted her to be.

She sighed. Nothing had ever come easy for her.

CHAPTER 12

Gerome paced his small office while two gentlemen he'd long worked with sat discussing the situation at hand.

"The guns have to be somewhere. Albert obviously hid them well from prying eyes. Unfortunately, he is dead now, and no one seems to have a clue where the weapons and whiskey are," the elder of the two men declared.

The young man nodded. "It's been nearly four months, and my people are getting anxious. They had hoped for an uprising before now. New immigrants seeking land grants will be here before we know it, and unless we can free up more land from the reservations, they'll have poor options to choose from."

"There's no guarantee we could get the government to act fast enough anyway," Gerome remarked. "We knew that early on."

"Yes, but at least with something to promise, we could secure a nice commission for ourselves to act on their behalf," the old man replied.

"Exactly." The younger man nodded. "And if there were conflict going on and the government was already inclined to take an active role, it would be easier to convince the new arrivals of our ability to benefit them."

"I'm doing all I can. It's evident Mrs. Pritchard knows nothing about her dead husband's affairs. I've discussed the matter with her at length, and she's completely unaware."

"But you assured us it wouldn't be difficult to manage this matter," the younger of the two men said, steepling his fingers. "I am finding that to be far from the truth. There are guns and alcohol out there that we anticipated using for our plan, and no one knows where to find them. Including you, Gerome. You've been searching since March, and still nothing."

Gerome gritted his teeth to keep from spewing expletives. After a moment, he took a deep breath and sat behind the desk. "I am well aware of our need, gentlemen. I am convinced that among Albert Pritchard's things are maps to the various caches. He once told me that he had a half-dozen or more places to hide stores of goods. He was good at what he did and had good friends among the riverboat captains. It's just a matter of learning the locations, and I believe that with a little more time, I will be able to secure that information from Mrs. Pritchard."

The old man shook his head. "You said she knew nothing."

Gerome met the man's rheumy eyes. "That doesn't mean she doesn't have access to the knowledge. She simply doesn't know what she's looking for and probably has put very little effort into looking for it because it doesn't pertain to her immediate needs. I believe it might benefit our cause to have someone search the house in her absence."

"You mean break in?" The older man was aghast. "Not only are the legalities daunting, but I understand she boards guests now. How would you ever manage it?"

"They all go to church on Sundays," Gerome said, smiling. "It shouldn't be hard to send someone to look around during that time. The neighborhood will be all but deserted. No one will be the wiser. I know a man who can slip in and out and never leave a sign of having been there."

The old man nodded and got to his feet. The younger man jumped up to offer assistance. "I suppose it is what we must do, but I want to know nothing about it. Report back to us as soon as you have news."

Stupid man. Gerome hated his dismissive nature and the attitude that Gerome would take all the risks and receive few of the benefits. There were times when Gerome would just as soon put a bullet between the old man's eyes than have to deal with one more day of his smug superiority.

Gerome sat at the desk for a long time after his cohorts had gone. He knew the warmth of the summer day made his office seem even smaller, but he was tired of having so little. Nancy was a wealthy woman—she just didn't know it yet. There was more than enough money tied up in the store and house, as well as all the guns. If he could just convince her to marry him, all of that would belong to Gerome. He would have the money he needed to promote his own causes and finance the political ambitions he had for the future. Fortunately, in the meantime, he had managed to slip those IOUs into Albert's paperwork. Hopefully no one would question the lack of names and signatures when he produced his own copy.

He sighed and looked at the calendar on his desk. It was nearly the Fourth of July. There would be a huge celebration for the country's independence. Perhaps he could convince Nancy to accompany him to the city picnic, where he was slated to speak. If he could put her on his arm and let others see them together, it might allow him to merit credit with the right financiers. That might lend further support to his causes.

Of course, there was Seth Carpenter to contend with. Carpenter had made it clear that he was interested in Nancy, and he had the benefit of having grown up with her. His family and hers were friends. Trust already existed between them, and the camaraderie of youth was certain to strike down the walls that Gerome would have to pull down brick by brick. It wasn't fair. He'd admired Nancy even while she was married to Albert, and he intended to have her for his wife.

He rubbed his thumbnail against his thick mustache. He was a handsome man. Many said so. He cut quite a figure in his carefully tailored clothes. People around him presumed he had money and backing, but those things apparently had never mattered to Nancy. She had never sought the life of a socialite. She was young and beautiful but completely ignorant of the power she could exert through those qualities. A part of him liked her all the more for her innocence, but a greater part knew that with the proper teacher—himself—Nancy Pritchard could become a force to be reckoned with. A force that he could use to aid his own cause.

Nancy found the evening to be the most pleasant she'd ever had with her tenants. Mrs. Weaver had come down from her seclusion to spend an hour in the sitting room with the other boarders, and after a while she even began sharing stories of her life as if they were all old friends.

"Of course, before the war, things were very different," Mrs. Weaver said between sips of tea. "There was a gentility among people that is lost now."

"But what about slavery, Mrs. Weaver?" Bedelia asked. "Did your people keep slaves?"

The older woman looked surprised. "Of course we did. All of our friends did. We ran very large plantations of thousands of acres. Someone had to work the land. It took hundreds of slaves. But we were good to our people."

"How can you consider it good to own another person?" Bedelia looked down her nose at Mrs. Weaver.

"The times were different," the old woman said, her voice barely audible. She set down her teacup. "Perhaps I shouldn't have come." She looked as if she were about to leave.

"Nonsense," Nancy declared before Bedelia could further insult the poor woman. "As you said, times were different, as was the culture. Did you know that the Indians also kept slaves? My father was out here many years before the wagon trains came. He was a trapper and loved the solitude of the land. He was also very good friends with some of the native peoples. Slavery is hardly isolated to white men. I believe we must all own our mistakes and wrongdoings, however. I am opposed to slavery, but I would not belittle Mrs. Weaver for choices her family made and institutions that she partook of because of her society."

"I don't seek to belittle but to properly berate," Bedelia said with a stern nod. "A tradition of evil is hardly an excuse to continue evil."

Nancy put aside her cup. "I agree. I do not want slavery for any man or woman. I was merely extending grace to Mrs. Weaver. She was good enough to join us tonight. This being her first time to spend the evening with us, she was quite gracious to share stories of her life. I don't want her to feel put upon."

The old woman adjusted her cap, then picked up her cup

and saucer. "Many of the household slaves were dear to me. I was nurtured and cared for by my mother—a dear woman who hated slavery. But I was also tended by Mama Abigail, a wonderful black woman who had also raised my papa." She fixed Bedelia with a frown. "It was not an easy situation simply to cast aside slaves. Before they married, my mother made my father promise he would set them free as soon as possible. When I married, there were less than half the number that had worked for us when I was born."

"Had they been sold or actually freed?" Bedelia demanded.

"Father freed them. When they were ready to leave, he gave each person twenty dollars in gold and their papers. Sadly, many returned because they had spent their money and yet found no employment in which to earn more." Mrs. Weaver dabbed her lacy handkerchief to her eyes. "I'm so sorry. Those days and the loss of my husband and family still bring me great sadness."

Nancy thought she might have to intercede, but to her surprise Bedelia softened her tone. "Nonsense. We are honored to have you here and for you to tell us your story, despite not having spent much time getting to know us. That could not have been easy for you, and we commend you for it."

Mrs. Weaver looked at Nancy in surprise. She looked as though she might say something, but Bedelia was already changing the subject.

"Sister and I wondered, Mrs. Pritchard, if we might cook for you on the Fourth of July. We realize there are picnics and parties going on and that perhaps you intend to partake in the celebrations. We have no such plans and would like to offer our help so that you may be free to do as you choose. I presume Mrs. Weaver will be here as well." She waited for Mrs. Weaver to acknowledge this. When the old woman nodded, Bedelia continued. "We would be happy to prepare meals for anyone who needs them that day, and this would give you time to enjoy the festivities."

Nancy was touched that Bedelia would extend such an invitation. Normally she would have shied away from anyone else working in her kitchen, but she smiled. "I would be honored. Thank you."

Bedelia gave a hint of a smile and nodded. "We shall keep to your schedule with breakfast at six."

Nancy shrugged. "I am not opposed to sleeping late on the Fourth of July."

The front door opened, and Clementine and Mimi entered the house with Seth. Nancy hadn't realized Seth would be joining them and suddenly felt self-conscious.

Mrs. Weaver seemed shaken by the appearance of a man and quickly got to her feet. "If you'll excuse me, I must retire." She hurried past the ladies and Seth, giving a little nod to them as she headed up the stairs.

"I hope we didn't cause trouble," Clementine said, staring after the old woman. "Had she been here long?"

Nancy collected Mrs. Weaver's cup and saucer along with her own. "She came down to join us shortly after we gathered. It was quite a surprise."

Bedelia took a cookie from the serving platter. "Indeed. She even shared stories about her youth and adult life in the South."

"Her people kept slaves," Cornelia said, following her sister's comment with an air of authority.

"But we decided that was no fault of hers," Bedelia added with a raised brow. "Didn't we?"

Cornelia gave multiple tiny bobs of her head and said nothing more.

"She's a very interesting woman," Nancy said, heading toward the kitchen with the dirty teacups. "Would you ladies care for tea? Seth, I can make coffee as well."

"No, we've had refreshments enough," Clementine replied. "Seth wanted to come in, however, to ask you about the Fourth of July."

Nancy was already in the dining room and called back. "I can't hear you. Come to the kitchen. We can speak there."

She was surprised when Seth rather than Clementine appeared. "My sister was trying to ask if you would like to accompany me to the Fourth of July festivities."

He ran his fingers through his auburn hair, combing it into order. He was far more handsome than she remembered from their time in Oregon City. In their youth he had seemed gangly and awkward, just as Gabe had. Seth had been charming enough but never what she considered handsome, what with his fair skin and freckles. Now his complexion had evened out and the freckles were less noticeable. His face had filled out in a most attractive way, and he all but took her breath away with his casual smile and cornflower blue eyes.

"What are you thinking?" he asked her, cocking his head. "I'd swear you were planning something."

Nancy coughed and turned away. "I was simply remembering something from when we were children. Now, what did you want to talk about?"

"The Fourth of July. Clementine suggested we make a foursome for the day. Gabe will still be in town, and she thought it might be fun for all of us to spend the day together. We can start in the morning and attend some of the festivities and then share a picnic and listen to some of the orators. In the evening we can go to the dance. It will be a great deal of fun. Please say you will."

"I've been a widow for barely four months. What will people say?" Nancy really didn't care, but she didn't want to appear too eager. She hurried to busy herself with the dishes.

"That's the joy of a large and growing town. No one will know or care. Your friends will be delighted to see you enjoying yourself, and strangers won't know your situation." He stepped to her side and gently turned her to face him. "Besides, the ladies of the house seem anxious that you be back among the living. Please say you will."

"All right. I will." She held up the cup still in her hands. "But between now and then I must wash my dishes."

"I can help."

"No. I wouldn't hear of it. Go enjoy yourself with the ladies."

"You're the only lady I want to enjoy myself with."

His words hit her in an unexpected way. What was he saying? Nancy couldn't bring herself to lift her face and meet his gaze. "I, ah . . ." She shook her head and put the cup in the sink. Why did she suddenly feel so weak in the knees? "I have work to do, and you should go."

"I will look forward to spending all day with you on the Fourth. In the meantime, you should know that John and I have closely examined all the books and papers you brought to us. It seems that financially you are solid and have no need to concern yourself with the future, but there are some debts to pay."

"Albert didn't believe in owing anyone. I find it hard to believe he had debts."

"We still haven't figured out whom the IOUs are owed to. There wasn't a name, just the amounts and dates. The way the paper was prepared looked rushed and haphazard, but it appears that whoever made the deal has the other half of the paper. No doubt he will present himself in time with his proof, and then we'll pay him."

"Gerome implied that Albert owed him, though it surprised me. You should speak with him."

"I will. Fear not." Seth smiled. "You're going to be fine, Nancy. Don't worry about anything. I intend to see you protected and taken care of. Of course, we desperately need to figure out more about the weapons and whiskey. It makes little sense that your husband felt he had to hide such things."

Nancy felt the blood drain from her face. She couldn't forget Mr. Hanson's threat to expose Albert's schemes to put guns and whiskey in the hands of the Indians. Worse still, to tell everyone that she was a part of it. What would happen if Seth found out about those things and believed Hanson?

Perhaps the time had come to confess what she knew. To tell Seth everything, even about the river journal and maps. After all, she'd had no time to go and investigate for herself.

Looking at Seth's sweet expression, Nancy wanted to believe that she could trust him. There was really no reason not to, but something inside her reared up and told her to remain silent. If she could figure it out on her own, then maybe she could take everything to the authorities at once and, in doing so, prove her innocence before anyone could accuse her.

"You look almost green. Are you all right?" Seth asked, taking a step toward her.

"I'm fine." Nancy put out a hand. "I'm fine, truly. Just tired. I should finish here and go to bed."

He watched her for a moment. "Nancy, if there is something I can do to help you more than I'm already doing, you need to let me know. Is that Mr. Hanson bothering you again? Berkshire?"

"No. No. I've seen nothing of Mr. Hanson." She waved him

off. "Leave me be so I can finish my work. Morning comes faster and faster these days, and I have a great deal to accomplish before I can go to bed."

She heard him move away and relaxed a bit as she put soap and hot water in the sink. But then she felt Seth's hands on her shoulders and nearly jumped into the air as she twisted to face him.

"I don't know why you're so fearful," he said, "but I meant what I said. I care about you, Nancy. And not just because of our youth. I want to be your friend."

They were much too close. His lips were just inches away from hers, and the fading scent of his cologne was intoxicating. For a moment Nancy gazed into his eyes and willed herself just to enjoy the moment. Perhaps Seth was the one man with whom she could have a future. Perhaps she could find true love with him. He said he wanted to be her friend—could he want to be more?

"Seth?" Clementine called as she approached the kitchen.

Nancy turned back to the dishes, banishing thoughts of a love life. The last thing she wanted was to give the household ladies fuel to stir the fires of matchmaking.

"I'm here," he said, stepping away. "I was just concluding our plans for the Fourth. Nancy has agreed to come."

"I'm so glad," Clementine replied, entering the kitchen. "I have enjoyed rekindling our friendship."

Nancy glanced over her shoulder. "I have, too, although I fear we've both been too busy to give it the time it deserves."

"Then we will make up for it on the Fourth," Clementine said, smiling first at Nancy and then her brother. "I'm off to bed, brother of mine."

"Yes, and I'm headed back to my apartment. Gabe will probably be wondering where I am."

Nancy dried her hands on a dish towel. "I didn't know he was staying with you."

"Well, he could hardly stay here with you and all your ladies," Seth said, laughing. "And I couldn't let him spend money at a hotel when I had a perfectly good extra bed. Besides, we've had a lot to catch up on."

"Come along, then, brother. I'll see you out." Clementine took Seth's arm and pulled him from the room.

"I'll see you on the Fourth," he called to Nancy over his shoulder.

She had wanted to walk him to the door herself, but since Clementine had volunteered, there was nothing else to be done. Nancy stood for a moment longer staring at the doorway before forcing herself back to the task of washing the dishes. She still felt weak in the knees from Seth's nearness and soft words. Could she have a future with him?

CHAPTER 13

Fourth of July dawned cloudy and overcast, causing Nancy to worry that it might rain all day. However, the rain held off, and some of the clouds moved eastward, leaving everyone in a festive mood.

Nancy dressed in a burgundy and black dress. It wasn't exactly mourning attire but was subdued enough that if she ran into anyone who knew her situation, it would pass muster. She was glad that Gabe was to be her escort. It was harder to condemn a woman stepping out with her brother rather than a beau. But when Seth and Gabe arrived, Nancy was surprised to find her brother eagerly taking Clementine's arm and leaving Seth to accompany her.

"You look lovely," Seth told her as they started down the porch stairs. "Did you sleep well?"

With the other couple walking several feet ahead of them, Nancy couldn't help but think that Bedelia Clifton would never approve.

"Nancy?"

She looked up. "Yes?"

"I asked if you slept well, but you appear to be lost in thought. Is something wrong?"

"I thought Gabe was to be my escort."

Seth looked wounded. "Do you have something against me?"

"Of course not, but as we discussed before, I am a new widow."

"Nancy, you've never struck me as someone willing to live a lie, and yet after eight years of marriage to a man you clearly didn't love, you're perpetuating exactly that by continuing to pretend you cared for him."

"I did care for him. How dare you say I didn't." She hadn't meant to snap. "I'm sorry. But I did care for Albert, at least to a degree. I never wished him dead. If anything, I wished him more alive. More loving." She hadn't meant to speak that last part aloud and quickly looked away.

"But you shouldn't have to go about in sackcloth and ashes. He's gone, but you're still here—alive and young. I don't think God has in mind for you to sit at home wearing black."

"How would you know what God has in mind for me?"

He grinned. "Well, I think it involves me."

Nancy threw him a sidelong glance. "Of course you do. Men always think they know what God has planned when it involves a woman. I have barely come to accept that God loves me and that I owe Him my trust and allegiance, but you already know my future."

Seth took her arm. "Don't be that way. I don't know everything about the future, nor do I mean to suggest I do. Let's just enjoy the day and see where it takes us. We're celebrating our Independence Day. Maybe you should look at it as a celebration of your own independence. You have been set free from a loveless marriage and the sadness of one lonely night after another."

Nancy stiffened. She'd never said anything to him about being lonely. Had she? She searched through their former conversations and remembered the night they'd gone to supper and then a play. She had told him. The memory made her cringe.

Up ahead, Clementine laughed heartily at something Gabe was saying and then began to gesture with her hands as she told him something in return. His roar of laughter left little doubt that they were enjoying their conversation together. Why was it that Nancy couldn't do likewise?

As they neared the park, band music could be heard. It sounded like a polka song, with the tuba blasting out an *oom-pa-pa* to a steady beat. Polka music was something new to the area thanks to the influx of Polish and Czech immigrants. Nancy had gone to a presentation and lecture on Polish culture the year before. It was there she had first heard and rather liked the festive music.

The crowds thickened as the foursome drew closer to the large park. Food vendors offered a wonderful assortment of foods, including some of the kolaczki pastries Nancy had sampled the year before. The filling was a mixed berry compote, and she had never tasted anything quite so good. Perhaps she could get the recipe this time. Just beyond the food carts, a group of costumed dancers were demonstrating the polka to the lively music provided by a small band. People were clapping in time and seemed completely caught up in the celebration.

"What would you ladies like to do first?" Gabe asked, calling back to Nancy and Seth.

"I'm content to walk around." Nancy could see that there were plenty of attractions. Besides the food vendors, there were others who were selling handmade items, and there were also magicians, musicians, and singers. Across the park, Nancy could even see a man running several dogs through a series of tricks, to the delight of a dozen or more children.

"That's fine with me," Seth replied.

Nancy felt him take a possessive hold on her arm and then noticed Gerome Berkshire approaching. The mustached man frowned as he gave Seth a once-over. She did nothing to alter his displeasure. If anything, she leaned a little closer to Seth. She didn't like the way Gerome made her feel. There was something odd about him that made her feel vulnerable and exposed. He had tried very hard to woo her, begging her to let him court her, but Nancy had no desire to agree. There was something foreboding about Gerome Berkshire, and the longer she knew him, the stronger that feeling came across.

"Well, I must say I didn't expect to see you here at the celebrations, Mrs. Pritchard. Weren't you just telling me it was much too early for you to be out publicly? That was your response to *my* invitation to today's festivities."

Gabe and Clementine quickly joined them. Gabe had apparently heard Berkshire's comment, because he spoke before Seth or Nancy had a chance.

"Is there a problem here? I believe my sister has the right to go out with her brother and family friends."

Gerome smirked. "Of course she does. I've been trying to convince her of that for weeks. A beautiful young woman needn't adhere to social conventions. Especially here in the West, where single women are harder to come by. There will be many a man happy to partner with you for dances and meals. Myself included."

"Well, I'm hardly in search of a partner, since I have my brother and friend at my side," Nancy said.

"Even so, perhaps you would consider allowing me to escort you to the luncheon where I am to speak. It would be my honor to have you there."

"I'm afraid that might give the wrong impression," Gabe declared. "You'll have to find someone else."

Gerome gave him a blank look, then glanced at Clementine.

Gabe put his arm around her shoulders and shook his head. "She's also spoken for."

"You've got that right," Seth said, tightening his hold on Nancy to an almost painful point.

"Well then, the loss is mine," Gerome said, tipping his hat as he bowed. As he straightened, Nancy noticed a change in his demeanor. "By the way, Mr. Carpenter, I have some work that you might be able to help me with."

"Legal work?" Seth asked.

"Yes. I wonder if you would like to stop by my place this week. It's time-consuming work, but I would pay you well."

"You'll need to speak with John Lincoln about it. Come to the office and make an appointment with him. He'll know better whether we have time for your needs."

"I thought perhaps you might earn this money for yourself on the side." Gerome grinned. "I'm sure you could use the extra money."

Seth frowned. "I work for John. I wouldn't consider doing something behind his back or on the side. He's a good man, Berkshire—an honorable and fair man. Talk to him about your needs, and I'm sure he'll give you a fair deal."

Nancy thought Gerome looked insulted. His dark eyes seemed to grow even blacker, and his face took on a ruddy hue. She looked at Gabe, who watched Gerome as he might a wild animal. She could tell he was sizing him up, determining how big of a threat he might pose. The last thing she wanted was for a fight to break out.

"I must have some of those pastries," she said, smiling at Seth. "Would you mind if we get in line?"

Seth hesitated only a moment. "I'm at your command." He gave her a smile and loosened his hold on her arm a bit.

"Good day, Mr. Berkshire," Nancy said and all but pulled Seth toward the line. "Come on, Gabe, you have to try these. They're amazing."

It wasn't until after they'd purchased their baked goods and found a table where they could sit and sample their fare that anyone spoke again.

"I wanted to punch that guy in the nose," Gabe said, popping an entire kolaczki in his mouth.

"Mr. Berkshire has that effect on people." Nancy hated to admit even that much, for fear it would start them back into ill feelings and ruin the day. "But thankfully we don't have to deal with him anymore. I'm so glad the day has turned nice."

Everyone glanced overhead. There were still clouds in the sky, but the sun was shining, and the rain was holding off.

"I heard there is to be a Founding Fathers play at eleven. What say we make our way to that?" Clementine suggested. "One of my friends is playing George Washington."

"Oh, that sounds like fun." Nancy smiled and sampled her pastry. It was just as good as she remembered, like a cookie that had been wrapped around its fruit filling. "I have to figure out how to make these. I don't think the filling will be all that difficult, but the dough is something special."

"I'll bet we can get someone to share the recipe," Clementine murmured between bites. "I'd like to be able to make these as well. Maybe once you learn, you can teach me too."

Nancy took another bite of the filled cookie. "Maybe one of your students this fall will be of Polish or Czech descent, and his mother would be willing to teach us both."

"We can only hope," Clementine said, snatching another cookie. "I know this will probably spoil my lunch, but they're so good."

The day passed much too quickly. They enjoyed the Founding Fathers play and then watched another performance by schoolchildren regarding the founding of Oregon. Lunch was a veritable feast of roasted pig, sweet baked beans, and so many other foods that Nancy lost track. By the time evening rolled around, she was more than happy to return to the house.

"Are you sure you two don't want to stay and dance?" Gabe asked. "I'm not much into it myself, but I don't want it said I was the cause of you gals not getting to enjoy yourselves."

"No. I'm supposed to be in mourning, remember?" Nancy's feet also hurt from spending all day walking around the park.

"And my feet hurt," Clementine declared as if reading Nancy's thoughts. "I shouldn't have worn these boots. They always did pinch, and now I've probably got a blister."

"Put vinegar on it," Gabe said, laughing. "That's what our ma would say."

They all laughed and continued toward Nancy's boarding-house. It was nearly dark by the time they reached it, and the warm glow of light emanating from the house made a cheery welcome.

"Would you two like to come in for coffee?" Nancy let Seth help her up the steps while she clutched a handful of her skirt.

"None for me," Gabe said. "Even though it's Saturday to-morrow, I have to be down at the mill, working. We've got to get a big shipment of finished lumber down to California.

After that, I'm headed home, so I doubt I'll see you again on this trip, sis."

"And I'm looking forward to my bed and a long sleep," Seth said with a grin. He dropped his hold on Nancy's arm when they reached the door. "I'm just going to bid you good night. Thank you for the wonderful day."

"That's what I was about to say." Nancy opened the front door. "I had a splendid time and am very glad I let you talk me into going."

"It was fun," Clementine chimed in. "I didn't realize just how delightful your brother could be."

"Of course I'm delightful. I'm also charming, witty, and dashingly handsome," Gabe added with a laugh.

"That he is," Nancy said, shaking her head. She kissed Gabe on the cheek.

"Hey, what about me?" Seth said, sounding pitiful.

Nancy surprised herself and him by going to him and repeating the gesture. She placed the briefest of kisses on his cheek, then stepped back with a smile. "Thank you as well."

Seth said nothing more, and Nancy felt a little overcome by her actions and the day. She had the strangest feeling of awakening from a dream. It was as if she'd been sleeping for years—dead to the world—and now she was coming back to life. She could almost feel the blood coursing through her veins.

"Good night," she whispered, then hurried into the house.

Without bothering to see if the ladies were in the front room, Nancy made a dash for her first-floor bedroom and kicked off her shoes. She thought about the day and how much fun she'd had. She hadn't enjoyed herself that much in forever. She'd never had fun like that with Albert. He wasn't one to enjoy such things, and business always kept him much too busy.

The thought of Albert and his business affairs caused her to go to the bedside table where she'd left his river journal. Picking it up, Nancy thumbed through to the pages of suspicious drawings. She paused on the drawing that looked familiar. She was certain it had to be that place they used to go. Tomorrow was Saturday. Maybe if she got her work done in time, she would saddle the horse and slip off to investigate.

"Your sister is quickly charming her way to my heart."

"I think you're completely gone on her," Gabe replied as they walked back to Seth's apartment.

"I suppose it would be foolish to say otherwise. She does have a way about her that I can't deny is extremely attractive."

"I think you two work well together," Gabe said. "I think she needs a man like you."

"I do too," Seth replied, laughing. "I never would have figured that scrawny, sad-faced little girl would be the woman I'd one day want to marry."

"Are you sure about it now?"

"Gettin' surer every day." Seth pushed his hands deep into his trouser pockets. "I never gave too much thought to settling down. I mean, I was never against the idea, but there was always my schooling or work. I was determined to be finished with school and secure in my job before I even bought a place to live."

"Well, you can't get much more secure than working toward a partnership," Gabe countered. "I'd say you're well enough established to take on a wife and family."

"And you wouldn't mind having me as a brother?" Seth asked, grinning.

"I can't think of anyone I'd rather have. That Pritchard fella wasn't worth the spit it would take to wet a stamp."

Seth paused to make sure his voice still sounded natural. "Did you know him well?"

"No. He wasn't inclined to let any of us know him very well," Gabe admitted. "He wanted nothing to do with the family. Pa and I both tried to reach out to him—to make him feel welcome. None of us wanted Nancy to marry him, but once the deed was done, we didn't want to do anything to come between them. We always tried to extend friendship, but Pritchard wasn't interested. He told us to mind our own business and left it at that. He didn't want Nancy having much to do with any of us."

"Perhaps he was afraid of someone finding out about his liquor and weapons business." Seth was surprised to find they'd already reached his apartment. He fished out his key and shook his head. "One thing is certain. Albert Pritchard was a man of secrets."

Gabe shrugged. "I suppose we all have them."

Seth frowned and thought of his reason for coming to Portland in the first place. Investigating Albert and Nancy Pritchard. Theirs had only been names on a page until Seth realized who Nancy truly was. Now that he knew, how was he ever going to explain his position to her?

Secrets indeed.

CHAPTER 14

They've written about Mr. Berkshire's speech in the newspaper," Bedelia announced at breakfast Sunday morning. "Did any of you attend on the Fourth?"

Nancy shook her head and passed a bowl of fried potatoes and onions. "I had no desire to listen to him drone on and on about his hatred of people of color. You would think he had been personally harmed by the emancipation of slaves." She sipped her coffee.

"I suppose it's not that surprising that so many hate other kinds of people," Mimi said, her fork halfway to her lips. "I find that folks are often afraid of things or people or even places that are unfamiliar. I believe if white people took time to get to know the black population, or the Indians or Chinese, they might change their tunes."

"I agree. One summer when I was about fifteen, I went to one of the Indian reservations to help my aunt and uncle." Nancy remembered it fondly. "I got to know some of the Indian women and children and learned about their history and their culture. It was fascinating."

"You lived with the heathens?" Bedelia asked, her voice a mix of disapproval and awe.

"Not exactly. I stayed with my aunt and uncle and cousins. They minister to the Indians and teach school. They have always had a love of all people, and I really admire that. I wish I could say I had always felt the same, but as Mimi mentioned, I suppose fear kept my heart guarded until I got to know them myself."

"Well, there are hardly enough black people in Portland to worry over. Yet Mr. Berkshire would see them all rounded up, severely whipped, and then put on a train for parts unknown," Clementine said, reaching for another biscuit. "The article said he spoke in a particularly distasteful manner about the integration of black children into white schools. He believes the black children would corrupt the thinking of the whites."

"Corrupt it? In what way?" Mimi asked.

Clementine shrugged. "I suppose in every way. Mr. Berkshire said black people are lazy because they aren't working. Yet he doesn't encourage white people to hire them. In fact, he suggests it be made an illegal offense to hire black people or Indians for positions white men can do. He truly doesn't see anyone but whites as deserving of jobs and education."

"I read that it was illegal to educate black slaves," Mimi said.

"It was in Georgia," Mrs. Weaver announced as she entered the room. "I apologize for being late." She looked at Nancy and nodded.

"You mustn't fret, Mrs. Weaver. We do not stand on ceremony here. Please have a seat."

Nancy was glad Mrs. Weaver had decided to join them. She had told Nancy the day before that she wanted to attend church, and Nancy had invited her to come along with her and Clementine and Mimi. Mrs. Weaver had admitted that she hoped to do exactly that. It was a show of trust, Nancy thought, that the old woman had become more social, and Nancy intended to do whatever she could to promote it. The fact that she had come to join them for breakfast was just another encouraging moment.

"You were saying that it was illegal to educate slaves," Bedelia reminded Mrs. Weaver.

"Yes." The old woman nodded, and her lacy cap bobbed. "But I didn't care to be a stickler for the law. If one of the black children showed interest, I taught them the alphabet. I even taught one child to read. My mother was all for such endeavors. She thought it foolish to keep people ignorant. She was of the strong opinion that knowledge equaled power."

"But would that not have been the precise reason white people refrained from educating their slaves?" Bedelia asked. "They would not want them having any power."

"Yes, I'm sure you're right on that account," Mrs. Weaver replied.

"Mr. Berkshire believes all blacks should be sent back to Africa—the land of their origin—yet never accounts for the fact that most were born right here in the United States and know nothing of their African ancestry or culture," Mimi threw in. "I can't imagine if someone suggested I go back to Germany where my ancestors were born. I can't speak German and certainly have no idea where I would go or what I would do."

"Not only that, but Seth and I were discussing the fact that many black people aren't even from Africa. How would you ever figure out where to send them?" Clementine asked no one in particular.

"I don't believe the blacks should be forced from Oregon," Bedelia interjected. "However, I can well imagine they'd have little to do with white people. They don't understand our culture, just as we don't understand theirs. It would be better for them to remain in their own communities amongst their own people. Like the Indians. Perhaps there could be a black reservation."

"Rather than take time to learn about one another?" Mimi questioned.

"Well, we would hardly have any reason to learn, would we? It isn't like we will ever be able to socialize together."

For a moment everyone looked at Bedelia.

"But why not?" Nancy asked.

Bedelia frowned. "Because we're not alike. We have nothing in common."

"Surely we have in common the things of life itself. Our families, homes, fears, and dreams," Nancy reasoned.

"I believe friendships are possible," Mrs. Weaver interjected. "But it is true that few people are accepting of such things."

The conversation dried up at that point, and it wasn't until the clock chimed eight that anyone seemed compelled to do anything but eat.

"I need to get to church early," Clementine said, dabbing her mouth and then setting her napkin aside. "I'm teaching Sunday School this morning."

"I am too." Mimi got to her feet. "I'll walk with you."

Clementine got up and grabbed her dishes. On Sundays everyone helped clear off the table and put the dishes in the sink to soak. Mimi followed suit, and together they headed for the kitchen.

Bedelia took a final sip from her teacup, then nodded at Cornelia. "Come, sister. We should be on our way as well."

That left Nancy and Mrs. Weaver to finish breakfast. Nancy

smiled at the older woman. "Since it's raining, I thought we'd take the buggy." She had decided to take the buggy rain or shine in order to accommodate Mrs. Weaver's frailty.

"That would be lovely, Mrs. Pritchard."

"I want you to call me Nancy." She smiled. "I'd like us to be friends."

Mrs. Weaver nodded. "I feel that we are. In fact, I have felt most welcome here."

"I'm glad to hear it. I'm afraid I haven't always been the most congenial."

"But of course not. You're a new widow and so very young. I can't imagine losing my husband at your age. It was hard enough as an old woman."

"I would think that would make it all the harder. After all, you had a lifetime of memories together."

Mrs. Weaver nodded. "And we were so very happy. My Robert and I fell in love when I was just thirteen and he fifteen. We were inseparable." Her eyes dampened. "The days are quite lonely without him, and but for—" She stopped abruptly. "Oh goodness, how I do ramble on." She finished her biscuit, then struggled to her feet. "Do we still plan to leave at nine?"

Nancy could see the old woman was rather flustered. Perhaps she wasn't yet ready to speak about her dead husband. "Yes. Nine. I'll bring the buggy around front."

Mrs. Weaver hurried from the room without gathering her dishes. Nancy didn't mind, however. This was only the second time she'd joined them on a Sunday, and she had probably forgotten the procedure the others had started.

Nancy got to her feet and collected the dirty plates. She couldn't help but think about the conversation they'd shared at breakfast. People like Gerome were so hateful toward the

Indians, blacks, Chinese, and anyone else who wasn't white. Albert had been the same way, and her husband's prejudices made her angry. Why did he hate the Indians so much? Her own family had actually suffered at the hands of Indians, yet instead of hating, her family held great love for them. Her father still made journeys to see his old friend Sam Two Moons, a Nez Perce who lived with his family in Canada. Her uncle Adam was even part Cherokee, although no one talked about it in public. There were all sorts of laws against races intermarrying, and Aunt Mercy had no Indian blood. Her marriage to Adam might be questioned should anyone realize his heritage.

With the table cleared, Nancy went to her room to finish dressing for church. She chose a gown of darkest green trimmed in black. She wore her black mourning hat but removed the veil. Had anyone seen her at the Fourth of July celebration, they might think her hypocritical to come to church draped in a mourning veil. Besides, she didn't feel like mourning. With each passing day, Nancy felt less and less given to dwell on the past and her loss. Her new walk with God had given her much to think about, and while she couldn't say she felt completely certain of His path for her, Nancy felt so much better just for having cleared the air, so to speak.

She picked up her Bible and hugged it to her breast. She still wasn't sure where one went from this point. She had asked God's forgiveness for her bad thoughts and attitude toward Him. She had asked Him to direct her steps and teach her from His Word. And while she had to admit she did feel as if a heavy blanket had been lifted from her shoulders, she was still rather uncertain what else she was to do.

"Lord," she whispered, looking toward the ceiling, "I've

never been all that quick to learn. If I'm not seeing what you're trying to show me, please open my eyes."

Church was a pleasant affair, and Nancy was glad when Clementine and Seth joined her and Mrs. Weaver in the pew. It gave her a sense of family and reminded her of all the years she'd gone to church in Oregon City, surrounded by her parents and siblings as well as aunts and uncles and cousins. Nancy had forgotten just what a strong sense of family church had always represented. Why hadn't she appreciated it then?

A memory of Douglas came to mind. Shortly before he died, she had been in charge of keeping him quiet in church one Sunday. Her mother was absent, delivering a baby or helping someone who was sick, and Nancy had taken charge of Douglas while her father oversaw James, who was a few years Nancy's junior and quite a handful. Douglas had curled up beside her and put his hand in hers, and there they sat for the entire service. He had been as good as a child could be. Afterward her father had told her that one day she was going to make an excellent mother. The memory was bittersweet. Why had there never been children for her and Albert?

After church, Clementine and Seth went their separate ways. It seemed the Lincolns had invited them to dinner at their house. Nancy loaded up Mrs. Weaver for the ride home. She was delighted when the old woman mentioned enjoying the pastor's choice of Scripture from Ephesians.

"It was always a particularly favorite book for my Robert," Mrs. Weaver explained as they made their way home.

"Do you have a favorite book of the Bible, Mrs. Weaver?"

The old woman nodded. "Goodness, yes. I love the Psalms. They inspire me to such heights of hope. What about you?"

Nancy had never thought about having a favorite book of

the Bible. It was upon pondering this that she realized just how surface-level her relationship with God and His Word had been. She had read a good part of the Bible as a matter of rote, but understanding had come hard, and she was never sure how this ancient book applied to her current circumstance. Today, however, in hearing the pastor teach from the first chapter of Ephesians, Nancy felt hope that things would change.

"I keep thinking on verse seventeen from today. I couldn't help memorizing it: 'That the God of our Lord Jesus Christ, the Father of glory, may give unto you the spirit of wisdom and revelation in the knowledge of him.'"

She needed a better knowledge and understanding of God and His Word. She needed the spirit of wisdom and revelation in the knowledge of Him.

"A wonderful verse, to be sure."

Paul had prayed that the Ephesians would have this. Dare she pray for it for herself?

At home, Nancy helped Mrs. Weaver from the buggy, then drove it around back to the carriage house. Racer, a thorough-bred mix, was happy to return to his comfortable stall. Nancy took a moment with the horse and remembered her youth, when she'd quite enjoyed riding. When had she gotten away from that? She had often gone for long rides after Douglas's death, but after marrying Albert, her habit had fallen away. She remembered once asking Albert if they might go riding, and he had told her that hardworking people had no time for such nonsense.

"Well, Racer, perhaps if you will tolerate the intrusion, I should like to go for a ride someday." The horse ignored her, far more intent on the fresh hay she'd served up.

Nancy smiled. She had planned to ride out the day before

and investigate Albert's drawings, but so much busyness had taken up her time with ironing and preparations for Sunday, and before she knew it, the day was waning. Tomorrow, however, she might be able to slip away. Especially once everyone got off to work. Even the Clifton sisters had their work at the church, sorting used clothes for the poor and making sure the garments didn't need mending.

Making her way into the house, Nancy heard Mrs. Weaver telling Mimi something in an alarmed voice. She'd never heard the old woman so upset.

"What's wrong?" she asked, entering the front room.

"Mrs. Weaver is adamant that someone broke into the house while we were gone," Mimi declared.

Nancy shook her head. "Why do you think that?"

Mrs. Weaver looked away and wrung her hands together. "I, well, you know that I always lock my room. Upon our return, the door was unlocked, and it looked as though my things had been gone through."

"Surely not." Nancy glanced around the front room. Nothing seemed to be missing. Had someone really come in while they were gone? If so, why? Were they seeking to rob the place? "Mimi, did you check your room?"

"Not yet. I just got back. Mrs. Weaver met me before I could go upstairs."

Nancy nodded. "I suggest we each go to our rooms and investigate. Should anything be missing, note it, and we will tell the police."

With that, Nancy hurried to her room and began to search for anything that looked out of place. She had begun to think that all was well until her gaze fell on the nightstand beside her bed. Albert's river journal was gone. Perhaps it had fallen. She went to the bedside and raised the thick quilt. Bending down, she looked beneath the bed, but there was no sign of the book.

She felt a shiver start at the nape of her neck and run all the way down her spine. Someone had come into her house and taken the book. She was certain of it. She was even more certain that the book would turn out to be the only thing missing. She bit her lip. Someone wanted the guns and whiskey badly enough to risk getting caught robbing her house. What else would they risk?

Nancy made her way to the front room, where Mrs. Weaver waited. The old woman caught her attention. She knew. She knew that Nancy had realized the truth.

Mimi returned as well. "I can't see that anything is missing, but I do believe Mrs. Weaver is right. Someone was in my room. I say this only because I had laid out some things on my desk, and they seem to have been reordered."

Nancy nodded. "Someone was in my room as well."

"Is anything missing?" Mimi asked.

"A book." Nancy felt her knees weaken and grabbed the back of the chair. "I didn't note that anything else had been taken."

"Who would break in to take a book? It would hardly have any value—unless of course there was something special about it."

"I don't know. It was my husband's."

But Nancy did know. She knew without a doubt that whoever had broken into her house was after those maps. Had it been that awful Mr. Hanson? She felt sick inside. What was she going to do?

CHAPTER 15

Seth and Clementine returned to the boardinghouse after spending a leisurely lunch at the Lincolns'. The conversation had been enjoyable and the company satisfying. If only Nancy had been included, it might have been perfect.

As they approached the boardinghouse, a light rain started to fall. Neither had remembered an umbrella, so they hurried their steps until they were all but running. Laughter spilled out of Clementine.

"I remember when we used to race to the house from the barn in the rain. Papa told us that for every step we took in the rain, we would get hit with at least one thousand raindrops."

Seth laughed and shook the rain from his blue worsted coat. "I remember that. I always wondered where he came up with that number."

Clementine nodded and reached for the door. "I did too. I once tried to count raindrops, but it didn't work out well. I was soaked and still couldn't figure out how to count the ones that hit my back." She pushed the door open. "Are you coming in?"

"I figured to. I hoped I might have a chance to speak with Nancy. There was no time at church, since she was determined to get Mrs. Weaver home."

"I'm sure she'll have time now. She's very good about keeping the Sabbath. She doesn't even cook much and instead uses food she's already made. I had never really thought about how Mother kept the Sabbath. She always seemed to have everything in order, though. Now, as I watch Nancy, I see what a chore it must have been, always doubling up the work on Saturday." Clementine stepped aside as Seth walked through the door. "Wait here, and I'll announce that you've returned with me."

He leaned back against the doorjamb once the door was closed. "Announce away."

Clementine smiled and left him in the foyer. Seth heard her tell someone that her brother had returned with her, and then it seemed there was nothing but upheaval. Everyone was talking all at once, and nothing made much sense. Clementine was soon back in the foyer. She looked concerned.

"They say that someone broke into the house while they were in church. I need to inspect my room to see if they were in there as well."

Seth felt his muscles stiffen. He glanced around the foyer and then settled his gaze on the steps. "Are they certain whoever it was isn't still here?"

Clementine shrugged as she headed for the stairs. "I don't know. You'd better speak with Nancy."

Seth went into the front room, where Mimi Bryant and Nancy were talking. "Clementine just told me that you think someone broke into the house."

"We don't just think so, we know they did," Nancy replied. "They took something."

"What was it?" Seth felt his anger stirred at the very thought of someone threatening the well-being of these ladies.

Before Nancy could answer, Bedelia and Cornelia Clifton returned from church. The elder sister immediately sensed there was trouble.

"What has happened?" Bedelia asked, going to Nancy.

Nancy drew a deep breath and glanced at Mimi. "I'm afraid someone broke into the house while we were all at church."

Cornelia gasped and put her hand to her throat. Bedelia, however, gave a no-nonsense nod. "We shall investigate our room and let you know what, if anything, is missing. As two single ladies of poor means, we hardly had anything of value, but there are strange people who steal things purely for the satisfaction of it. Come, Cornelia."

She made her way from the room as Clementine returned. Bedelia paused as if sensing there was a report coming.

"I have nothing missing." Clementine looked at Seth. "But someone was definitely in my room."

He frowned. Given the trouble Albert Pritchard had gotten himself into, he had little doubt this was about him. Now he needed to know what they had taken from Nancy. He led her to the kitchen.

"What did they take from your room?"

"An old river journal Albert kept." She bit her lip and looked at the floor. There was something she wasn't telling him.

Seth took hold of her arms. "Nancy, don't you trust me, even after all this time?"

She said nothing right away. When she finally looked up, there were tears in her eyes. "I want to. I know there's no reason I shouldn't. I'm sorry I've been so unwilling."

"Trust me now, then. I promise, I have only your best interest at heart." He pushed aside his growing guilt at not being honest with her about his investigation.

She nodded. "I believe that. You know about the guns and whiskey and that Mr. Hanson asked after his. Threatened, in fact. That night he was here waiting on the porch, he made it clear that he would . . . well, he told me that the guns and whiskey were to be sold to the Indians."

"Why would he admit to something like that?" Seth asked, having already formed an opinion of Hanson's declaration.

"I don't know. He threatened me too. Said I needed to find out where the stuff was. I told him I would go to the authorities because I wanted no part in anything illegal. He told me if I dared try, he would make sure the authorities knew I was—I was—" She couldn't seem to speak.

"A part of it?" Seth asked.

"Yes." She shook her head. "I swear I'm not. I knew nothing about it, but the authorities would have no reason to believe me over Mr. Hanson."

"They'd have every reason, Nancy. You're an upstanding Christian woman. You have people who have known you for a long time who would vouch for you. No doubt Hanson thought that if he threatened you with the truth of what Albert was doing, you'd be motivated to find what he needed."

This was the only conclusion Seth had been able to come to, but it made perfect sense. Hanson had asked Nancy to investigate and find his cache of weapons, but she hadn't found them nor given any indication that the matter was of importance to her.

"I feel so stupid. I found Albert's journal, but at first it seemed like nothing. It was an older book from his days on the river. The cover was royal blue," she said as if that made a difference.

178

"He had made charts of the Willamette and Columbia, noting currents and water depths, snags and such. Each map was dated and noted with longitude and latitude. But then at the back, I found other maps. There were quite a few—a half dozen or so. They weren't identified with longitude and latitude, although I thought I recognized one of them as a place where Albert had taken me on a picnic several times. I've been intending to make my way out there to see what I could find."

"You were going to go there alone?" Seth asked in disbelief. "Nancy, these men are dangerous. No doubt they are watching you."

"They probably killed Albert, didn't they?" She sounded like a scared little girl.

Seth wasn't about to lie to her more than he already had. "Probably."

"Do you suppose they'll know what the maps mean?"

"I would imagine so. It seems to me that they broke in with the sole purpose of finding that journal. Maybe one of them knew about the book. Maybe Albert told them about it. It might even be Berkshire. After all, they had some sort of partnership. It wouldn't surprise me if Berkshire fronted some of the money. Maybe that's what the IOUs are about. Not so much a loan, since Albert didn't believe in such things, but rather his investment in the guns and whiskey." Seth's thoughts churned. "Who knew you'd found that book?"

"No one. I didn't even mention it to the ladies."

She looked so distressed that Seth couldn't bring himself to reprimand her. "Well, if they have what they want, then perhaps they'll leave you alone now." He wasn't convinced of that, however.

Her eyes widened. "Surely they will. I have nothing else. I

know nothing. You have to believe me, Seth. I never knew about the guns and whiskey. My aunt and uncle work on a reservation. I would never approve of giving guns and whiskey to the Indians. I know how hard it has made life. Aunt Mercy is always talking about the problems associated with liquor on the reservation."

"Yes, and people seem determined to use it to ruin them. If they can manipulate the Indians into starting an uprising, the government's response will be swift, and the Indians will suffer for it."

"Albert never told me what he was doing. Foolish man. Foolish." She buried her face in her hands.

Seth couldn't help himself. He pulled Nancy into his arms and held her. "It's going to be all right, Nancy. You'll see. I won't let anyone hurt you."

"But you don't have that power," she said, looking up.

Her lips were just inches from his. Seth had never wanted to kiss someone more than he wanted to kiss Nancy right now. He was fairly certain it was a poor time to do so, however, and stepped away from her.

She stared up at him for a moment, then turned away as if embarrassed. "What should I do? Should I send for the police?"

"No. I think we let them believe they pulled it off without anyone being the wiser. We need to figure out exactly who took the journal. I feel fairly confident it was Hanson or Berkshire."

"Gerome?" Nancy's brow furrowed. "Why do you think he's involved?"

"You said he was bothering you for what Albert owed him. Berkshire hates the Indians more than just about anyone in the city. If anyone was going to start a war with them, it would be Berkshire and his cohorts."

"But how would they benefit from arming the Indians and

starting a war? How is that going to aid their cause?" she asked, hugging her arms to her body.

"Whenever the Indians dare to fight, the government punishes them. Usually by stripping away more land. I have a feeling this is about enticing the Indians to go to war so that the government will force them onto a smaller reservation farther from white settlements. Berkshire could be part of a group that pretends friendship with the Indians only to instigate bad feelings toward the local settlers. There are groups out there that band together to see that the Indians are denied every possible benefit—not that the government has given them much in the way of concessions."

"Aunt Mercy and Uncle Adam say it's appalling how the Indians are treated. They are promised blankets, materials to build homes and furniture, food and medicines, and then receive poor substitutes and worthless items that cannot possibly benefit them. I remember once she said they were to receive wool blankets, but when they arrived, they were so moth-eaten and poorly woven that they were hardly usable."

"I've heard similar stories."

Clementine joined them in the kitchen. "The ladies are all in a dither. The Misses Clifton are terrified the burglars will return after nightfall and harm them in their sleep." She smiled. "I think they worry about potential danger."

Seth nodded. The eccentric sisters were always worried about something, it seemed.

Nancy looked at Seth. "I don't know what to do or even suggest."

"I do. I will spend the night. I can sleep on the porch if needed. Come, we'll talk to the ladies and see what compromise will be acceptable."

Nancy followed him and Clementine back into the front room, but Seth could see by the look on her face that she didn't believe his solution would be agreeable.

"Ladies," Seth said, motioning them all to draw near, "I know you are worried about this situation. I personally don't believe that you are in any further danger. The book that was stolen was the very article I believe the thief was seeking."

"Who steals a book?" Bedelia asked. "It could hardly have been worth much."

"In this particular case it was worth quite a bit." Seth saw no reason to tell them everything, but it was important they feel safe. "Nancy had been asked about this book, but her knowledge of it was limited. She happened upon it and didn't realize that this was what the man sought."

"What man?" Bedelia demanded. All gazes went to Nancy.

Seth wasn't going to let the matter fall on her shoulders. "A former customer of her husband's. He was looking for proof of an order he had purchased. It's all being managed by John Lincoln and myself, and I cannot go into more detail at this time. However, I want you to know that I will take personal responsibility for you ladies and this house. I will stay here tonight to ensure that you all feel safe."

The ladies glanced at one another. Mrs. Weaver spoke up first. "I think that would be a wise idea. Just in case the man tries to return."

"It's hardly appropriate to have a man in a houseful of women to whom he's not related," Bedelia began. "However, given our fears, I cannot protest. It would be a comfort to know someone was here keeping watch."

Seth knew she was the one to win over. "I could sleep on the porch if that makes you more comfortable."

Bedelia frowned. "The porch? But you would never hear if someone were actually in the house. No, I believe you should sleep here on the sofa. Our bedrooms are all upstairs, except for Nancy's." Her frown deepened as she looked at Nancy. "You have a lock on your door, don't you? Perhaps Mr. Carpenter's sister could share your room tonight."

Nancy nodded. "I am not opposed to that. I am just as afraid of this situation as you are." She looked at Clementine, who nodded her approval.

"It's settled, then." Seth smiled. "But I need to leave you ladies for a short time so I can collect a few things."

"I hope one of those things is a firearm," Bedelia declared. Cornelia gasped and put a hand to her mouth.

Seth nodded. "Indeed."

"Just don't go shooting one of us if we venture downstairs in the night," the spinster declared with a hint of a smile on her lips.

"Perhaps just for tonight," Seth said, looking at each woman, "you could all refrain from venturing downstairs. That way, if I hear anyone moving about, I will know I'm free to shoot."

"He's right, of course," Bedelia replied. "We must all remain upstairs once we retire. It will be to everyone's safety, including Mr. Carpenter's."

Seth might have laughed out loud, but he had the strangest thought that he wouldn't put it past Bedelia Clifton to have a gun of her own. And while he truly didn't believe Hanson, Berkshire, or any of their hirelings would be back, he certainly didn't want to have a shootout with the spinster.

After all, she might win.

Nancy found it almost impossible to sleep knowing Seth was just down the hall in the front room. Clementine, on the other hand, slept like a log. She didn't so much as roll over. Staring at the ceiling, Nancy wondered if Seth was right and Gerome Berkshire was at the head of all this trouble. He had made a pest of himself since Albert's death, and even before. She had always felt uncomfortable with his attention and wondered why Albert never seemed to notice.

She didn't know when she fell asleep, but when she awakened hours later, Nancy felt surprisingly rested. She also realized that they'd made it safely through the night without any intruders. At least she hoped that was the case.

Careful not to awaken Clementine, Nancy slipped from the bed and dressed quickly in a brown skirt and ivory-colored pleated blouse with a high collar, buttoning up the front. Used to tending to her own needs, Nancy combed out her long brown hair and plaited it into a single braid that she wrapped into a knot at the nape of her neck and pinned into place. She looked simple and modest. Would Seth like what he saw?

"Mmm, what time is it?" Clementine murmured from the bed.

"Early. I need to start breakfast. Go back to sleep." Nancy unlocked and opened her bedroom door just as the grandfather clock chimed the hour. "It's five, to be exact."

Clementine rolled over and pulled the covers high. "I'll be up shortly."

"I'll have breakfast on the table by six as usual."

But before Nancy could reach the kitchen, she caught a whiff of coffee and something else. She frowned. Who was cooking in her kitchen?

She came through the dining room and into the kitchen and

found Seth standing over the stove, humming. She paused to watch him for a moment, smiling at the very domestic sight. He'd apparently decided to attempt breakfast. In truth, he looked surprisingly at ease.

"Albert would have been struck dead before lowering himself to cook," she said, announcing her presence.

Seth didn't even turn around. "Then he didn't have a mother such as mine, who declared that every young man should be able to cook for himself in case he found himself waiting well into adulthood for the right woman to marry."

Nancy giggled. "My mother used to say something like that to my brothers. Gabe and James are quite adept in the kitchen. In fact, I hate to admit it, but their biscuits might even be better than mine."

Seth glanced over his shoulder. "That I find highly doubtful." He went back to tending the skillet. "Did you sleep well?"

Grabbing her apron as she crossed the room, Nancy shook her head. "Not at first. It seemed strange to have you here and even harder to accept that someone had broken into the house. Your sister, however, slept like the dead."

He turned and frowned. "Didn't you trust me to keep you safe?"

Nancy tied her apron around her waist. "Of course I did, but it was disconcerting to know there was a man in the house and that the house is apparently easy to break into." She came to the stove and saw that he'd just put bacon into a skillet and was frying it up. "Here, let me."

"No. I want to prove to you that I'm fully capable. The coffee is brewing and should be ready soon."

"Then I'll start making biscuits and bread. I have never seen women who love their bread and rolls as much as this bunch do."

Seth laughed and turned his attention back to the skillet. "Do you suppose there might be cinnamon rolls?"

Nancy smirked and reached for her jar of ground cinnamon. "I think that could be arranged."

"Your baking is the best I've ever had. I can't imagine your brothers are capable of anything better. Your biscuits are as light as a cloud."

Nancy smiled as she took out her mixing bowls. "Be that as it may, bread isn't really what's occupying my thoughts at the moment. What do you think I should do about Albert's journal?"

"Nothing."

She looked at him, but he ignored her. "Nothing?"

"I don't want you to do anything about any of this. You don't understand these men. If they're part of the bunch I think they are, then they're very dangerous sorts."

"You seem to know an awful lot about them for having just come to the area."

"Not at all. Any law-abiding man who has paid attention to what's going on in the area knows these things. Your brother and I talked at length about it. He said your aunt and uncle have been battling to keep whiskey off the reservation. It always leads to trouble and yet it's always so readily available. I just know that when men put their minds together to create a problem where none should exist, they are generally motivated by greed, and greedy men are dangerous."

Nancy shrugged and retrieved the flour from the pantry. "I suppose that makes sense. Still, I know where one of those maps led. I want to find it for myself and see what's there. Those men may have Albert's journal, but they're going to be as confused as I was."

"Not necessarily. You said that the maps were drawings of

the rivers. There are a great many men in Portland who know every inch of the Willamette and Columbia. They may well take one look at those maps and recognize the place without need of longitude and latitude."

"I suppose you're right." Nancy had been so perplexed by the maps that she presumed everyone would have the same difficulty, but what Seth said made good sense. There were a great many rivermen in the area, and from the details that Albert had put in, someone was bound to identify the location.

"What I think you should do is tell me where Albert took you picnicking, and I'll check it out myself," Seth said.

"Why can't I help you?"

"Because, as I said, these men are dangerous. I don't want you putting yourself into a position where you might get killed."

"Like Albert."

"Yes."

She frowned. "I never even knew he had left the house until the police showed up at my door to tell me he'd been fished from the river." She shook her head. "Had we shared a room, I might have been able to stop him from going. From being killed."

"It wasn't your fault, Nancy."

"I know. But I feel there must be something I can do to help find his killer. Don't I owe him that much?"

She stopped and looked at Seth, who was watching her. He came to her and placed a hand on her arm. "No. I don't think you owe him anything. You gave him eight years of your life, and this is how he repaid you. He lied to you and involved himself in who knows what dangerous activities. He didn't care about the risk to you, but instead willingly associated himself with men who, unless I am mistaken, were responsible for ending his life. Men who could do the same to you, or worse.

Nancy, this isn't a child's game. Promise me you won't go looking for trouble."

"I never go looking for trouble." She smiled, hoping it would ease the worried look in his eyes. "It just always seems to find me. If that weren't the case, I wouldn't be here now, talking to you in the kitchen at five in the morning. Speaking of which, I need to get my bread and biscuits made."

"And cinnamon rolls," he said, grinning.

"Yes, and cinnamon rolls," she replied with a smile, hoping he didn't see the worry she felt.

If Albert truly had been murdered, then what was to stop his killer from coming after her? Perhaps he was the one who'd broken into her house. The one who could just as easily do it again.

CHAPTER 16

Despite assuring Seth that she would do what she could to avoid trouble, when Gerome Berkshire came calling with an invitation to a birthday party being held in his honor, Nancy saw it as the perfect opportunity. Seth was convinced Berkshire was a part of the weapons and whiskey conspiracy and perhaps had even instigated the break-in at her home. If she spent the evening in his company, maybe he would accidentally tell her something. Something to help her understand if he'd had a part in Albert's criminal activities.

"It would be such an honor to have you with me for my birthday," Gerome said, sitting opposite her in the front room. He balanced the cup of tea she'd given him with the grace and elegance of man used to such finery.

"Where is this party to be held?" She didn't want to appear too eager, but if she could spend a little time with Gerome, maybe he would reveal what he and Albert had planned.

"At the home of Samuel Lakewood and his wife, Deborah. It will be only the finest of society," he assured her.

"And who might accompany us?"

"Accompany us?" He looked confused.

"Yes, to act as chaperone." She took a sip of her tea. "I must guard my reputation, after all. It's bad enough that I've broken with tradition and not held to a year in mourning."

"Yes, but you're an adult and a widowed woman. It's not like you're a young maid, innocent of the affairs of man." His smile verged on leering.

"Perhaps it's because I'm not a young maid innocent of the affairs of man that I feel the need for a chaperone." She kept her expression serious. "I believe a Christian woman should guard her reputation at all costs, whether she's a maid, wife, or widow."

Clementine came into the front room. "Oh, I'm sorry. I didn't know you were entertaining. I'll find another spot to read."

"Nonsense," Nancy said, spotting in Clementine a perfect partner for her plan. "Mimi has just stepped out to get her book. We don't need privacy. Mr. Berkshire just invited me to a birthday party in his honor. I wonder if you would consider going with me as my companion."

Clementine looked surprised but then nodded. "I might, if I knew when the event is to take place."

"Friday evening. Mr. Berkshire said he would call for us at seven."

Nancy could see that Gerome was anything but glad about this, but he said nothing.

"I believe I can go with you. As far as I recall, my calendar is clear," Clementine said, sounding only slightly hesitant. "Is it formal?"

"Of course," Gerome replied, his tone edged with unmistakable disgust. "Do you honestly suppose it would be otherwise?"

"Your attitude is hardly called for." Nancy gave him a reproaching glare. "Schoolteachers don't often go to formal affairs. Neither do I. I was going to ask the same thing."

He regained his composure and apologized. "I'm sorry. I'm on edge, since there have been rumors of Indian troubles. I hesitate to mention such things, however, as I don't want you to be afraid to come to the party."

"There are always rumors of Indian troubles." Nancy smiled. "But as for your party, Clementine and I will be appropriately gowned and ready for you at seven on Friday. For now, however, I have other work that needs my attention. I hope you understand."

He put his cup and saucer aside. "Of course. I'm delighted that you agreed to accompany me." He glanced at Clementine, who stood silently watching him. "And you too, Miss Carpenter."

Nancy showed him out and then returned to the front room, where Clementine could no longer remain silent.

"What in the world was that about? I thought you were . . . well, I didn't think you liked him."

"I don't. However, he knows something about what was going on with Albert, and your brother believes he might well have been behind the burglary here at the house."

"That's hardly a reason to spend an evening with him. Seth didn't want you doing anything to endanger yourself."

"That's why you're going to accompany me. But please say nothing to Seth. There are just some things I feel I must do, and I know your brother wouldn't approve. If you can't help me, then I'll go alone."

"Seth would never forgive me. Besides, I'm intrigued enough by this entire affair to want to satisfy my own curiosity." She smiled. "And I suppose we can't get into too much trouble at a formal birthday party given by one of the town's privileged and elite."

Nancy laughed. "That was my thinking. Frankly, I'm far more concerned about Gerome trying to steal a kiss than putting my life in jeopardy."

Clementine shrugged. "I'm not sure what to wear, though. I have nothing that is really formal."

"I have an attic full of gowns in storage, and we're very nearly the same size. We'll figure something out."

Friday night arrived sooner than Nancy had expected. Throughout the week, she had considered at least mentioning the outing to Seth but always changed her mind. He was sweet on her and would never approve of her stepping out with Gerome, even for the purpose of learning more about his business dealings with Albert. Not only that, but Seth hadn't really been around. He'd come once on Wednesday to escort Clementine to an evening function, and that had been Nancy's only real chance to speak to him. Besides, if Clementine had said nothing to him, then surely it wasn't that important. After all, Nancy could hardly keep her friend from telling her brother about the event. Since Clementine had deemed it acceptable to refrain, Nancy didn't feel so bad.

At least that was what she told herself. Nancy still couldn't help but feel some guilt. She knew Seth didn't want her involved, but the way she saw it, Albert had already involved her long ago, and now Gerome was perpetuating that arrangement. When Seth found out, he was going to be upset with her, but she would find a way to justify it and smooth things over. When they were young, Seth had been very logical in his arguments, so she would use logic to persuade him that she had done right. They both thought Gerome had played a role in this matter, so taking the opportunity to spend time with him in circumstances where his guard would be down seemed wise. Of course, Nancy understood that there was some risk, but surely having Clementine with her would negate that.

Seeing that time was getting away from her, Nancy hurried to dress. She chose a green silk gown that she'd never worn. It had arrived just days before Albert's death, and she hadn't even bothered to try it on. Now, as she modeled it in front of her mirror, she was happy to see that the fit was perfect and the color alluring. It drew out the green of her eyes and looked lovely against her creamy complexion. The bodice was more modest than some of her other evening attire, and that was the way she wanted it. The last thing she needed was Gerome and his friends ogling her throughout the evening.

Next she battled her hair, pulling it high atop her head. She secured it with two ivory combs Albert had given her for her twenty-fifth birthday, then heated the curling iron to manage some of the escaping hair. This was the only time when she really missed having a maid or at least a mother or sister around to help.

Finally, just before seven, Nancy finished the last curl. When she looked in the mirror, she was pleased with the outcome. She drew a deep breath. Hopefully she could escape the house without any complications. She had asked Clementine if Seth was wise to their plans, and Clementine had assured Nancy that he was busy with work and that she had told him nothing. The Clifton sisters were also occupied with a lecture at the Methodist church this evening, so they wouldn't be there to criticize Nancy's departure. That left Mimi and Mrs. Weaver, and neither of them would cause any trouble.

A light knock sounded on her bedroom door, and Nancy went quickly to see who it was. Clementine stood on the opposite side, gowned in a pale lavender evening dress. Her red-brown hair was fashionably yet simply arranged with part of it pinned up and the rest left to cascade down her back in curls.

"You look beautiful!" Nancy said. "That gown looks like it was made for you. Perhaps you'll attract the eye of a wealthy bachelor." She grinned. "I believe I'll make that dress a gift to you. I never looked as grand."

"That's generous of you, Nancy. I don't know that I should accept it, though, and I definitely don't want the gown if it attracts the likes of Berkshire's friends. Besides, I thought you knew I find your brother rather intriguing."

"Gabe?" Nancy laughed. "No, I hadn't really thought of that. How marvelous. I would love to have you as a sister."

"And I you. I think it might very well suit us to marry each other's brothers."

Nancy felt her cheeks grow hot. "I, well, I don't know about that."

The front door knocker sounded, echoing down the long hallway. At the same moment, the clock began to chime.

"Well, he's prompt, if nothing else," Nancy said. She went to her bed and picked up her gloves and wrap. "I'm ready if you are."

Clementine nodded and followed Nancy to the front room. Mimi had already let Gerome into the foyer, and when he spied Nancy, he all but pushed Mimi aside. "I'm sorry I wasn't here earlier. I had late business matters to tend to."

"Well, you did say seven." Nancy pulled on her gloves.

"Yes, but it would have been nice to have a little time to visit." He looked at her and shook his head. "You are without doubt the most beautiful woman in all of Portland. That green is an ideal color for you."

"I believe you have overlooked Miss Carpenter." Nancy motioned toward Clementine. "She is quite breathtaking."

Gerome turned to Seth's sister. "My dear Miss Carpenter, I do apologize for my neglect. I was so enraptured with Mrs. Pritchard that I quite overlooked your radiance."

"That's quite all right, Mr. Berkshire," Clementine replied.

"I must say fortune is with me this evening, for I am privileged to take not one but two beautiful women as my guests." Gerome looked back at Nancy. "I am quite honored."

"Well, one doesn't have a birthday every day," Nancy said, wrapping her gauzy shawl around her shoulders. She hoped to move the conversation to another topic. "Do you suppose we should be on our way?"

Gerome seemed momentarily uncertain, then nodded. "I wouldn't want to be late, since I am the guest of honor."

He said little on their way to the Lakewood house. He again praised both women for their stunning appearance but seemed otherwise preoccupied. Nancy didn't mind. At least she didn't have to pretend to be enthralled with his chatter.

The Lakewood dining room was as beautifully set as any Nancy had ever experienced, and the food was incredible. Nancy found herself trying to figure out the ingredients of each dish in the hope of remaking it at a later date.

"Are you enjoying yourself, my dear?" Gerome asked her. She had been seated next to him near the head of the table, while Clementine had been given a place some distance away.

"The meal is delicious."

"And the company even more so," he said, giving her a leering grin. "I am glad you agreed to come. It makes the event

more special. Our first of what I hope will be many more outings in the future."

Nancy said nothing as she pretended to be focused on her
lamb. It wasn't long before Mr. Lakewood called everyone to
attention in order to toast the man of the hour.

"We are here, of course, to honor Gerome Berkshire on
the occasion of his birthday, but also to applaud him for his
diligent work to secure Oregon for white settlers and their
descendants."

"Hear, hear," several men called as they pounded their fists
against the table in approval. The women smiled tolerantly.

"Gerome has worked for the benefit of all in this matter
and even now has agreed to accompany me to Salem to fight in
support of the anti-black laws that are being widely ignored."

There were murmurs and nods. Lakewood continued, but
Nancy felt compelled to ignore him. Instead she tried to memo-
rize the names of the people she'd been introduced to when they
first arrived. It was possible that each and every one of these
men was involved in Albert and Gerome's scheme.

When Lakewood finished, he bid Gerome to stand and receive their well wishes. They drank to his health and success
and then turned the floor over to him to speak.

"Thank you. I'm honored to be here tonight, especially with
one of the most beautiful women in Portland by my side." He
smiled down at Nancy, much to her displeasure. She hadn't
wanted to be singled out in any way, and now he was doing
exactly that. At least he had the good grace to say that Nancy
was only *one* of the most beautiful women in Portland. With
ten other women seated around the table, it would have been
the height of rudeness to say otherwise.

"Many of you don't know Mrs. Pritchard well, but I hope

in the future to share her company more often, in which case you'll get to know and care for her as I have."

Nancy wanted to crawl under the table but remained fixed in place, a hint of a smile plastered to her face.

"As many of you know, our efforts of late have been focused on encouraging the government to rid the state of not only the black population but the Indian as well. We have more than our fair share of reservations stealing precious land from hardworking white settlers. It is my intention to share with our legislators a plan to see these reservations dissolved and the Indians moved to other locations where reservations are much less intrusive, like the territories of Montana and Dakota. With few white settlers vying for land in those areas, it is my reasonable belief that they will make the perfect location for reservations.

"Oregon is a smaller area and rich with potential for farming and logging. We have more than enough industry along the rivers to entice a greater population of white settlers, and there is no room for people of color who have little intent to work."

Nancy noticed most of the men nodding in agreement. Gerome droned on for several more minutes before finally changing the subject.

"But enough of that for now. I want to thank my host and hostess, Mr. and Mrs. Lakewood, for this celebration of my birthday. It deeply touches me and, in the absence of my own family, leaves me with a sense of purpose and belonging."

Mr. Lakewood stood again and motioned to the serving staff. They rolled in a tea cart with a large round cake, and Mr. Lakewood started everyone in singing "For He's a Jolly Good Fellow."

Nancy sang along with the others but kept her voice low. She wished she had refused the invitation and stayed at home.

Obviously these men were supportive of Gerome and his view-points, but whether or not they were also involved with her husband's underhanded affairs remained to be seen. It was clear that proving it one way or the other was going to be difficult at best.

The cake was cut, and when the final piece was served, Mr. Lakewood turned to the table. "I know it may seem less than proper, but I believe it completely acceptable for the ladies to retire to the music room with their cake. My daughters Anna and Elizabeth would very much like to entertain you on the piano and harp. Meanwhile the men may join me in the library for brandy and cigars, and of course they, too, may bring their cake."

It was a relief to be free of Gerome. Nancy left her cake uneaten and made her way to Clementine. "I'll be so glad to leave here."

"We could go early. I wouldn't even have to feign a head-ache," Clementine declared.

Nancy could only agree. "Mine started the minute Gerome arrived at my front door."

"He is pompous and full of himself," Clementine continued as they followed the ladies into the music room without their cake. "They all are."

"Are you enjoying yourself, Mrs. Pritchard?" Mrs. Lakewood asked. Without waiting for Nancy to reply, the older woman continued. "I was surprised when Gerome told us you would be his companion for the evening. You are such a new widow."

"You were quite gracious to extend the invitation." Nancy offered nothing more.

Mrs. Lakewood looked at her for a moment, seeming not to know what to say. Finally, she nodded and turned to one of her friends for conversation.

Clementine and Nancy forced back giggles as they made their way to chairs at the back of the room. Soon enough the music started, and while Nancy enjoyed it, she would much rather hear what the men were discussing over their brandy and cigars.

By the end of the second number, Nancy's headache had increased to the point of misery. Leaning over to Clementine, she said, "I don't think I can bear another number. If you don't mind, I'd like to find Gerome and see if he would take us home."

"That's fine by me."

Clementine rose with Nancy and followed her from the room. In the large drawing room beyond the music room, they both paused.

"I wonder where the men have taken themselves." Nancy glanced around. "Lakewood mentioned the library." She paused to listen. "Do you hear anything?"

Clementine moved closer to the hallway entry. "Sounds like they're farther down the opposite way. I think I hear men's laughter."

Nancy followed her and listened as the sound of men's voices increased. Thankfully the long hall was carpeted and muffled the sound of their footsteps. It wasn't long before they stood outside closed double doors. The conversation and amusement of the men rang loud and clear from the opposite side.

"Dare we listen in for a moment?" Nancy asked, pressing closer to the door.

"It is of course difficult to say what the effect will be on the general populace," one of the men was saying. "But it is my belief that few will concern themselves with the matter."

"So you are all agreed that the public whipping of any and all blacks would benefit our cause?" This sounded like Lakewood.

There was a rousing chorus of approval to this suggestion, and then Gerome spoke up. "I believe once we prove Portland is intolerant of people of color, we will see them leaving voluntarily. That will make it far easier on us while we fight to get the laws enforced."

"My friend is right. He is also here to speak to us about our most serious matter." Nancy strained to hear as Lakewood lowered his voice. Clementine all but pressed her ear to the door.

Gerome continued. "We have been delayed receiving the guns we were promised, but I assure you that the problems we were earlier facing are no longer a concern. I have recently come into knowledge of the whereabouts of our rifles and whiskey. Once we get these items collected and distributed to the reservations, our man will see that the hatred already festering there will bring about results. Mr. Bridges, do you still have volunteers to aid in killing the heathens?"

"I do. I also have my brother-in-law set to put the army in motion. It won't take long to get everything under control, and with you and some of the others working in Salem, I feel confident we can motivate the legislature to the proper action with the federal government. No one wants another Little Bighorn, but we will stress the possibility of exactly that to our senators and congressmen."

"It would probably serve our purpose to have a few dead settlers to point to. Especially women and children."

Nancy felt ill. How could they speak so casually about killing women and children of any color? She pulled back and looked at Clementine in disbelief.

Unable to listen to more, Nancy moved away from the door and down the hall. It was perfect timing, as one of the house servants came along at that moment.

"Excuse me," Clementine said. "Could you find Mr. Berkshire for us and ask him to meet us in the foyer?"

"Of course, miss." He took off in the direction they'd just come.

"Hopefully he won't be too disagreeable," Clementine said as they waited.

It was only a few moments before Gerome appeared. His forehead was furrowed and his brows drawn together. "What's wrong?"

"I have a terrible headache," Nancy said. "I wonder if you might have your driver take us home. I wouldn't want you to leave the party. After all, it is your birthday."

"Of course." Gerome motioned to the young uniformed man who'd followed him. "Call for my driver and see that the ladies get their wraps."

"Yes, sir."

The man left quickly, and Gerome turned back to Nancy. "My dear, I'm so sorry that you are under the weather."

"It's sure to pass. I apologize, but I know that if I don't return home to rest, it will only become worse."

"I'll see that she is well cared for," Clementine added. "Thank you for such a lovely evening, and I hope you had a memorable birthday."

"It was quite memorable," he assured them.

It was only a few moments longer before the young man reappeared. The butler came, too, with Clementine and Nancy's shawls.

"I will call tomorrow and make certain you are on the mend," Gerome declared as he helped the ladies out to the carriage.

"Please don't bother on my account," Nancy said. "I'm sure to be quite well after I rest."

She climbed into the closed carriage and settled onto the leather upholstery as Clementine followed. Once the carriage was in motion, she heaved a sigh.

"Those people make me sick. I cannot believe the hatred they hold. Hatred so fierce they would kill innocent people to see their purposes served." She barely whispered her words, lest the driver overhear.

"I know." Clementine shook her head. "They are ruthless."

Nancy was uncertain what to do. She knew she should probably say something to Seth. After all, she had promised to trust him. From what had been said at the party, the men planned to see their ideas put into action very soon. Albert's guns and whiskey had been the only thing missing, and now they had maps to locate those items.

"Will you tell Seth?" Clementine asked as if knowing the turmoil going on in Nancy's head.

"I know I should. I know, too, that he'll be upset that I went to the party. He asked me not to put myself in danger, and now I've done that as well as endangered his sister. He won't look kindly upon that."

"I think you must tell him."

"I just don't know what to think about it all. It's clear those men were part of an organized group that intends to see the demise of all people of color. I believe Albert was part of their group—or at least he was their merchant. I have no idea if he had other parts to play, but he must have approved of their plans, or he would never have agreed to sell them the guns and liquor."

"Maybe he didn't know what they planned to do with it."

"I doubt that. Otherwise he would have had no reason to hide them. Neither are illegal to buy and sell, except if one intends to sell to the Indians. It's my guess that Albert knew the quantity of guns he was purchasing would be called into question and he would have to account for where they were sold. He and Gerome probably devised this plan with the help of those other men. It's too horrible to imagine the killings they plan, but equally terrible to imagine their desire to see the Indians driven to even smaller reservations hundreds of miles away." Nancy shivered. "What a horrible, heartless man I married. How could I not know?"

Clementine patted her gloved hand. "Because horrible, heartless men are good at hiding the truth."

The carriage came to a stop, and the driver soon opened the door. He helped Clementine down first and then Nancy. He tipped his hat at them both and then bounded back up to the seat and snapped the lines.

Nancy drew a deep breath and tried to figure out what she would do next. Unfortunately, she didn't have long to contemplate, as Seth appeared from the shadows of the front porch.

"What in the world are you two doing, stepping out of Gerome Berkshire's carriage?"

CHAPTER 17

S eth could hardly contain his anger. He took hold of his sister's arm and then Nancy's and dragged them both up the sidewalk and steps to the front porch. "Sit, both of you, and tell me what's going on."

"There's no need to lose your temper, Seth," Clementine began.

"I'll be the judge of that."

Nancy took a seat in the wicker rocker and pulled her shawl close. "It was Gerome's birthday, and I felt sorry for him. He invited me to his party, but of course I couldn't go without someone accompanying me, so I dragged Clementine along."

"Didn't I make it clear that I believe he's dangerous?" Seth demanded. "That I believe him to be up to his neck in this ordeal with the guns and whiskey?"

"He is. In fact, quite a few of Portland's social register seem to be," Nancy countered. "We overheard discussion about that very thing, although no one knew we were listening."

Seth paused, startled into silence for a moment. "Who was discussing this?"

Nancy began listing off names, starting with Lakewood and ending with Berkshire. "They are all involved."

Clementine nodded.

Seth took the seat nearest Nancy, his mind whirring. This could be huge. "What did they say?"

"That their plan was delayed while they were waiting to find their missing guns, but Gerome assured them he had recently come into knowledge of their whereabouts," Clementine answered before Nancy could. "So obviously he has the stolen book."

"They plan to cause all sorts of trouble—even kill innocent people," Nancy added.

"Two of whom could have been you." Seth couldn't put it any blunter than that. "I can't bear the thought of having to explain to our folks—or yours, Nancy—that I knew there were dangers and did nothing to keep you from harm."

"Seth, I'm sorry," Clementine began. "I didn't mean to worry you. It was a simple birthday party, and we were with other women. No one was going to do anything to harm us there. I saw no reason to think it was dangerous."

"Nor did I. Now, however, we know Mr. Lakewood and his friends—bankers, lawyers, manufacturing owners—are all involved in this plot to start a war with the Indians. I want to know what we can do to stop them," Nancy said, sounding upset.

"You"—Seth pointed at them both—"don't do anything! It would be absolutely foolish for you to try to stop those men."

Nancy got to her feet. "I don't deserve nor will I sit here and listen to your criticism of my decision to go tonight. It gave us proof that we need to stop these men. Furthermore, you aren't my brother or my husband."

Seth stood as well and held out his hands in placation. "I may not be either of those, but I care deeply for you. I don't want you to end up like your husband—floating in the river because you dared to cross the wrong person."

Nancy shivered. "Do you honestly think that's what happened?"

"Who can say why, but I do believe he was murdered, and probably by one of those men you deemed safe enough to spend your evening with."

Nancy's ire returned, and she spun away from him. "I thought it would be helpful, and I was right. I'm sorry if you don't support my decision."

She stormed into the house, letting the screen door slam behind her.

"Nancy!" Seth called.

Clementine took his arm. "You'll never get her to understand by yelling."

He sighed. "Neither of you seems to understand just how dangerous this situation is."

"And how do you suddenly have such an intimate knowledge of this terribly dangerous situation?" Clementine asked.

He shook his head. "I can't say."

"So you know even more than you're letting on." Her voice was almost accusatory. "I thought you were acting rather strangely."

"Don't say anything to Nancy or anyone else. I can't explain it all right now, but in time I promise I will."

Clementine looked at him for a long moment, then started for the door. "I think you've handled this poorly, and if I were you, I'd show up tomorrow with flowers and an apology."

Nancy paced her bedroom floor. Seth Carpenter had some nerve, scolding her like a wayward child. She'd only tried to help—to do what she could in a place and time that seemed completely safe.

She plopped into a chair and reached down to remove her shoes. Why couldn't he understand that she only wanted to help? Gerome Berkshire would never have allowed Seth to get close enough to overhear his plans.

A sigh escaped her. Why should Seth get so upset anyway? *Because he loves you.*

There was no one speaking the words, but still the statement lingered. Perhaps it was just wishful thinking.

"Do I want him to love me?" she whispered.

Getting to her feet, she began to unfasten the hooks that held her bodice to the skirt. She had come to care for Seth. She knew that. She had told herself over and over that it wasn't love, it was merely the comfort of familiarity. Now, however, she felt uncertain. Had she fallen in love with him?

She didn't like to consider it. For years she had lived without love and had done very well. When occasional feelings reared their head, Nancy had easily tucked them aside and reordered her emotions. She had known her lot in life, and it wasn't to be adored and loved by her husband, and therefore she could not be loved and adored by anyone else.

"But Albert is dead," she reasoned.

She finished undressing and pulled a white lawn nightgown over her head. Next, she went to her dressing table and began to pull the combs and pins from her hair. Still she contemplated her heart. She had only just accepted that God loved her. She had finally come to see that He could forgive her. That He *wanted* to forgive her. How could she possibly add the love of a man to the madness that was her life?

Nancy brushed the tangles from her hair. Would that she could brush out the troubles of life as easily.

"Father, I just don't know what I'm supposed to do. My life is a jumble of feelings that I can't seem to properly sort. I listen to the pastor preach that I must trust and obey you in everything, that I must love you with all my heart and soul and mind. But I don't know how to do that. Please help me. I don't know how to love you in a proper way, and I don't know how to love Seth either."

Seth took his sister's advice the next morning and went searching for flowers first thing. Thankfully there were several street vendors with flower carts on the outskirts of the city who had bouquets for sale. He purchased a small bunch of various blooms and headed back to his apartment. It was still too early to show up at Nancy's. The other ladies would no doubt make much ado about his appearance, and before he knew it, one of the Misses Clifton would be chiding him for his improper attention to social etiquette.

He was contemplating just how long he'd have to wait when he reached his block and saw that Gabe Armistead was waiting for him on the steps outside his building. Seth grinned. Gabe was the perfect answer. No one would question his showing up in the early hours of the morning with Nancy's brother in tow.

"Gabe! What brings you here?" Seth bounded up the steps and gave his friend a hug.

"I just had a hankering to visit. Seems I can't get a certain redheaded girl out of my mind."

"Oh dear. Sounds like you are smitten." Seth grinned.

"Maybe. I need a little more exposure to be sure," Gabe replied, laughing. He pointed at the flowers. "I think those are probably for my sister. Guess you're smitten too."

"Could be." Seth looked down at the bouquet, remembering their harsh words the night before. "Actually, I'm glad you're here. There's something I need to talk to you about. Come upstairs. This is going to take a while, and by the time I finish, it will be an acceptable hour to go calling."

They went upstairs and settled into Seth's apartment. "This may seem a strange tale, but I hope you'll give me a chance to explain when you hear what I've done and how it involves your sister."

Gabe gave him a look that was somewhere between disapproval and concern. "I hope it's nothing untoward."

"Not exactly." Seth got up and began to pace his small sitting room. "When I was back east, I was approached by a man named Elijah Brady. He works in the Bureau of Indian Affairs. He told me they've been having difficulties with rifles being given to the Indian tribes in various locations in the Northwest. They suspected a man named Albert Pritchard of supplying the weapons, as well as alcohol."

"Nancy's Albert?"

"Yes. I didn't realize it at the time. The reason they came to me was that Mr. Brady learned I was from the Oregon City area. When he told me he needed someone to go to Portland to investigate Albert Pritchard, I mentioned that it would be easy enough for me because my sister was taking a teaching position there. He explained what was involved, and I agreed to come. I had no idea Nancy was married to Albert."

Seth continued. "I learned that Pritchard had died and left behind a widow. Brady suggested that she might be involved as well and that we needed to investigate her and learn what we could about Pritchard's associates. When I came to Portland, I nosed around and discovered that Nancy Pritchard had gone to John Lincoln to manage her late husband's affairs."

"So you went there and got a job?" Gabe asked, clearly still not quite understanding.

"I went to John, and I suppose it was the Lord telling me to trust him, but I explained to him why I was in Portland. I told him that I understood he'd taken on Albert Pritchard's will and that I needed to pretend to work with him so that I could have access to all of Pritchard's papers. I explained that it might well save the lives of hundreds, if not thousands, and he agreed to hire me on.

"When I realized who Nancy was, I knew she would never be involved in anything like we suspected Pritchard of doing. John Lincoln told me he had known her nearly all the time she'd lived in Portland—even attended church with her—and that he didn't believe she knew anything about her husband's underhanded affairs."

"Does she have any idea what's going on?"

"She knows her husband was involved in buying weapons to give to the Indians—whiskey too. She knows it was done with the desire to entice the Indians to start a war. She also knows that Gerome Berkshire is involved. Against my wish that she not get involved, she went to a party being held in his honor last night. She dragged Clementine along as well, because she thought they might learn something more about the people involved. And, to be fair, they did. I now have a list of names."

"She's always been rebellious," Gabe said, shaking his head. "She always thinks she knows best."

Seth nodded. "If she continues to investigate on her own, she could end up getting herself and my sister killed, and that would make me very unhappy."

"Wouldn't make me or our family too happy either," Gabe replied. "So what do you want me to do?"

"Nancy thinks she knows where one of the caches might be. She said the layout of the map looked familiar. It's a place Albert used to take her for picnics. Most likely he was already hiding weapons and wanted to do business while they were there, because he'd leave Nancy alone near the site for quite some time. Anyway, I'm thinking we get Nancy to draw us a map, and you and I go check it out. But I have to ask that you say nothing to Nancy about my work. I wasn't supposed to tell anyone, but I felt it important to be honest with John and now you. I need a partner in this."

"What about being honest with Nancy?" Gabe raised his brows. "Doesn't she deserve that?"

"I can't. At first it was because I didn't know whether or not she was involved, but now I feel like if I tell her, she'll be angry and maybe do something foolish."

"Like go to a party where all the men in attendance are planning an Indian uprising?" Gabe shook his head. "I know you love her. I can hear it in your voice when you talk about her. But you have to have honesty in order to have trust, and you can't have love without trust."

Seth rubbed his chin. He knew Gabe was right, but there was no way he wanted to tell Nancy and risk her life. Worse still, he was afraid to tell her and risk her rejection.

"I'll tell her in time, but right now we have to find that cache. No doubt Berkshire and his associates have the book. Apparently he implied as much last night. If they do have it, they're going to find those caches. I want to get to the one Nancy remembers and see if we can't follow them to the others. When it's all over and done with, I'll tell her everything. I promise."

"I believe you. I just hope it won't be too late," Gabe said, his voice filled with concern.

Seth hoped it wouldn't be either.

"Gabe, what a surprise!" Nancy hugged her brother. "Are you still growing? I swear you're taller." She looked beyond him to where Seth stood, flowers in hand.

When their eyes met, Seth extended the bouquet. "I believe I owe you an apology for my behavior last night."

Nancy nodded. "You do." She took the bouquet and smelled the flowers, watching him all the while.

"I'm sorry. I was just very concerned about your decision to go with Berkshire."

She glanced over her shoulder toward Gabe. He'd taken himself inside, however, so she didn't need to worry about him overhearing.

"I want to see if I can find the cache," she said.

Seth shook his head. "You can't, Nancy. It's far too dangerous. Those men have the maps now. They'll know where to go, and you can't be out there with them. I'll go. Gabe and I will both go. We just need you to draw us a map."

"Gabe? You've involved Gabe in this?"

"I felt it was important to have help. That way we can watch each other's backs."

Nancy knew it was the wise thing to do. The problem was that she wanted to be involved. Seth's tone of voice, however, made it more than clear that he wasn't about to let her come along.

She remembered that Seth was a man of logic and reasoning. "Why wouldn't three of us be even better? I can carry a gun as well as Gabe. The same man taught us both to shoot."

"And you think you could kill a man?" Seth asked, narrowing his blue eyes.

"Well, if he was about to kill you or Gabe, I think I could."

Seth shook his head. "Nancy, I don't want anything to happen to you."

"And I don't want anything to happen to you! I don't think I could bear it." She had never meant anything as much as she did that statement. She was still struggling with her feelings, but Seth Carpenter had taken an important place in her heart, and she didn't want to send him out to die.

He stepped forward and, to her surprise, touched her cheek. She didn't move for fear he'd stop. She liked the warmth of his hand on her face. Her breath quickened as she contemplated whether he might kiss her.

"Nancy . . . please don't make this more difficult. I care for you. Surely you know that by now."

"I care for you, too, Seth." It wasn't exactly a declaration of love, but she felt confident that was what he intended it to mean. She intended the same.

"I need you to do as I ask. Please just trust me and Gabe to get the job done. I promise that no matter what happens, I'll tell you everything."

She frowned and pulled away. "All of my life people have been ordering me about and demanding I go or stay at their command. I'm sick of it."

"As I understand it, you never listened to them anyway and

did pretty much as you pleased." Seth's expression dared her to argue. "I'm not trying to order you about. I'm asking. Begging, really. Please do this for me. Please."

Nancy looked down at the flowers. Part of her wanted to throw them back in his face, while another part was touched that he cared so much about her well-being. "Fine. Come to the dining room, and I'll draw you a map."

She left him to follow her and made her way inside. She put the flowers in water, then went to Albert's office for a pencil and piece of paper.

"I know this isn't easy for you."

She looked up to find her brother's frame filling the doorway. "No, it's not. I don't understand why I can't be a part of this. I am, after all, the one whose husband was up to his neck in it. I deserve to know what's going on and to try to right his wrong."

"Which you are doing by helping us."

She came to him with paper in hand. "I'm tired of being left out of things."

"Your husband did that a lot, didn't he?" Gabe asked, his voice sympathetic.

She met his dark eyes and nodded. "Yes. Yes, he did. He wasn't at all the man I thought he was. I couldn't admit that to anyone then, but now I can. I was foolish to marry him, just as everyone said."

"But you loved him." Gabe smiled.

"I did," Nancy admitted, shaking her head. "At least as much as I understood love. I think mostly it was infatuation with a life that allowed me to have some say over my destiny and choices. Albert promised to give me free rein, and he did. Of course, that freedom came at the cost of love and was never really freedom at all."

"I'm sorry for that. You deserved better. I think this time around you'll have it."

"This time around?"

He chuckled. "I know you know that Seth has feelings for you. I think you've completely captured his heart. And from the way I've seen you watch him, I think he's captured yours, as well."

Nancy could see her brother was serious. "When did you become an expert in such matters?"

He laughed all the more. "I'm not claiming to be an expert. I just see the way you two look at each other. I hear it in your voices when you talk to each other."

She smiled. "Well, only time will tell, but I think your perception is skewed by your own romantic desires. Seems to me you have special feelings for a certain redheaded boarder of mine."

"Could be," Gabe said, stepping away from the door so Nancy could exit. "Maybe once we get all your troubles squared away, I'll be able to pursue my own interests."

Seth awaited them in the dining room, and once Nancy had drawn out the map as best as she remembered it, the men were ready to leave.

"You'll come back and tell me what you've found?" she asked.

"If we find anything," Seth replied. He gave Nancy a smile. "But I promise I'll come back and let you know what's going on."

Nancy looked at the clock. "It's nearly noon. Why don't you stay for lunch? The Clifton sisters won't be here, nor Mimi, so it will probably be just us. Mrs. Weaver might come down, but she rarely does, and if she knows anyone else is here, she most assuredly won't."

Gabe looked at Seth and grinned. "I could stand to wait until after lunch."

"I suppose it makes sense not to go out on an empty stomach," Seth agreed, smiling. "Very well, you've convinced us. Lunch first and then we're off."

CHAPTER 18

N ancy hurried to prepare something to eat. She had a roast in the oven that would take care of supper that evening and leftovers for Sunday, but she hadn't given lunch any real concern. Checking her supplies, she finally settled on throwing together some smoked salmon with fried cabbage and potatoes. She knew her brother and Seth had a sweet tooth and was grateful there were still quite a few oatmeal cookies in the cookie jar.

She set the table in between stirring and chopping. Seth and Gabe had apparently gone back out to the porch, because she heard nothing from them in the front room. Wondering if they wanted coffee or something cold to drink with their lunch, she made her way toward the front door. The front room windows were open to let in the air, and they let in conversation, as well.

"But if you don't tell her the truth about why you came here in the first place, she's going to feel betrayed. And I can't say I would blame her," Gabe said.

Nancy froze in place. What was he talking about?

Seth spoke, his voice hardly above a whisper. "I will tell her, just not yet. I don't think she'd understand, and I want to make sure I get these guys before I try to explain my duties. My superiors made it clear that I wasn't to tell anyone why I was here, and I've already violated that agreement by telling you and John. I felt I had to with John—after all, he was hiring me to work for him. I didn't want to give pretense to that job and then just walk away once I was able to get to the bottom of Albert and Nancy's involvement in this mess."

Nancy felt sick. She leaned back against the wall and tried to draw a decent breath. Seth had lied to her. He was obviously far more involved in whatever Albert and Berkshire had going on than he was telling her. Not only that, but he'd included her as part of the scheme.

He used me and he believes me to be involved.

The thought echoed in her head. He had used her to accomplish whatever it was he was trying to do.

"I know my sister," Gabe continued. "Being honest with her now will go a long way toward her forgiving you."

"I can't tell her yet. I will, though. I care too much about her to perpetuate the lie any longer than necessary."

So he admitted he was living a lie. Nancy swallowed the lump in her throat. Well, let him live a lie. Two could play that game. She didn't need him or anyone else. At least Gabe cared enough to try to resolve the issue, but even he thought it had been all right at some point to keep the truth from her.

Nancy straightened and drew a deep breath. She wasn't going to let them defeat her. She walked to the door with a smile plastered on her face. "Lunch is ready," she declared.

Gabe looked at her and smiled. "Good, because I'm starved."

"Plotting and conspiring will do that." She turned back to the house. "I'll see you both in the dining room. I need to let Clementine and Mrs. Weaver know."

Nancy could barely sit through the meal. Her brother and Seth offered high praise for the food, but she hardly heard their words. Clementine thankfully kept the conversation going with stories about one thing or another, while Mrs. Weaver had decided to remain in her room. Gabe seemed to hang on Clementine's every word. It was obvious he had fallen hard for her. Nancy hoped there were no lies between them.

Seth seemed content to focus on Clementine's stories. No doubt he would do anything to keep Nancy from bringing up her desire to join him and Gabe on their search. Perhaps his guilt made him occupy himself with his sister's adventures so he didn't have to face Nancy with the truth. No matter. Nancy wanted only for lunch to end so she could be rid of them both.

She wondered exactly what Seth was here to do and who had hired him to do it. She wondered if he had originally planned to arrest her. Perhaps he was a law official from back east with the power to take prisoners. She shivered but did her best to continue the pretense that all was well.

The sadness of Seth's betrayal was really beginning to sink in by the time they finished. Nancy excused herself to check on Mrs. Weaver, and thankfully Bedelia and Cornelia arrived at about the same time. Nancy offered to prepare them a plate, but the ladies had eaten earlier.

"We are quite satisfied," Bedelia said, noting the men at the table. "Gentlemen, I hope you enjoyed your luncheon."

"We did," Seth declared. "I also want to let you know that I spoke with someone at the police station. They're having an officer walk through the neighborhood each evening for a few weeks. Like me, they believe the thieves got what they came for, but they're happy to send a man in order to ease your minds."

"That is quite reassuring," Bedelia replied. "Though I still don't understand what they wanted with Mr. Pritchard's book."

Nancy had had enough. "My late husband was involved in hiding weapons. The book contained maps of where those weapons are to be found, and the thief knew this. He came with the sole purpose of getting it."

"Weapons? Whatever was Mr. Pritchard doing with weapons?"

Seth gave Nancy a look that suggested she say nothing more, but she was angry and no longer cared what he thought. "He wanted to give them to the Indians and start a war. Apparently, there are a great many men who want to do this, and Albert was determined to assist them. Now, if you'll excuse me, I need to see if Mrs. Weaver would like anything more. I'm sure if you have further questions about the weapons, you can ask Mr. Carpenter. He seems to know all about it."

She put several cookies on a plate, then hurried from the room, knowing that if she didn't, she might very well confront Seth about his lies and what he was really doing in Portland. She wanted to cry and rant at the same time. How could she have been so stupid? So blind? Why hadn't she guarded her heart better?

"Mrs. Weaver? I'm here for your tray," Nancy announced after knocking on the door.

She could hear the woman moving about and waited patiently until she slid back the bolt. Mrs. Weaver opened the door and gave Nancy a smile.

"Lunch was delicious, Nancy dear. I was far hungrier than I anticipated." She let Nancy in to retrieve the tray. There wasn't as much as a crumb of food left.

"I brought you these cookies, but I could get you something more."

"Oh no. This was just fine, and the cookies will finish things off nicely." Mrs. Weaver took the plate from Nancy and put it atop her dresser. "You treat me so well. I am a most grateful tenant."

Nancy put aside her heartache and smiled. "And you are a gracious one as well. If you find yourself hungry later, there are more cookies and of course fresh bread and butter in the kitchen. We'll be having roast beef for supper."

"That sounds wonderful. Thank you, Nancy." Mrs. Weaver waited for Nancy to pick up the tray. "I believe I'm going to take a nap."

Nancy nodded and headed for the hall. She heard Mrs. Weaver close the door behind her and slide the bolt back into place. She also heard the old woman speaking in a murmur, as if reminding herself of some task she needed to do. Bedelia said the older woman often talked to herself.

"Well, at least in speaking to herself, she knows she won't be betrayed," Nancy muttered.

By the time she made her way downstairs, Seth and Gabe were ready to go. Her brother came to her first.

"We'll be back as soon as we can. Remember your promise to stay out of trouble."

"I always remember my promises." Nancy couldn't even bring herself to smile. "I know what's expected of me."

Gabe studied her for a moment. "Are you all right?"

Seth didn't give her a chance to reply. "Don't sulk. I promise you'll get every detail once we figure out what's out there."

She met his blue-eyed gaze. She wanted to call him a liar and tell him that she knew he was deceiving her but forced herself to remain silent. She felt so weary and tired that all she could think of was getting away from all of them.

"I'm going to take a nap. Clementine, I'll see to the dishes later."

"Sister and I can manage the cleanup," Bedelia said, coming from behind Nancy. "You appear under the weather, and I believe rest would be good."

Nancy didn't care what the older woman thought, but it was a good excuse. "Thank you." She left them all staring after her. She didn't allow herself to feel guilty or concerned about the worry in Seth's face. Let him worry. She hoped he was eaten up with guilt.

Once inside the sanctuary of her room, Nancy fell onto her bed and stared at the ceiling. She wondered where God was in all of this. Again, she felt as if He'd let her down.

"I'm trying, Lord. I'm trying to understand and trust you. I'm trying, but it comes so hard when things like this keep interfering. I thought he cared." Her voice was barely a whisper. "I thought he really loved me. Instead, I'm nothing more than a means to do his job."

She felt a heaviness settle over her. For the first time in years, she longed for her mother. Grace Armistead always offered sound advice and reason, but more than that, Nancy knew that her mother could offer spiritual comfort and insight. Not that Nancy had ever let her give it in the past.

Nancy sighed. "I want to go home." The words surprised her, but she didn't deny they were exactly how she felt.

She glanced at the clock. She knew there was a riverboat that would leave for Oregon City around four. Why not be on it? Why not go home and allow her mother to console her?

She got up and sat for a few minutes on the edge of the bed. She would have to arrange with Bedelia to run the boarding-house. She knew the spinster would love being put in charge.

Nancy could even offer to discount her rent. That would please the penny-pincher even more. Other than that, she'd say nothing to anyone—especially not to Clementine, who would just reveal her location to Seth and Gabe.

Nancy found Bedelia cleaning up in the kitchen while Cornelia gathered things from the table. Nancy caught the attention of the elder of the Clifton sisters and motioned her to the pantry. "I have a favor to ask."

Bedelia raised a brow. "Do tell."

"I need to leave for a few days. I was wondering if you would manage the house. I will discount your rent in return."

Bedelia was instantly interested. "Where are you going?"

"I'd rather not say. I don't want anyone to know and try to follow me."

"Such as Mr. Carpenter?" Bedelia asked in a knowing tone.

"Yes. Or even my brother. I just need some time away. I will be with family, but that's just between you and me."

"Of course. I will carry your secret to the grave."

"There's a roast with potatoes and carrots in the oven for tonight's dinner and tomorrow's noon meal. There is freshly baked bread, we have numerous canned vegetables, and the icebox is full of milk, butter, and cream. Feel free to use whatever you need. And don't worry about cleaning the rest of the house. I won't be gone more than a couple of days."

"Very well. I will see to everything." Bedelia looked almost sympathetic. "Is there nothing else I can do?"

Nancy fought to keep from tearing up. "Pray. Pray God will help me understand exactly what He wants from me and what I'm supposed to do."

Oregon City wasn't all that different despite eight years pass-ing since Nancy had seen it last. She had always claimed to be too busy to travel back, and thankfully no one had died, forcing her to return for a funeral.

She'd taken the riverboat to Oregon City, but she wasn't sure how she would get out to the farm. It was Saturday, after all, and Uncle Lance and other family members who worked in town were probably already gone, if they'd been there at all. She thought of her great-uncle Edward's family. They might be willing to give her a ride, or she could just rent a horse from the livery.

She was still considering exactly what to do when she heard someone call her name.

"Nancy? Is that you?"

She turned and was surprised to see her cousin Faith. "What are you doing here? I thought you were attending college in Salem."

Faith brushed loose wisps of brown-black hair from her tanned face. "I was, but there are no classes in the summer. I came home to enjoy my time off with family. I was just in town selling some of the yarn Mother made. What are you doing here?"

Nancy shrugged. "I've spent eight years avoiding this place and its people. I figured it was time to come home and make peace."

Faith gave her a hug. "You have always been one of my favor-ite people. I'm glad you've come and that I get you to myself first. Do you have a ride to the farm? Do they know you're coming?"

"No—on both counts."

"Good. Then we will have the ride to talk, and you can tell me all about life in Portland."

"I have a boardinghouse," Nancy blurted.

"How interesting!"

"It's for ladies only, and I have a rather eclectic group. Mrs. Weaver is the oldest, and she's been a widow for about five years. Then there's a widow whose husband died just last January. Clementine Carpenter is also boarding there."

"Clementine? Weren't the two of you good friends when you were still at home?"

"Yes, and we're good friends again." Nancy decided to say nothing of Seth. "Last but definitely not least are the Clifton sisters, Bedelia and Cornelia. They are spinsters and quite the pair."

"It sounds like you definitely intend to stay in Portland."

"I do. I like it there."

"Well, rumor has it the college is moving the medical portion to Portland next year, so perhaps I shall see more of you."

"I think it's amazing they allow women to attend college, much less medical school. Will you truly be a full-fledged doctor when you graduate?"

"That's the plan. I've never minded being a midwife and healer like your mother, but having this schooling under my belt will allow me a certificate as well."

"Well, I hope they do move the medical school up to Portland."

"Maybe I could even room at your place," Faith said, her tone animated.

"I would like that very much." Nancy realized that she truly meant it. It would be very enjoyable to have Faith living at the house. Faith had always had an amazing way of looking at life.

"Then, we shall see what God has in store for us." Faith hugged Nancy again. "Now come on. The wagon is just over there in front of Brody's General Store. I had to pick up some things as well as deliver the yarn. They should have everything loaded by now."

Nancy wasn't sure what to think. Faith Kenner was different from the rest of the family. She had a wild and adventurous spirit that Nancy had always understood. When Faith had announced that she wanted to become an educated doctor rather than follow in Nancy's mother's steps as an herbal healer and midwife, Nancy had thought it wonderful. The rest of the family had been less certain of Faith's decision, and of course it was questionable what college she would attend and whether they would admit her, since she was a woman. But there was no holding back Faith Kenner. She was a woman who knew her own mind and went after what she wanted.

Nancy climbed up onto the wagon and waited while Faith spoke to the general store clerk. Several people with familiar faces passed, but they didn't seem to know Nancy, and she made no attempt to know them. She nodded in greeting as passersby met her glance but otherwise said nothing. Hopefully Faith would hurry and keep her from having to engage in any conversations.

"Well, that's that. Now we can head home," Faith said, climbing into the driver's seat beside Nancy. She released the brake and slapped the lines almost in one fluid motion. Once they were headed up the road for home, she turned to Nancy. "I was truly sorry to hear about your husband. Sorrier still that I couldn't come home. I was busy with testing and other studies."

"I know. Your letter explained as much. Frankly, everyone could have stayed away, and I would have been just as happy."

Faith nodded. "I know how that can be. Sometimes a person just needs the silence."

"Exactly."

"And how is it now?" Faith asked, keeping her eyes on the road.

Nancy looked down at the Willamette River. It seemed so much busier than she remembered. "Now I finally feel the need for a dose of home. My mother in particular."

"Your mother is an amazing woman, but you already know that."

Nancy considered her words. "I don't think I do. At least I don't think I allowed myself to know it. I've been so angry and unloving. All I ever wanted from the time I was young was to be away from all of them."

"Why was that?"

Nancy shook her head. Faith was five years Nancy's senior, but in many ways she was years beyond that. Faith had always seemed so mature for her age, probably because of the complications of her past. Few ever spoke about it, but Nancy knew that her cousin was the result of Hope's captivity with the Cayuse at Whitman Mission. Hope had gone south to stay with friends of the family long before her pregnancy had started to show, and thus most people thought Faith was the daughter of Isaac and Eletta Browning and that Hope had only been there to assist Eletta. Years later, when Isaac and Eletta died, Faith had come back to Hope, and she and Lance had welcomed Faith into their family. Nancy hadn't learned the truth until she was nearly seventeen. Faith herself had brought up the subject once when the women were canning vegetables together. Nancy had been shocked to learn her cousin was half Cayuse. With her intense blue eyes, no one would think of her as Cayuse.

"I'm not sure I really understand it myself," Nancy finally

answered. "I'd say that I never felt as if I fit in, but saying that to you seems silly."

Faith laughed. "I find that only the person involved can make their life fit. I probably wouldn't have fit had I relied on others for my comfort and assurance. Instead, I just decided that I was going to make the best of the situation and enjoy what I had."

Nancy envied Faith's ability to rise above her circumstances. "You're braver than I ever was. Smarter too."

"Nonsense. We all have the ability to reason and alter our choices. God gave me no more or less than He gave you."

"I'm still wrestling with God. Not as much as I was, but I'm still confused and not sure I'm doing it right."

"Doing what right?"

Nancy shrugged. "Being a godly woman, I suppose."

Faith glanced at her and smiled. "It isn't complicated, so don't make it that way."

"What do you mean?"

"Well, we decide to accept Jesus as our Lord and Savior, but that doesn't mean He's not Lord and Savior if we say no. Just like I could refuse to accept that Dobbin is a horse." She nodded toward the old sorrel pulling the wagon. "I could say he was a dog, for instance, but that wouldn't make him one."

"Of course not."

"Well, it may sound shocking, but what you decide doesn't change the truth. God will still be God. He wants us to come to Him, to love Him, but it doesn't keep Him from loving us. The Bible says, 'But God commendeth his love toward us, in that, while we were yet sinners, Christ died for us.' God loved us enough to do that even though we were against Him."

"But surely I have some responsibility in saving myself from hell."

"Christ gave His life and died a brutal death to save us. What more can you do?" Faith paused to let that sink in and then continued. "Don't get me wrong, we do have certain responsibilities. We are to come to Him—to yield ourselves in obedience. And daily we should strive to be like Him—not to save ourselves from hell, but to draw nearer to Him. Only He can save us."

"You make it sound so easy."

"Well, it needn't be difficult. Jesus said in the Gospel of John that He is the way, the truth, and the life, and that no one cometh to the Father but by Him. It's always and ever about Him. 'For by grace are ye saved through faith; and that not of yourselves: it is the gift of God.' Have you ever had to do something in order to earn a gift?"

"No. I suppose not."

"God loved you enough to die for you, Nancy." Faith glanced at her and smiled. "Just cherish the thought of that kind of love."

Her words stayed with Nancy even after they'd changed the subject to speak on other things. When Nancy saw the homestead come into view, her eyes filled with tears. There was something special about coming home. Something she'd never allowed herself to believe or consider before now. She dabbed at her tears with the back of her sleeve and soaked in the sights and sounds. She was home, and for once it felt right. For once she was going to cherish not only God's love but her family's love as well.

"It's so good to have you here," Nancy's mother said, squeezing her daughter's shoulders as they embraced.

"I'm sorry for not giving you any warning."

"Nonsense. That never matters. Though your father is off on one of his treks and your brothers aren't here."

"But I am," fourteen-year-old Meg declared with her hands on her hips. "And I want to hear all about life in the big city. Have you been to any plays or operas? How I long to go to an opera." She danced around the room, her braids flying out behind her. "I'd love to see the ballet."

"I did go to a play not long ago," Nancy admitted. "It was lovely and very funny. The theater in Portland is said to be some of the finest in the West."

"And did the ladies wear Worth gowns and jewels?" Meg asked with a sigh.

"I did see one or two gowns that were sure to be Worth, but I saw a whole room of them at a birthday party just last night."

"You did? I'm positively green with envy."

"Envy is a sin, Meg," Mother reminded her youngest.

"Oh, bother. I'm just a sinner, then. I try not to be," Meg said, giving Nancy a look of contrition. "But sometimes it just worms its way into me. Tell me about the Chinese. Do they really go about in their native costumes?"

"They do. Well, some of them do," Nancy said, doing her best to remember. "It's been a while since I was in Chinatown, but once when I was there I sampled their food. It was very unusual."

"Oh!" Meg gave an even bigger sigh. "I wish I could see it for myself. I'll positively perish out here on the farm before I get a chance to see Portland, much less the world."

Grace took hold of her youngest as she danced by. "Margaret, I know you have chores to do. Why don't you get them done, and then you'll be able to spend time this evening visiting with your sister about all these things?"

Meg frowned. "You're so lucky to be grown up and not have chores."

Nancy laughed. "I have chores. I run a boardinghouse and have plenty of work to do."

"Well, at least you're the one in charge. No one orders you around like they do me."

"Meg, you are breaking my heart," Mother declared, folding her arms across her chest. "Perhaps you'd like to spend next Saturday helping me sort the attic."

Meg's eyes grew wide. "But next Saturday is Sarah Armstrong's birthday party."

"Then maybe you should make yourself scarce and do the work you have to do so that I forget about wanting to clean the attic."

Nancy watched as Meg hurried from the room. She could remember her mother saying such things to her when she was Meg's age and complained about the workload.

"She's such a handful," Mother said.

"Worse than me?" Nancy asked, then quickly followed up, "Don't answer that. I know I was a beast of a child."

"You weren't a beast of a child. You were just very wounded and hurt by the loss of your brother." Mother took a seat across the table from Nancy. "We all were."

"We never talked about it much." Nancy remembered the pain more intensely here in the house where Douglas had died.

"I tried to talk to you about it, but . . ."

"But I pushed you away. And probably said ugly things that I'd rather not remember."

Her mother gave her a sympathetic smile. "I just remember how much you were hurting and how I couldn't help you."

Nancy hadn't imagined that her mother could see anything

past her own pain. "It hurt so much. I blamed God and wanted nothing more to do with Him. He was cruel, I thought. Cruel to take such a sweet little boy away from the family who loved him so dearly. I wanted nothing more to do with Him."

"And I clung to Him even more. In my brokenness I saw no other hope." Her mother paused. "I wish I'd had more strength in order to be there for you—to comfort you and encourage you. I knew you were devastated, but then I learned I was expecting Meg."

"I was angry when I found out," Nancy admitted. "I thought it cruel to take Douglas only to give us another baby. I didn't want to know the new baby. I didn't want to care. It hurt too much."

"My poor Nancy." Grace wiped the tears that came but never looked away.

"Mother, I'm truly sorry for the way I've behaved toward you and Father. I've tried to set things right with God, but I'm still not sure I'm on the right course. I must surely do something more than ask for forgiveness."

Her mother smiled. "A surrendered heart will show in your actions. Perhaps that's what you want to see in yourself. But just remember that you can't save yourself by some course of works. God only asks that we come to Him, yielded and trusting. Believe me, those two things are hard enough."

Nancy nodded, unable to stop thinking about Seth and what she'd overheard. "Trust is very hard," she murmured. "Probably the hardest thing of all."

CHAPTER 19

W ell, it's empty," Seth said, closing the door to the small shed. It wasn't much larger than six feet by six feet and hidden so well by the overgrown brush and trees that they had nearly missed it.

"Do you suppose they beat us to it?" Gabe asked.

"Possibly." Seth scanned the surrounding area. "But on the other hand, it doesn't look like anyone's been here in some time. And you said there weren't any tracks."

"True enough. Maybe Albert didn't have anything stored here. Maybe he was waiting for a shipment."

"Could be." Seth moved toward the river. "My guess is that someone brought him the supplies via the river and then offloaded the goods down here." There was a fairly smooth rocky outcropping that Seth figured could easily be used as a makeshift dock. "After that, Albert brought it up here and stored it."

Just then they heard the sound of horses on the road. Knowing the road's position above the river would make it easier to spot them, Seth and Gabe hurried to disappear into the brush. They ducked down into the vegetation just as the party came to a stop above them. Seth had no doubt this was Berkshire or at least his hirelings.

"Spread out. It has to be in this area, according to the map," someone declared.

Seth and Gabe stayed hidden while the newcomers spread out and started looking for the cache. The men weren't sure of the area and stopped several times to consult the map. It was a full hour before they spotted the small building, and all the while Seth feared he and Gabe would be spotted, or someone might find where they'd hidden their horses.

"It's over here," one of the men called.

The others came running, but Seth didn't recognize any of them save one. Newt Hanson brought up the tail end. From the way he barked out orders, he was apparently in charge.

"I'll go in first," he told the others. "You keep your guns handy and an eye out for anyone who means to interfere."

A light rain had begun to fall, dripping down through the trees and brush. Seth didn't dare so much as draw a deep breath. No doubt if he and Gabe were discovered, Hanson and his men wouldn't be welcoming. Worse still, Seth wasn't sure what Hanson's attitude would be when he found the building empty.

"Nothing here. Let's move on to the next one."

Hanson's lack of concern made Seth curious, but there was nothing to be done about it. Perhaps Albert had told his cohorts that not all of the caches would be full at the same time. Maybe these men knew that it was completely questionable whether any of the storage cabins would hold what they were looking for.

The men quickly formed ranks and climbed back up to the road. Seth and Gabe remained in place until the sound of horses and wagon faded.

"Wanna track them?" Gabe asked.

"Of course. Are you up to that?" Seth grinned. Gabe was probably the best tracker in the region, second only to his father, Alex Armistead.

Gabe rolled his eyes. "I think I can manage. We'll give them a bit of a head start, but since they don't seem to be anticipating any real trouble, I doubt they'll try to hide their progress."

Seth got up and dusted the brush off his pants. "Let's get to it, then."

They had hidden their horses down by the river about a quarter of a mile away. Seth had been afraid one of Hanson's men might trail down that way and find them, but thankfully the men had stuck to a tight radius around the cache's location.

The horses seemed unconcerned as Seth and Gabe rejoined them. They'd been enjoying the grass and had little interest in the men. Seth untied his horse and climbed on. Gabe did likewise.

"They headed north along the river," Seth said.

Gabe nodded. "There are quite a few little islands in the river between here and Portland. If I were going to hide something, I might use one of those."

"I thought of the same thing when Nancy mentioned that the maps were all drawn around the river. But there are lots of good hiding places in the rocky outcroppings, coves, and brush."

"The islets might have been more worrisome when the river levels were higher than usual or flooding, but even so, Albert would have had plenty of time to move the guns to higher ground."

Seth had also considered that. "Pritchard had been doing this for quite a while. My guess is that he had friends from his days on the river who helped with deliveries and keeping it quiet. Nancy said Albert spent quite a few years on the river doing just about every job. The fact that he kept river charts suggests that he even piloted boats at one time or another. With his knowledge of the river and the area, he wouldn't have had any difficulty putting together the hideouts and the people he needed to assist him."

"Which is why he was so successful."

"Until he managed to cross the wrong man."

Seth had read the report on Pritchard's death. He'd sustained a heavy blow to the back of his head. It was dismissed as being inflicted when he fell, but Seth felt with some certainty that human hands had done the deed. Pritchard was in someone's way, or he had outrun his usefulness. Either way, it had cost him his life.

They tracked the men to the next cache. With the sun beginning to set, Seth and Gabe had both wondered what the men intended to do. They were well upriver from Portland, and with no sign of a town nearby, there wouldn't be a hotel or even a livery in which they could spend the night. It wasn't long before it became clear that the men intended to make camp and utilize the cache's small building for shelter.

"I guess we'll be sleeping out under the stars," Gabe said, squatting down behind a bush. "At least the rain stopped."

Seth shook his head. "I wish I'd thought this out better. I didn't bring much in the way of supplies."

"I don't think we're all that far from Mikelsson's Trading Post," Gabe replied. "I could ride there and back in a couple of hours, probably, and get us some food, blankets, and whatever else you think we need. We'll have to run a cold camp or risk being spotted up here."

"Yeah, I already figured that too." Seth put his binoculars aside and reached into his coat pocket. He pulled out several bills. "Use this. I get expense money from the government for anything I need in order to do the job properly." He smiled. "I think that might allow you to include dessert as well as supper."

Nancy awoke the next morning before it was even light. She stretched out in her old bed, remembering her youth and the loneliness she had known. The last time she'd been here was the night before she'd run off to marry Albert. It seemed like a lifetime ago. How foolish she had been.

Getting up, Nancy tried to pray. She thought of all the things Faith and Mother had said to her regarding God. It seemed like every time she started to pray, her thoughts were only of herself. She was going to make a real effort to focus only on God. But what should she say?

"Lord," she began in a hushed whisper as she took a hair-brush to her hair, "I want to think about you and what your will is. I'm sorry I keep thinking of myself and my problems. If I understand correctly, I can pray about those things too. Mother assured me that you want us to bring our cares to you. However, I want to dwell on you—to honor you and thank you for all you've done for me. I don't know that I even have the words."

She put the brush aside and began to plait her hair. "I know that you have been there for me even when I turned away from you. You have always been so faithful, and I thank you for that."

A smile came to her lips. It wasn't so hard to ponder God when you thought of the good things He'd done.

"I know you have done so much for me over the years. Things I never even noticed, and I thank you for those things—the times you protected me from harm, the times you prompted me to do good."

She continued to whisper her thanks while dressing. The sun was coming up over the horizon, and for a moment she halted by the window to look out over the pasture. It was serene. She thought of the years she had played in those fields, taken long walks, or helped herd sheep. She had known a good life on this farm. She'd had good parents who loved her and brought her up to fear God. Why had she been so heartless and cruel to them?

"I'm a wretched person, Lord. I don't deserve your mercy. I don't deserve love." Tears came unbidden. "I loved my brother more than I loved you. I loved myself more than others. How can you love me?" She hugged her arms close. "How could anyone love me?"

She made her way downstairs, fearing that if she remained alone, she would start crying in earnest and might never stop. To her surprise, Nancy heard voices coming from the kitchen and paused. Should she avoid whoever was there?

"Nancy, is that you?" her mother called. "Come join us."

Nancy peeked into the kitchen and found her mother, Aunt Hope, and Faith sitting at the kitchen table with Bibles open before them.

"I'm sorry. I didn't mean to interrupt."

"Nonsense," her mother said, pushing back the chair beside her. "We have a time of prayer and Bible reading each morning and would be honored if you joined us. We planned to invite you but wanted you to be able to sleep in this first morning. When we finish up here, we'll head to church. I hope you'll come with us."

Nancy smiled. "Of course."

She took a seat, and Aunt Hope touched her hand. Nancy turned to face her. Hope smiled. "You've been crying."

In the past, Nancy would have tried to hide it. "Yes. I suppose I was."

"Want to tell us about it?" her mother asked.

Nancy considered for a moment. There had been a time when she would have hidden her feelings from her mother for fear of . . . what? The truth?

She sighed. "I was trying to take Faith's advice and focus my prayer on God and all that He's done for me. Instead it just reminded me of how wretchedly I treated all of you and how undeserving I am of love. It's no wonder I've been without it for so long."

She quickly lowered her gaze. She hadn't meant to say that. Now her mother and the others would want to know what she meant. They'd want all the details about Albert and why Nancy felt unloved.

"Often we have so much love around us—given to us—but we push it away," Aunt Hope said. "I was like that for a long time, so certain I couldn't be loved. Convinced I was undeserving of love."

"I went through that too," Nancy's mother admitted. "I had hardened myself to be able to deal with the difficulties of life, and in hardening myself against the pain, I hardened myself against love, as well."

There were no questions. No condemnation. Just sympathy and understanding. Nancy shook her head. "I'm sorry for the way I've behaved. I truly am. I hope you'll forgive me."

"Of course. That was done long ago," her mother declared while Aunt Hope nodded. Faith said nothing, but her smile suggested there was no longer any reason for Nancy to bear the burden she'd been carrying.

"Still, there's something troubling you. What is it?" her mother asked. "We can pray about it."

Nancy thought of Seth and shook her head. "I was foolish and gave my heart too easily."

"To your husband?" Aunt Hope asked. "Is this about losing him?"

"No." Nancy shook her head. "It's about Seth Carpenter." She didn't know why, but she suddenly felt compelled to tell them everything. "He came to Portland with his sister. She boards at my house."

"Yes, we knew he was there. His mother told me at church several months ago. Gabe was so excited to see him again."

"Seth hired on with the lawyer I engaged to settle Albert's affairs. I thought it was just coincidence, but recently I learned that Seth is there on a job for the government. He's there investigating my husband—late husband."

"Investigating him for what?" Faith asked.

Nancy shared what she knew about Albert's dealings and brought the conversation back around to Seth. "The trouble is, he made it seem like he cared for me, and I fell for his lies. I lost my heart to him completely."

"What makes you suppose it to be a lie?" Mother asked. "That hardly sounds like the Seth we knew."

"But that Seth was back east for a long time. He could have changed completely. Apparently he did, because I, too, thought him trustworthy."

"Then why suppose he isn't?"

"Because everything I just told you about him working with the government to search out my late husband's illegal activities is something he never bothered to tell me. He kept it hidden. And he suspected I was involved! I only learned of it because

Gabe was trying to talk him into being honest with me, and I overheard."

"Gabe knew?" Mother asked.

"Apparently. Although I don't know how long he's known. He was trying to convince Seth to be honest with me, which I greatly appreciate. But Seth didn't want to."

"It doesn't mean that his feelings for you are a lie," Faith said matter-of-factly.

"Why not? Everything else is. Why should that one thing be true when he lied about everything else?"

"Well, we're here to pray," Faith reminded them. "So let's pray about this as well. I think, given your feelings for him, that it's important that you give him a chance to explain. We can pray that you'll have not only the opportunity but the words and open heart to receive his explanation and determine the truth."

"I think Faith makes a good point," Mother said, reaching over to take Nancy's hand. "Why don't we pray?"

Church was surprisingly pleasant. There was a new minister, but he was quite good at teaching the Word and had a gentleness about him that instantly put Nancy at ease. After services, she spoke with most of the congregation—old family friends and neighbors. The one family she hadn't thought about encountering was Seth's.

"We were sorry to hear about your husband," Mrs. Carpenter said. She gave Nancy a hug. "I've been praying for you to find comfort."

"Thank you. God has definitely been good to me." Nancy felt awkward speaking to Seth's mother. She was still so hurt by what he'd done.

"Clementine tells us that your boardinghouse was an answer to her prayers. Her biggest concern was where she would live."

"It was our biggest concern as well." The male voice belonged to Mr. Carpenter, and Nancy was startled by how much Seth resembled his father.

"She is a very welcome addition." Nancy tried not to show her discomfort. "It's been wonderful to rekindle our friendship."

"Clem mentioned Seth spending a fair amount of time there as well," Mr. Carpenter said with the same boyish grin that Nancy had come to love on his son.

"Yes, well, we do get our fair share of visitors." Nancy glanced toward her mother, who was speaking to the pastor. "If you'll excuse me, I believe Mother is ready to go."

She hurried away before the Carpenters could say anything more. Hopefully she hadn't offended them.

"There you are," her mother said. "Pastor Willis, this is my daughter Nancy."

The older man smiled. "I'm pleased to meet you. I've heard so much about you from your folks."

Nancy smiled and shook his hand. "I very much enjoyed your sermon, Pastor Willis."

"It's hard to go wrong when you preach straight from the Word. I find using anything other than the Bible to be a tedious experience that results in very little."

Nancy nodded, uncertain what to say.

Thankfully, Mother interceded. "Well, we should be on our way."

They bid the pastor good-bye and paused only momentarily to speak to others on their way to the wagon.

"I'm so glad you came with us today," Mother said as they

climbed onto the wagon. "Now, if we can just find Meg." She looked across the churchyard.

Nancy spied her sister talking to several girls who looked her age. Nancy gave Meg a wave when she glanced up, and although Meg looked less than happy to leave, she gave her friends each an embrace, then ran to the wagon. Nancy reached down to help her sister up.

"I wish we could stay and visit," Meg said. "Sarah was telling me her plans for the party."

"It'll be here soon enough," Mother declared, "and then you won't have to worry about getting the details."

Nancy couldn't help but smile as Meg settled into the seat behind them. She might have been very much like her little sister had Douglas not died. Social and outgoing, excited about the latest fashions. Nancy had lost far more because of her brother's death than she had ever realized.

"Are you going to stay for a long time?" Meg asked after Monday morning's prayer and Bible reading.

Nancy shook her head. She knew she would soon have to think about heading home.

"No. I have a home in Portland. I run a boardinghouse for several ladies. Most are of limited means and depend on me to provide for them."

"Who's taking care of them now?" Meg asked, flipping back one of her braids. "Why can't they just keep managing it for you so you can stay here?"

Nancy saw that her mother seemed to have the same question in mind. "Because it's my responsibility, and I like it there. I only came here for a couple of days to sort through some problems."

"What kind of problems?" Meg stopped eating and cocked her head to one side. "Mama says we should always help one another with our problems. Can I help?"

Nancy shook her head. "I wish you could. Instead, why don't you tell me what you've been up to these last eight years?" It was hard to look at the dark-headed, dark-eyed girl and not think of the years that had passed. Meg had been a child when Nancy had left—just a couple years older than Douglas when he'd died. She'd avoided having much to do with her new sibling for fear of dealing with the loss should anything happen. She considered Meg. She was a petite and pretty little girl—well, not so little anymore. She was fourteen, and before Nancy knew it, she would be grown.

"I go to school and work. That's all I ever get to do." Meg gave a dramatic sigh.

"Didn't you say there's a birthday party for one of your friends on Saturday?"

"Yes, but that's rare. Folks can't always afford to have a party." Meg looked momentarily downcast, then perked up. "But Sarah's folks are rich. They'll give her a good party. That's why I just *have* to go. Besides, Sarah is my best friend."

"Well, attending the party of a best friend sounds very important."

"Oh, it is. Sarah said I can help her open her presents. I get to write down everything that she gets and who it's from so she can send thank-you cards to everyone. She has special stationery just for that purpose. Isn't that marvelous? I wish I had special stationery."

"Perhaps you shall one day." Nancy smiled at her sister's dreamy expression. Would that fancy stationery could fix all of her problems. "What did you get Sarah for her birthday?"

"Mother suggested I embroider a pair of pillowcases for her hope chest. Would you like to see them?"

"Of course."

Meg jumped up from the table and made a mad dash from the room.

Nancy chuckled. "I didn't mean she had to get them right now."

Mother laughed. "Everything with Meg is *right now*. She has more energy than I can muster. But she keeps us laughing and reminds us of our blessings. She's definitely fonder of your father than me. Mostly because he always brings her treats when he goes to town or travels. She's so spoiled by him that I have to be the one to stand firm."

"That hardly seems fair." Nancy remembered it had been the same for her, however. "I guess children will take advantage of whoever benefits them the most. I recall being the same way. I suppose I owe you a big apology."

"Here they are," Meg announced, bringing the folded pillowcases into the kitchen. "I worked very hard on them."

Nancy inspected the embroidered flower border. "The work is very well done, but the test is to see the back." She turned the edge of the pillowcase to reveal very neat and orderly stitches. "You get a star for making the back as lovely as the front."

Meg beamed. "Thank you."

Later in the day, Meg took Nancy on a tour of the sheep barns and to the pen where the lambs were being kept. Weaning was in process, and Meg informed Nancy of everything that had been done and was going to be done. Then she took Nancy to her favorite places around the farm. Some of them had been Nancy's favorites.

To Nancy's surprise, however, Meg walked to the tiny family cemetery. Nancy had never even considered visiting this place.

"I love it here," Meg said, pushing open the little wooden gate. "It makes me feel like God is right here with me."

Nancy walked to Douglas's grave, which was marked with an engraved stone. His name and the years of his birth and death were all that was given. Not far from where he'd been laid to rest was a grave belonging to the infant daughter of Aunt Hope and Uncle Lance. Thankfully there were no other graves.

"I come here sometimes and bring flowers. I didn't know Douglas or Aunt Hope's baby Charity, but they're still family, so I like to come and remember them."

Nancy was touched by her sister's heart. She hadn't returned to Douglas's grave since the funeral. "Charity Kenner died at birth, so no one really got to know her, but Douglas was a sweet boy, and everyone loved him."

"That's what Mama says. Do you know she still cries when she talks about him?"

Nancy didn't think about her mother's pain often, but she knew that the pain she felt over Douglas had brought her to tears for many years. She had always selfishly thought her pain was greater than anyone else's.

"I don't imagine a mother ever stops hurting over the loss of a child," Nancy murmured. How she wished she had been more comforting to her mother instead of turning away from her—from all of her loved ones—after Douglas died.

Meg cleared some grass away from the headstone and smiled. "Mama said I was her consolation. She said God sent me specifically to bring joy back to our family. She almost called me Joy—did you know that?"

Nancy shook her head. "No, I don't think I did."

Meg looked up at her. "I wish she had. I like the name Joy."

"Well, it's clear that you're full of joy." Nancy smiled, but the feeling was bittersweet. Meg might also have been her consolation. Instead, Nancy had thrown away the chance of happiness in her sister's company because of her fears of loss.

"I wish we could have been close," Meg said, straightening. She fixed her gaze on Nancy. "Mama said that losing Douglas broke your heart and you were afraid to love me."

Nancy hadn't expected this conversation and felt embarrassed. What could she say to her sister? It was true, but to admit it was to see her shallow and wretched heart for what it was.

"I was afraid," Nancy barely murmured. "I'm still afraid of so much."

Meg took Nancy's hand. "You don't have to be. The Bible says perfect love casteth out fear. Perfect love is God's love for us. Did you know that?"

Tears came to Nancy's eyes. "I think I'm learning it."

Meg hugged her older sister. "Don't be afraid anymore, Nancy. I love you and God loves you."

Nancy wrapped her arms around Meg and let her tears fall freely. Out of the mouth of babes came healing.

By the time evening rolled around and supper was called, Nancy had been completely reimmersed in Armistead-Kenner Farms. She felt her spirit had been set free from its prison as she reacquainted herself with her family. Her time with Meg at the cemetery had given her more healing than she'd ever thought possible. Still, she was concerned about going back to Portland to face Seth. She loved him, but obviously he didn't feel the same way.

At dinner with her aunt and uncle, cousins, and parents,

as well as the vivacious Meg, Nancy watched the camaraderie between her family. Faith's brothers Sean and Ed were absent, since they had married and lived elsewhere with farms and families of their own, but her youngest brother, Brandon, who was the same age as Meg, was happy to entertain them with stories of his summer escapades.

"I caught an even bigger fish than Pa did," he said, holding his hands out to demonstrate its length. "It was huge, at least two feet long."

"That fish gets bigger every time he tells the story," Uncle Lance said, rolling his gaze heavenward.

"It was a whopper. You said so yourself," Brandon protested as he pushed a lock of brown hair back from his face.

"Something was a whopper, that's for sure," his mother said before Uncle Lance could answer.

"I sure miss James. I hoped he'd come home for the summer," Mother said, "but I think there's a young lady."

Lance laughed. "There always is."

Nancy smiled, but the comment reminded her of Seth. She wondered if he'd found the cache of weapons and if that had given him the proof he needed. She wondered if he would wrap up the investigation and leave before she returned home, or if he even knew she was gone. Most of all, she wondered how she was ever going to stop loving him.

CHAPTER 20

Seth used the binoculars to better observe what was going on below. They had the advantage of the high ground this time, and while they couldn't make out everything going on below, they knew that Hanson's men had found another cache and that this one had some of the goods they were seeking.

"They're loading the wagon," Seth told Gabe in a hushed voice. "Where do you suppose they mean to take it all?"

"Hard to tell, but my guess is back to Portland and then to whatever reservation they've targeted."

"The same one your uncle works with." Seth lowered the binoculars. "The whole reason I'm here is that we traced the shipments from his reservation back to Portland."

Gabe's eyes narrowed. "You think Uncle Adam knows about this?"

"Unfortunately, the evidence suggests it."

Gabe shook his head. "Then your evidence is wrong. My uncle would never do anything to incite the natives to war. His family lives on the reservation, for grief's sake. He's not going to have the Indians running amok with guns."

"Are you sure about that? I mean, how well do you know him?"

"Very well, and I know my Aunt Mercy even better. She'd throttle him if he turned in that direction. No, your information is dead wrong. Those two are completely devoted to helping the Indians survive life on the reservation and learn how to live with the white man. It's gotta be somebody else."

"I wish I could be as confident of that as you are."

There was some commotion down below as the men loaded the final crates. Seth held up his hand to silence Gabe and listened as one of the men gave the order to move out.

Since Seth and Gabe had already gathered their things and packed them on the horses, they sat hidden until the wagon and riders had cleared the area and pushed on. Giving Hanson's men a good head start, Seth and Gabe followed at a leisurely pace, careful to keep themselves hidden and off the main road as much as possible.

It wasn't long until the trail led to the river again, only this time it was to a ferryman and what appeared to be the only river crossing for miles in either direction.

"I think it's best we wait up here out of sight until they're well across. We can watch with the binoculars and see where they head once they're on the opposite side of the river."

"They leave a trail big enough for a child to follow," Gabe said, shaking his head. "I don't think we have to worry about keeping them in view."

Seth nodded and lifted the binoculars all the same. He had already identified Newt Hanson but was trying to figure out if he knew or had seen any of the other men. The flat, open ferry gave him a clear view, and since none of the men seemed inclined to hide their faces, he could do a lengthy study of each one. At least until they reached the other side.

"Hey, one of them isn't going aboard," Gabe said, pushing Seth down. "Looks like he's coming back this way."

Seth had been squatting by a stand of small trees in order to keep out of sight. Gabe's push sent him to his backside, and Gabe hurried to duck into the brush beside him. Thankfully they'd hidden their horses farther into the trees.

The rider didn't notice them as he flew by on his mount. Seth wondered where he was going in such a hurry. Was he taking word back to Portland? Was he summoning more help?

"Where do you suppose he's going?" Gabe asked.

"I was just wondering that myself." Seth shook his head and got back on his feet. He raised the binoculars again.

The ferry hadn't yet reached the other side of the river. Seth was impatient and wished he dared to let his horse swim the river. Such a choice would be foolish, though. The horse was rented, and Seth knew nothing about its capability.

An hour later, it was Seth and Gabe's turn on the ferry. Thankfully a few other folks had joined them, so they wouldn't stand out. It was always possible the ferryman knew the men who were collecting the guns and whiskey.

Once they reached the other side, Seth let Gabe take charge. The tracks were easy to spot most of the time, but Seth was glad for his friend's ability. Once they reached the road, their fellow passengers headed north, while Seth and Gabe went south. At least they didn't have to worry about the others obscuring the tracks.

They rode for five or six miles before Gabe motioned toward a scrawny path. It was hardly big enough for a wagon, and Seth wasn't sure they should follow on horseback.

"Why don't we find a place to hide our mounts," he whispered.

Gabe nodded. "There was a spot back up the road. It looked like it headed pretty deep into the trees."

They found the location again and explored the area until Seth was satisfied it was the perfect spot to tie off their mounts. He and Gabe picked their way through the trees, keeping the edge of the road in sight until they were back at the narrow trail. They moved as silently as possible toward the river. There was no way to know exactly what they'd find when they reached the bank of the river.

They cleared the brush almost abruptly, and Gabe reached out to pull Seth back. He put his finger to his lips when Seth opened his mouth to protest. A quick shake of Gabe's head left Seth certain that something was wrong.

"I'm going across the path to the other side," Gabe whispered. "You stay here. I can hear talking, so they haven't gone too far."

Seth nodded and squatted down out of sight. It seemed like it took forever for Gabe to return. He was so good at keeping silent that he was nearly upon Seth before he realized it.

"The wagon is parked at the water's edge about fifty yards downstream. There are two men with it. The others have gone out to an island. It's pretty good-sized. I think we could go on down the river a piece and cross to the island at the far end. We ought to be able to sneak back upstream and see where they are. My guess is that the cache is on the island."

Seth nodded. "Sounds about right. Go ahead and lead the way."

Seth was more than a little frustrated when the men settled in for another night. There had been no action of any kind except for the discovery of the hidden cache on the island. Seth had gotten close enough to see for himself that the building was in poor repair. No doubt floods and lack of upkeep had left the cabin in a bad way. Nevertheless, Pritchard or someone else had stored enough crates inside that the men were still loading the wagon as night fell.

"Joe, take that wagon back to town, and Slim, you go with him. See Berkshire and find out where he wants it unloaded, then get back here by dawn."

Seth tensed at the mention of Berkshire's name. So he was right about Gerome's involvement.

"But, boss, that's gonna take all night."

"I don't care. Just get it done. You know what's expected, and you're being paid, same as the others. We've got a lot more here than we can possibly take in one load. The ferry will stop for the night in another hour. So get this load across and find Berkshire. Figure out where he wants this stuff stashed, then get back here so you can cross the river at first light. That way we can load up the rest."

Seth edged away from the cabin and retraced his steps, careful to brush away any tracks, as Gabe had shown him.

"Well?" Gabe asked when he returned.

"They're taking the wagon out of here. Getting it back across on the last ferry, then planning to be back here at dawn to cross over and get the rest of the crates. Apparently that dilapidated building holds more than it looks."

"What do you want to do about it?"

"Well, I heard Hanson mention Berkshire, so I know for sure he's involved now. The men are supposed to take the wagon to him and see where he wants everything stored. I think we need to get word to the army. This is too much for one man, or even two."

"We aren't that far from Oregon City. We could get word to the army there and then stay the night with my folks. They'd love to see you."

"My folks are in town and have room for both of us," Seth said, scratching his stubbly jaw. "Your folks are way out in the country."

"Either way, it'll give us a warm bed and hot grub. We can still get word to the army tonight and then send your superior a telegram in the morning."

By the time they reached Oregon City, the town was closed up tight for the night. The only exception was the saloons, and those were of no interest to Gabe or Seth. The sleepy army sergeant who took down the message was less than congenial, but Seth couldn't blame him. His day had probably started before dawn and would do so again tomorrow. Nevertheless, he assured Seth that he'd get the information to Portland. Seth felt a lot better knowing the army would be able to take over watching for the wagon and the guns. He felt a sense of satisfaction knowing that when the men showed up with the wagon at Berkshire's place, the army would be there.

Seth and Gabe made their way to the small two-story house where Seth had grown up.

"Looks like everyone's gone to bed," Gabe said as they approached. There wasn't a single light showing from any of the windows.

"The back door will be open. We'll slip upstairs. You can have Clem's room. I know she wouldn't mind." Seth grinned.

Nancy joined her mother for morning devotions just as Hope and Faith arrived. They read from Romans, then prayed for each family member before starting on the surrounding neighbors and friends. Nancy had enjoyed her stay very much but knew it was time to return to her home, and she hoped to get a ride from her uncle Lance. As the prayers concluded and the ladies began to talk about the day, she brought this up.

"Is Uncle Lance going into town today?"

"Yes," Aunt Hope replied. "He's still working most every day in his office. Why?"

"It's time for me to go home. I promised Bedelia I'd only be gone a day or two and, well, I've found what I came here for, so it seems only right that I return."

"And what were you looking for?" Aunt Hope asked.

"I don't think I can put it into words," Nancy said, smiling. "I was upset and angry that Seth had betrayed my trust, and I was still trying to figure out what God wanted from me. And what I needed from Him."

"And you managed to sort through all of that in this short time?" Faith asked with a smile.

Nancy let out a sigh. "It's not all sorted, but I do have better understanding and clarity. I feel more confident of who God is and what He wants of me."

"Well, that's a perfect start," Mother declared. "I find that when I can better understand God and His will for my life, everything else falls into place."

"It's not perfect, but I feel hope, and that's more than I had before." Nancy gave her mother a smile, then looked at her aunt and cousin. "And I feel that I have a better understanding of my family. Hopefully we shall all grow closer and closer."

"Of course we will. But why go back?" Mother asked. "Surely your boarder can continue to manage for you. You could stay with us for a while and rest. You look weary."

Nancy shook her head and started to answer, but the back door opened behind her, and Gabe announced his presence. "Morning, Ma. What's for breakfast?"

Mother beamed. "Gabe, what are you doing here? I thought you were going to be gone for a while."

Nancy stood and turned to face her brother. Unfortunately, Seth was right behind him. They locked gazes, and she frowned. She fought the urge to run.

"Nancy?" Seth said in disbelief. Even Gabe looked at her in surprise. "When did you get here?"

"I owe no explanation to liars and deceivers," she said, barely able to breathe.

She left the room with her head up and her shoulders back. She wouldn't let this situation destroy the fragile peace she'd found.

Thankfully she'd left her bags by the front door. Pausing only long enough to take them in hand, she headed outside.

"Nancy, wait," her mother said, following her.

"I can't. I don't want to speak to either of them."

Mother came to where Nancy had paused mid-step. "You don't have to leave like this."

"I'm not upset with you or anyone else. I just hate that Seth has lied to me and that only now, when he figures out that I already know what he's done, will he be compelled to be honest. Not because it's the right thing—only because he's been caught in his deception." Nancy fought back tears.

"But I'm sure he had a good reason for it and that you two can work through this. I don't approve of lying, as you well know, but I find it impossible to believe that you two can't reconcile."

"You don't understand, Mother. I've fallen in love with him."

Nancy shook her head. "I've fallen in love with a lie. Please just let me go. I want to go home."

Behind her mother, Nancy heard the screen door open and turned to see Seth there, wearing a questioning look.

"Good-bye, Mother."

Nancy headed for Aunt Hope's house across the yard. She hoped—prayed—that Seth would just stay where he was and leave her be. Otherwise she wasn't sure she could bear it.

CHAPTER 21

Nancy, wait," Seth called.

She kept walking, knowing that if she stopped to face him, she might fall apart. Her heart ached. She hadn't meant to fall in love with him, but it didn't matter. She had, and now she had to find a way to live without him.

"Nancy, we need to talk." He was directly behind her.

He would keep following her if she didn't address this. She had no choice but to stop. She put her bags down and straightened. Drawing in a deep breath, Nancy turned to face him.

Please, God, give me strength.

"Why did you call me a liar and deceiver?" Seth asked.

His blue eyes bore into her, and she swore he could see right down to her soul. "Because you are. You have been since you first showed up accompanying John Lincoln."

Seth frowned. "What are you saying?"

She shook her head in exasperation. "I heard what you and Gabe were saying on the porch just before you left. This has all been part of a secret job for you, figuring out Albert's illegal activities. And figuring out mine as well. I hope you weren't too disappointed to learn that I was just as clueless as everyone else.

The silly, stupid little wife who had no idea what her husband was doing—or her friend, for that matter. I suppose ignorance is no excuse, however. My husband was willingly breaking the law, and I lived under his roof—his wife, doing his bidding. So, will you put me in jail?"

"Nancy, that's not the way it is."

"Did you or did you not come to Portland purposefully to investigate my husband's activities?"

"I did." He looked uncomfortable.

"And did you or did you not keep that from me and instead pretend to be my friend?"

The embarrassment left his expression. "I didn't pretend. We've been friends since we were children."

"Yet despite our friendship, you lied to me." She tried not to notice how rugged and handsome he was with his light growth of facial hair.

"Nancy, I had a job to do and was sworn to secrecy. I told John only because I felt I needed to be completely aboveboard with him. I didn't tell anyone else until I confided in Gabe, and I only did that because I needed his help. This wasn't about me setting out to lie to you. Or to hurt you."

"So you needed to be aboveboard with John, but not with me."

"Yes, because at first you were part of the investigation. When I first came, I didn't know who Albert was married to. You could have been part of the entire operation."

"Fine." She turned around and picked up her traveling bags. "I should have known better than to expect you to apologize or understand the wrong you've done."

She headed toward her aunt's house, but Seth took hold of her bags and pulled them from her hands.

"Stop and give me a chance to explain. I'm sorry for the deception. I never set out to hurt you, and I don't want to hurt you now. I love you."

She whirled on him. "Liar! Love doesn't deceive like you did. You could have told me everything—you should have. You learned things from me about Albert and knew full well that I had no idea what he'd done. You could have taken any of those opportunities to confess why you were here instead of letting me go on believing you cared."

"But I do care! I didn't anticipate falling in love with you, Nancy, but that's exactly what happened."

"Well, I'm sorry for you."

His lips curled slightly. "Are you going to stand there and tell me you have no feelings for me?"

Her eyes narrowed at his smugness. "I have feelings, all right. I have feelings of anger, resentment, betrayal, and frustration. I'm full of feelings."

"What about love?"

How dare he push for a confession? "You've done nothing but deceive me. You thought I was helping to start a war with the Indians. Why in the world would I fall in love with you?"

He dropped the bags and closed the distance between them, taking hold of her shoulders. "That's not an answer but another question."

Then he lowered his mouth to hers.

His actions shocked Nancy and she froze, giving him a chance to slip his arms around her and pull her closer. His long, passionate kiss was unlike anything she'd ever known with Albert, and try as she might to feel nothing, Nancy found herself returning it.

When he pulled away, he lifted her chin and forced her gaze

to meet his. Nancy looked at him, willing her heart to stop pounding so hard.

"Tell me you feel nothing for me. Tell me you haven't fallen in love with me. Tell me that honestly, and I'll leave you alone."

She felt betrayed all over again, but this time it was her heart and mind betraying her rather than Seth Carpenter.

Pushing him away, Nancy turned and ran for the safety of her aunt and uncle's house. Tears poured from her eyes, blurring her vision. Why did she have to love him? Why? He had hurt her. He had lied to her. Why couldn't she just hate him?

She knocked on the front door of the house and pushed it open. "Uncle Lance?" She was barely able to speak.

Her uncle came from one of the other rooms. He was dressed smartly in a gray suit and gave her a broad smile until he saw her tears.

She threw herself into his arms. "Please t-take me to town."

"Nancy, what's going on?"

"I need to go home. I need to leave this place."

Seth knew better than to chase after Nancy. He felt terrible that he had taken advantage of her. He felt terrible for not being honest with her, but at the same time, his job depended on secrecy. Otherwise they might never catch the men who were overseeing plans for the insurrection. Seth's superiors had never felt that Albert Pritchard was the man in charge. They knew he played a role but that there were others with more power and money than he had. Those were the men they really wanted to catch red-handed. Pritchard had only been a pawn. Unfortunately, Nancy had become one too.

He stood for some time, staring at the Kenner house and

wishing he could help her understand that he only wanted to protect her from harm—that he truly did love her. He loved her so much that he could not imagine a future without her.

Seth picked up Nancy's bags and headed back to her parents' house. He placed them by the porch steps, knowing she would soon want them.

"You look like you've lost your last friend," Grace Armistead said.

He hadn't seen her sitting there. "I feel like it."

"Want to talk about it?"

He sighed and made his way onto the porch where she sat. He leaned back against one of the posts. "She thinks I purposefully deceived her, but it was never like that."

"Why don't you tell me what it was like?" Grace's expression was full of motherly tenderness.

"I was approached by the government. They knew me through the association of some of their lawyers. They knew I was from Oregon and that I knew the area of Portland in particular. They told me what was going on with the Indians. This came about shortly after Chief Joseph had been caught. Some of the reservation tribes were upset and felt that they should make a stand. It became clear that they were getting weapons and whiskey from someone, and we needed to figure out what was going on. I was hired to come here and investigate what few leads they had. I was to say nothing to anyone, because we couldn't be certain who was involved and who wasn't."

"I see. And I take it Nancy's husband was one of the men involved."

"Yes. We were fairly certain about him, and when he was killed, we felt confident he had crossed one of the other partners."

"Killed?" Grace put a hand to her throat. "I thought he fell in the river and drowned."

"That's what most folks think, but we're fairly certain he was killed. He sustained a bad blow on the back of his head, and while it's possible he could have hit his head on something in the river, the doctor felt he was dead before he was in the water."

"I see."

Seth crossed his arms and shook his head. "I didn't know Nancy was his wife until I met John Lincoln. Someone had mentioned that Albert Pritchard's widow hired him to settle the estate. When I realized it was Nancy, I felt confident she couldn't have been involved, but still, I had to be sure."

"And now you are?"

"I am. I have been almost from the beginning. I couldn't imagine Nancy involving herself in something like that, but then again, eight years can completely change a person."

"Especially when that person was already changed," Grace murmured.

"Yes." Seth knew he should probably say no more, but he felt compelled to explain his heart to Nancy's mother. "As I spent time with her, I lost my heart to her. She told me how miserable she was with Pritchard—how alone she felt. She never went into much detail, but the few things she did say left me with little doubt that she never had a happy marriage. However, she was determined to make it work, and he, in turn, lavished her with everything but love."

"My poor girl."

"Albert Pritchard only cared about his own purposes. He wanted a beautiful wife and an expensive house filled with beautiful things so he could show off to the world just how successful he was. He could never reach the social status of the elite, but he found ways to make himself useful to them and so be allowed into their society on occasion. He hated people of color, as many of the elite did, so when the opportunity came to help their cause, Albert made certain he was indispensable. Only somewhere along the way, he crossed someone or otherwise made himself unnecessary, and they killed him."

"What are you going to do now?"

Seth frowned. "About Pritchard or Nancy?"

Grace smiled. "I'm fairly certain you cannot tell me everything about your duties where my former son-in-law is concerned. I'm talking about Nancy. You're in love with her, if I'm not mistaken."

"Yes. I've never been in love with anyone before now. I always guarded my heart, but when I started spending time with Nancy, I guess I just thought of us as old friends and failed to see the danger." He smiled. "I fell hard, I'm afraid."

"And Nancy?"

"I know she loves me. Right now she's angry because I wasn't honest with her about all of this, but I think in time I can earn her forgiveness. After all, we belong together." He grinned.

"You may have to give her time. She's always been stubborn, and when she feels embarrassed or misused, she tends to spite herself in order to punish others."

Seth nodded. "I'll give her whatever time she needs, but I won't give up on her. I know we were meant for each other, and I hope someday she sees that as well."

Grace got to her feet. "It looks like we're going to have company." She waved. "Hello, Lance. Come join us."

The older man bounded up the steps. "This must be the young man who made our Nancy cry." He frowned at Seth. "She says you're a liar and a deceiver. A cad of the worst ilk."

"Seth, you remember my brother-in-law Lance Kenner, don't you?"

"I do. He gave me my passion for law." Seth held out his hand, and for a moment he wasn't sure if Kenner would take it.

Finally, the older man did, and his expression softened. "Seth, it's good to see you again. Your father told me some time ago that you were working back east."

"And so I was. Now I'm in Portland."

Lance nodded and looked at Grace. "Nancy insists I take her to town so she can catch the boat for Portland. I presume she wants to escape this young man."

"She thinks the worst of me, but I assure you, I don't deserve it." Seth hoped Kenner might believe him, but even if he didn't—God knew the truth.

"Yes. She wants to go back to her boardinghouse. Please take her. I know we won't keep her here." Grace sounded disappointed. "Are you heading back to Portland, as well, Seth?"

"I am. I doubt she wants to be on the same boat with me, but it will probably turn out that way. Perhaps I should go ahead of you, secure my place, and stay out of sight. I don't want to further upset her."

"I'd like knowing you were on the same boat," Grace replied. "Travel isn't without risks."

Seth nodded. "Then, you can count on me. I'll keep watch over her as best I can."

Nancy was relieved to be back home. When the hired cab dropped her at the house, it was dark and chilly outside. The driver helped her down, then carried her bags to the porch. For a moment Nancy stared at the front of her house. It was such a beautiful home. The glow coming from inside was welcoming. This was where she belonged.

She paid the driver, then picked up her bags. She heard laughter coming from the front room as she entered the house. It sounded like Mimi and the others were enjoying themselves. Nancy put her bags down and breathed in the rich aroma of whatever they'd had for supper. It had been a long day, and she hadn't eaten anything. Even so, she didn't feel up to company.

"I thought perhaps our burglars had returned," Bedelia said, coming to the foyer.

"Burglars probably know better by now than to mess with the ladies of my boardinghouse." Nancy shivered. "Goodness, I wasn't expecting such a chill in the middle of summer."

"Why don't you come sit by the fire? We have a nice blaze going and were just discussing a new quilt pattern Mimi learned from a friend."

Nancy had little desire to spend the evening talking about quilts. "I think first I shall go to my room and get cleaned up."

"That's probably a good idea. I have some supper if you're hungry. We had a hearty beef stew with leftover roast. I could warm you a bowl if you like."

"That sounds marvelous. Thank you, Bedelia. I can see that everything is in perfect order. I appreciate that you managed things so well for me."

Nancy didn't wait for Bedelia's reply and instead picked up her bags and hurried down the hall to her room. Fighting off tears, she laid a fire and was soon rewarded with a hearty blaze. The warmth did her weary heart good, and for several minutes all she did was stand in front of the fire with her hands extended.

She had tried all day not to think of Seth and his kiss. She was troubled beyond words at his declaration of love. How could he love her and still have lied to her? Even when Gabe had encouraged him to be honest with her, Seth hadn't wanted to.

"Lord, I don't know what to do. I do love him. At least I think it's love. I can hardly bear the deception, however. It's bad enough knowing what Albert did behind my back, but now Seth has done all of this, and even though it was for the side of good, how can I forgive him?"

She stared at the flames and then sank to her knees. She bowed in silent prayer, hoping that somehow God would take the pain from her heart and give her clarity about what to do next. Nothing made sense at this point, and each thought of Seth brought more pain than the last.

For several long minutes she did nothing but beg God for understanding and help. For so many years she had believed Him to be indifferent, even cruel, but her mother and Mary Taylor had convinced her otherwise. How she longed to feel His love—His comfort. Didn't He care that she was hurting?

She heard a noise and raised her head to find Bedelia standing in her doorway with a bowl of stew in her hands. Without a word, Bedelia put the bowl on the mantel, then lowered herself to the floor at Nancy's side.

Bedelia bowed her head and clasped her hands together. "'Where two or three are gathered together in my name,'" she whispered.

Nancy nodded and closed her eyes as the tears fell. The peace she longed for washed over her. God did care, and He was there with them. Somehow, He would see Nancy through the pain.

CHAPTER 22

ancy was surprised and a little disappointed, if she was honest, that Seth hadn't attempted to see her since she'd returned to Portland. She'd been home almost a week, and even though she felt certain he would have returned to town by now, she'd neither heard Clementine mention him nor seen him at the house.

It was just as well. She wouldn't have received him.

At least that was what she told herself.

"I'll be just down the block at Mary Taylor's house," she told Bedelia and Cornelia. "We're sewing for the poor today, and I will probably be gone until late afternoon. There's a pot of ham and beans on the back of the stove for lunch. There's also fresh cornbread on the counter."

"I'm certain we'll be fine," Bedelia answered as Cornelia bobbed her head. "And we'll see to Mrs. Weaver."

"That's so kind of you, but she told me she would come down for her food today." Nancy glanced at the clock. "Oh dear. I'd best hurry."

She was in her sewing room, collecting her things, when someone knocked on the front door. She frowned even as her heart began to race. Was it Seth? Had he come to apologize and press her to forgive him?

She went to the foyer just as Bedelia was opening the door. "Mr. Lincoln. How nice to see you again," Bedelia said. "Mrs. Pritchard is just preparing to leave."

Nancy hid her disappointment. She had intended to send John a letter of dismissal for his role in the deception with Seth but hadn't gotten around to it yet. Now she would have to do it in person.

She stopped just inside the foyer. "Mr. Lincoln." She gave a curt nod.

"I apologize for stopping by unannounced," he said. "I hope you might give me a moment, however, as it regards the sale of your husband's business."

Nancy nodded. "Very well. Please come to the front room." She led the way and tried to remain calm. "Have a seat."

"Thank you." He chose the wingback chair, and Nancy took the rocker.

While Mr. Lincoln opened his satchel, Nancy couldn't help but speak. "I hope this concludes our business. I'm afraid, given what I've learned about Mr. Carpenter's deception, that I no longer feel I can put my trust in your firm."

John Lincoln nodded. "Seth told me what transpired, and I have anticipated your decision, although I hope you will give me a chance to explain and apologize."

Nancy didn't want to be rude to a man who had been so gracious to her over the years. "Of course."

John drew out a few papers, then put the satchel aside. "I was against his keeping the truth from you—at least in the beginning."

"Only in the beginning?" Her tone was sarcastic. "Well, at least there was some point when you thought it wrong."

"I've always thought it wrong to a degree but at the same time understood the importance of secrecy. I assured Seth at the start that you were innocent of any wrongdoing. I told him we had been friends at church for the entirety of your marriage and that I had never known you to do anything that might suggest conspiracy with your husband's illegal activities. I also explained that my wife was well acquainted with you and would also vouch for your character. Still, he felt it necessary to refrain from sharing his purpose with you. He said there was great danger in what he was doing, and he didn't wish to put you in harm's way."

"How thoughtful."

John's expression became even more serious. "I am sorry, Nancy. It was not my desire to deceive you. I have done my best to have no part in it. Seth investigated all matters associated with your husband, and I simply handled the things you asked me to handle. Which is why I'm here today. I finalized the sale of your husband's store." He extended the papers to her. "You will see there at the bottom the price that was paid for the building and inventory. That amount has been deposited into your bank account."

Nancy noted the large sum. It was far more than she'd anticipated. "Thank you. That seems a very fair price."

"Indeed. The offer was generous."

She pretended to read the papers for a few long moments. She wasn't sure what else to say to John. A part of her wanted to completely dismiss him from her business, while another knew that he was sincere in his apology for having gone along with Seth.

"Does this conclude the business of my husband's estate?" she finally asked, forcing herself to meet John Lincoln's gaze.

"It does. We feel we have met all financial obligations owed by your husband, with the exception of the IOUs. Mr. Berkshire did approach me to declare himself the one owed. He produced the other half of the IOU and explained it was just their way of doing things. Do you want me to pay him?"

Nancy wanted it all to be done with and nodded. "Yes, by all means. Pay him and let the matter be laid to rest. I don't know what arrangements he and Albert had together, but I want it all concluded. I want no further need for a lawyer. I simply want to live my life quietly."

John got to his feet. "Then I will settle the matter this afternoon."

"And settle your fees, as well," Nancy said, also standing. "I trust that the charges will be fair—even though I should probably question everything, given all that has happened. I find, however, that I'm weary of the entire matter. Now, if you'll excuse me, I am joining the ladies' sewing circle today, and I'm already late."

"I apologize for having delayed you." He gave her a slight bow and headed for the foyer with his satchel tucked under one arm. He picked up his hat and turned to Nancy as she opened the door. "I do hope you know how sorry I am for all of this. I wanted to make myself useful to you, and I'm afraid I have only managed to cause you pain and doubt. Please forgive me."

Nancy felt her heart yield to his sincerity. She didn't want to hold a grudge. "Thank you for your apology. You have my forgiveness, for what it's worth."

"It's worth a great deal, my dear." He smiled. "A great deal."

Nancy waited until he was in his carriage and heading down the street before closing the door to return to collecting her sewing things. Only then did she realize she was still holding the papers John had handed her. She folded them and put them in her skirt pocket. There was a definite relief in knowing the store was sold and the money was in the bank. She was somewhat set for the remainder of her life—if she was a wise steward and managed her spending in a frugal manner. She didn't want to end up like the Clifton sisters or Mrs. Weaver. Even Mimi struggled to keep a tight hold on her spending. Nancy had never worried about money—not as a child and not as Albert Pritchard's wife. She certainly didn't want to worry about it as an old woman on her own.

She thought of Mrs. Weaver living in a boardinghouse after having owned a plantation. She'd once had wealth and the best of everything that money could buy, and now she was at the mercy of a boardinghouse owner. Life could change in the blink of an eye.

Seth's face came to mind, and the thought seemed all the more poignant. One minute she had been certain he would be a part of her future, and now she knew that wasn't to be. With a sigh, she made her way to Mary Taylor's house.

The ladies of the sewing circle were delighted to see her and even happier to barrage her with questions about her love life. Nancy tried to assure them that she had no love life and further had no desire for one. Mrs. Mortenson brushed aside her comment, insisting that Seth Carpenter was a perfect fit for her. She reminded them that with his sister at Nancy's boardinghouse, it made it easy for them to court. Nancy tried to dismiss the idea, but Mrs. Mortenson would have none of it.

"Nancy, my dear, you cannot keep such grand news from us. Do tell us how things are progressing between you and Mr. Carpenter. Has he kissed you yet?"

Nancy felt her cheeks flush hot at the memory of his kiss. She quickly looked at the needle and thread she held.

"Oh, I daresay he has kissed her. Look at her face. She's positively gone ruby."

"My dear Agnes," Mary Taylor said, "perhaps we could allow Nancy some privacy. After all, this is a transitional period of time that is difficult for any woman."

"Pshaw!" Mrs. Mortenson declared. "I can tell that she's positively bursting to tell us everything."

Mary shook her head. "Before we discuss personal matters, I wanted to share some Scripture reading and a prayer. After all, we are devoting this work to the Lord, and it seems only right that we spend a bit of time thinking of Him."

Mrs. Mortenson could hardly argue against this. She gave a nod and leaned back in her chair.

Nancy appreciated Mary's defense of her but knew it wouldn't be long before Mrs. Mortenson was back demanding answers. But Mary was no one's fool. When she finished with the Bible reading and prayer, she asked Nancy to help her in the kitchen.

"I've given my staff the day off, since I knew we'd be quite spread out with our quilting," Mary explained as they made their way to the kitchen. "I hope you don't mind."

"Not at all. I'm grateful for the rescue." Nancy glanced around the kitchen. "You've had it painted." The blue and white colors were very appealing.

"We did indeed. We settled matters with the dairy investment, and I pressed Mr. Taylor to move forward on our various projects here. I have always wanted white cupboards, and Mr. Taylor was not opposed, so we hired a young man to paint the cupboards white and the walls blue. Do you like it?"

"Very much. I wouldn't mind making the same change in my kitchen. I've never been fond of green. Especially that dirty sage color they used. And it has been over eight years since it was selected. I think it might be nice to have a change."

"Would you like the young man's name?"

Nancy shook her head. "No, I have David, who helps with the horse and yard. In fact, he has an entire family of siblings who come and help him. I think they are looking for work, so I don't mind hiring them on. Especially now that I have Albert's affairs decided."

"So it's concluded, then?"

"Yes, and I am comfortably set and needn't worry about having to return home. Although I did make a trip there last week."

"How did that go?"

Nancy joined Mary as she poured hot water into the teapot. "It went well overall. I was glad for the time with my mother and sister. My father was away on a trip and my brothers were elsewhere, but I had time with my aunt and uncle and two of my cousins. I even talked to Mother about God and all that I'm going through. She was very helpful. I should have talked to her years ago."

Mary smiled and replaced the kettle on the stove. "I'm so glad. It's always a blessing to be at peace with family and God."

"I want to be at peace with God, but I don't understand something that has happened. Something God surely knew was going on—since He knows everything."

"And what is that?"

"Seth Carpenter has been deceiving me. He came here on a mission to find out what my husband was doing. I can't explain it all, but Albert involved himself with something, and it was illegal. Seth was part of a secret government investigation. Although now that I'm telling it, I suppose I shouldn't be."

"I will keep your secrets, Nancy. Fear not." Mary smiled. "But in what way was Mr. Carpenter deceiving you?"

"He was doing all of this investigating without being honest with me about it. He befriended me and made me think he felt . . . well, something more for me. It brought about feelings I hadn't anticipated, and now I find it's all based on lies. Why would God allow such a thing when I had just decided to trust Him again?"

"What a strange question."

Nancy shook her head. "Why should that seem strange? I believe God is all-knowing, so He must have known what was going on. He knew, too, how difficult everything has been for me where He is concerned."

"You sound as if you believe God owes you something."

Nancy cocked her head to one side and put her hands on her hips. "Well, I surely can expect the truth from God. Can't I?"

"God is truth, Nancy. But this sounds more like He has disappointed you again—didn't manage things the way you wanted—and so you are uncertain that you will continue to extend Him the trust He deserves. You can't offer love and trust to Him one moment then withhold it the next just because He hasn't responded in the way you think He should." Her tone was chastising.

Nancy was surprised by her sternness. "I . . . well, I wasn't going to withhold my love and trust." Was she?

"You need to understand that things in this world will happen, and sometimes they will seem unjust and unfair. But, Nancy, God works well outside the realm of man, and we need to put our faith in Him, even when things don't look like we think they should. This isn't a game played by a child. You either take a stand to trust God and believe in His word, or you choose not to believe Him or trust Him. There is no middle ground."

Nancy knew she was right, and the guilt of it pierced her heart. Just because Seth had disappointed her didn't mean that God had treated her falsely.

"I'm sorry. You're absolutely right. I'm afraid I am a rather spoiled and selfish child."

Mary smiled and put her arm around Nancy's shoulder. "God sees into your heart, Nancy. Give Him your fears and doubts. Trust Him to deliver you from those who are false and unkind. Rest in Him, even when it seems impossible. Remember—He is the God of the impossible."

Seth heard John Lincoln come into the office. He waited only a moment for John to get to his office before heading after him. The office secretary wasn't yet in, and Seth wanted to speak to John in private before Cyrus arrived.

"Do you have a moment?" he asked, coming to stop in the doorway of his employer's office.

"Seth, come in. What can I do for you?"

"Well, I came to let you know I'll be leaving. Nancy knows about the investigation, so I needn't hide behind this position, and you've been more than gracious to let me remain as long as I have."

"I didn't do it out of graciousness, Seth. I was impressed with your performance, and I'd be glad if you stayed on. There's more than enough work for both of us, and it seems there is more coming in every day."

Seth stared at the stately man for a moment. "You'd keep me on?"

John smiled. "Of course I would. I wouldn't have brought you on in the first place if I didn't think you could handle the position. Why are you of a mind to run off? Do you have a better offer?"

"No." Seth shrugged. "I just figured you wouldn't want to have me around. I mean, you were generous to let me work here in order to be at the heart of Albert Pritchard's affairs, but now that that's over . . ."

"Have you found out everything you need to know?"

"Well, not everything, but a good portion. The army is watching some of the men I exposed. There's still a lot to do, and we may never be able to get the top man. He's no doubt protected by layers of secrecy."

"Then, it sounds like you still have a job to do. Can you work for me and continue your investigation?"

Seth leaned back against the doorjamb. "I'm not sure. I haven't heard from my contact yet as to whether they want me to continue working on this matter. Now that quite a few people know the truth of why I came here, I don't know that I'll be all that effective."

"So you will need a regular job," John said, nodding as if that settled the matter. "And I will need a partner. I believe the situation will resolve itself if you stay on. I have little tolerance for the way some men abuse people of color—especially the Indians. I will be happy to work with you as you strive to find those responsible."

"Thank you, John. I'd be honored to stay on with you."

The older man smiled and gave his bearded chin a stroke. "You should probably know that Nancy Pritchard has dismissed me now that the store has been sold. She's quite upset about the deception."

"Yes, I know." Seth shook his head and straightened. "I mean to resolve that situation soon as well."

"And how do you intend to do that?" John asked.

"By marrying her, of course."

CHAPTER 23

"M r. Berkshire, what are you doing here?" Nancy asked. It was nearly eight o'clock in the evening and well past the time for visitors. In fact, she had thought perhaps Clementine had forgotten her key and was knocking to be let back into the house after her evening out.

"Nancy, it's imperative that we speak. In fact, I'd like for you to come with me so that we won't risk being overheard." Berkshire looked fit to be tied. He was sweating profusely despite the cool evening air. Nancy couldn't help but be intrigued, but she shook her head.

"I can hardly do that, Mr. Berkshire. It wouldn't be appropriate."

"We can't worry about that now. I need your help." He took ahold of her wrist and pulled her through the open doorway. "You must come with me."

Nancy decided not to protest. She wanted to know what was going on, so she let him drag her down the steps and to his carriage. What could have upset him so much? Did it have to do with Seth's investigation?

"Gerome, this is hardly the way to treat someone whose

help you need," Nancy protested as he all but picked her up and pushed her into the enclosed carriage. She needed to keep up appearances, after all.

Once he was inside, he knocked on the roof to signal the driver and then closed the carriage door. "I'm sorry, but this is life and death."

Nancy scooted to the far side of the carriage. "Whose?"

"Mine, for one," Berkshire replied. "That Carpenter character is causing me problems. He got the army to confiscate one of my wagons, and I need your help to get him to stop."

"I can hardly tell Seth Carpenter what to do or not do. He's nothing to me."

"That isn't true, and I know it. I've seen the two of you together."

"In the past perhaps you did, but that is no longer our current state." She didn't know what Gerome knew, and she didn't want to give him any additional information. She might resent Seth's actions and lies, but she wasn't going to help a man who wanted to start an Indian war.

Her comment seemed to leave Gerome momentarily perplexed. For several seconds he said nothing at all, but then he started again with even more gusto. "I don't care what your current state is with that fool. I want to know what he knows."

Nancy couldn't resist. "About what?"

Gerome slapped her across the face. "Stop it. This isn't a game. I know Carpenter is on my trail. I know he's been investigating your husband's affairs, particularly the guns and alcohol."

She tried to think through the blaring pain in her head. "Of course he is . . . or was. John Lincoln asked him to investigate Albert's purchase of guns and liquor." She rubbed her cheek. "And if you ever lay a hand on me again, Mr. Berkshire, you'll regret it."

"Shut up. I'm not afraid of your threats, but you'd do well to heed mine. I can cause your family a great deal of trouble."

Nancy folded her arms across her chest. She wanted to give him a piece of her mind but decided it was probably best to say nothing and see where the conversation led.

"Good, I'm glad you see that I'm serious." Gerome shook his head. "I want to know every detail. Who is Carpenter working for?"

She shrugged. "John Lincoln. Everyone knows that."

"Besides him. Who else?"

"Who else would he want to work for when he already has a full-time employer?"

Gerome looked at her for a moment. The carriage was dim, and the way they were positioned cast a shadow across his face. Nancy tried not to shiver as a tingling went down her spine.

"You know nothing about his investigation?" he asked.

"Of course I know about his investigation." She figured it was better not to lie. "Albert was involved in the illegal sales of firearms and alcohol. He didn't sell them at the store, which would have been perfectly legal, but instead was dealing them in a nefarious manner. Mr. Hanson told me it had to do with getting weapons to the Indians. Albert hated the Indians, though, so I didn't understand why he would want to do that." She shook her head. "What has that got to do with you? I know he owed you money and some goods, but I can't imagine, with your political ambitions, that you would ever connect yourself with people who are trying to cause problems with the Indians."

Gerome shifted and gave a tug on his suitcoat. "Of course not."

"So this is about the money Albert owed you, right?"

"He did owe me money. He owed me a great deal, and I mean to have it."

"And who is trying to stop you? Honestly, Gerome, you drag me out of my house and then slap me simply because you want your notes paid back? John Lincoln told me about the IOUs. He already has a draft made out to you. You only need to see him." She gave her best performance. "I don't understand why you think so poorly of me. I would never keep you from your money. If Albert owed you, I don't even need proof. I trust you to be honest about the amount. You needn't be cruel to me."

Gerome settled back against the leather seat. "I'm sorry, Nancy, but this isn't just about the money. There's trouble brewing, and your husband is at the center of it."

"My husband is dead. He can hardly be causing you trouble now."

"He's caused nothing but trouble. Look, some very wealthy investors are going to be unhappy unless a certain project of ours continues. They have plans to see this through to completion."

"What has that to do with me? I've found no weapons or whiskey, if that's what you're after, and the only clue I had to where they might be hidden was stolen from my room." She watched him closely to see how he reacted.

He glanced away, shaking his head. "This isn't about the weapons and whiskey, it's about money. I gave a great deal of money to Albert, as did other investors. They are growing impatient for a return on their investment. It's clear by now that Albert never had a chance to order the full number of . . . goods he was supposed to bring in."

Nancy wanted so much to ask if they hadn't found what they were looking for in Albert's caches, but she knew it was best not to continue agitating Gerome. She tried to sound calm, almost bored with the conversation.

"Again, what has that to do with me? If you have a claim, see my lawyer. I know nothing about Albert's business dealings."

"But you have his money."

"Yes, as his widow, I have inherited his earthly goods. However, if you and your friends have some claim against me, then go see John Lincoln. I had no idea you were so involved with Albert. I thought you were simply good friends. Either way, you know very well that I have never troubled myself with any of Albert's dealings. Yet you act as though I was in the middle of everything."

"It doesn't matter what you say. I'll make certain the authorities believe you were involved if you don't help me. In fact, I'll see your entire family ruined . . . maybe even dead."

Nancy swallowed the lump that had formed in her throat. Would he really try to kill the people she loved? For what purpose?

"I don't know what you want," she said, no longer acting. "I don't know what I'm supposed to be able to help you with. If you want money—"

"I want you! You will marry me as soon as we can get someone to do the job. That way I'll have access to everything else I need."

"Marry you?" Nancy shook her head. "I'm not marrying anyone."

"You will unless you want to see your beloved aunt and uncle arrested for inciting the Indians to war."

Nancy couldn't keep from smiling. "I presume you mean my aunt Mercy and uncle Adam. They have long and tirelessly worked with the Indians on various reservations in the state. Their reputations precede them. You can't throw accusations against them that any legal authority would believe."

His eyes narrowed. "That's where you're wrong, Nancy, my dear. I know you want to think the best of them, but the truth will speak for itself. They have long been assisting me and my friends."

Nancy stiffened. She couldn't imagine there being any truth in his statement, and yet he seemed perfectly sincere.

"I see I finally have your attention." He rubbed his mustache and smiled. "We always think we know someone, but deception is easy when people trust you."

Nancy thought of Seth. She had wanted to believe only the best about him. Just as she did her aunt and uncle. But what if Gerome was telling the truth? After all, except for the funeral, she hadn't seen her aunt and uncle in years. What if they'd only allowed her to see the façade they'd created? They wouldn't be the first white people to work with the Indians only to deceive them.

"You have been raised to believe one thing about them while something entirely different was going on. I know, because I've been a part of it. Those guns Hanson was after were meant for me, and I was going to pass them along to your dear uncle, as I've done before."

His confidence sickened her. "I don't believe it."

"Believe what you will, but it's true, and if you don't marry me and help me, I will see to it that the authorities know of their involvement, as well as the involvement of other members of your family."

"What other members?" She couldn't believe she'd actually asked the question, but she waited in silence to see what he might say.

"It's enough that you know there are others."

The carriage had come to a stop, and Nancy could see that they had returned to her house. All she wanted to do was jump from the carriage and run to the safety of her room. Instead, she felt compelled to hear what Gerome had to say. He intended to cause her family trouble, that much was clear. Would he really continue unless she married him? What proof did she have that he would stop if she did?

Gerome grabbed her wrist and squeezed unmercifully tight. "You will say nothing about my involvement in all of this and do exactly what I command." He shrugged. "And who knows, in time you may be glad for this—glad that I made you wed me. I think we could be quite good together, and you would fit perfectly into my society."

"I can't marry you," she said despite the pain.

"Yes, you can, and you will, or there will be bloodshed the likes of which you'll never forget. And when I'm done with your family, I'll come after you." He dropped his hold. "I'll come for you tomorrow at ten o'clock. Don't make me wait."

For a moment Nancy couldn't move. She felt helpless and more frightened than she'd ever been in her life. Finally, she gathered her courage and exited the carriage without another word to Gerome. She hurried up the walkway as tears formed in her eyes.

What in the world was she supposed to do now? She had no one who cared. No one to be her champion.

Take it to the Lord, a voice whispered in her thoughts.

"If I'm not mistaken, it sounds like Nancy has returned," Clementine told her brother. She and Seth were in the kitchen, chatting with the elder Miss Clifton.

"Maybe she'll explain why she left in such a hurry," Bedelia remarked as she finished making herself a cup of tea. "It must have been an emergency of some sort. Perhaps the Taylors sent someone for her. I'm sure she'll tell us all about it."

The trio made their way through the dining room to the hall just as Nancy flew past. She was sobbing, and it cut Seth to the heart. Something was horribly wrong.

"Clementine, go see what happened," Bedelia urged. "Perhaps someone has died."

His sister nodded and followed Nancy to her room. Seth followed Clementine, careful to keep a few feet of distance between them in case Nancy came back into the hall.

"Nancy, may I come in?" Clementine asked as she knocked on the door. The door inched open. Nancy hadn't closed it completely.

Seth nodded toward the room. "Go to her," he whispered.

Clementine did as he suggested while he and Bedelia waited in the hall. He glanced at the older woman, who stood quietly sipping her tea.

It was only a few minutes before Clementine returned. "I can't understand a word she says. She's crying too much."

"Let me try," Bedelia said, moving past Seth.

"No." He gently caught Bedelia's arm. "I'll go."

"That's hardly proper." The spinster frowned and looked at Clementine. "Unless you go with him. In fact, we should probably all go."

"I'll go alone. The door will be open, and you can wait here to assure yourself that all is proper."

He left the older woman standing in the hall with her mouth open in surprise.

"Nancy?" he said as he entered her bedroom. He saw her across the room in front of her fireplace. She didn't even acknowledge him but wept softly into her hands.

He crossed the room in three long strides. "What's wrong? What's happened? Did someone die?"

She looked up, and her tear-filled eyes searched his face. "Someone is going to, I'm afraid."

"Who?"

She shook her head. "Why should I tell you anything? You'll just use it against me or tell me more lies."

He took her damp hands in his. "I promise you, no more lies. No deception. Whatever I know, I'll tell you. Please just trust me to help you now."

She shrugged. "I don't suppose it matters anymore."

"What are you saying?"

"Gerome demanded I tell him everything I know about your investigation, including who you work for."

Seth tried to remain unaffected by her words. "What did you tell him?"

"I told him you work for John Lincoln and that you investigated Mr. Hanson's claim that Albert owed him firearms and alcohol. Mr. Hanson demanded his goods, so we were both doing our best to find the shipments, but the only thing I had to help was stolen from my room."

"And you said nothing more?"

Nancy straightened. "I told him I knew Albert owed him money, and he said yes, that Albert owed him a great deal. I suggested he could collect it from John. Apparently, it's not that simple, however. Apparently, there are other investors and a great deal of money has exchanged hands. He believes Albert never ordered the 'goods' they've been expecting."

"So what they found at the caches was less than they anticipated," Seth said thoughtfully.

"Then he demanded I marry him so he could have full access to everything."

"Marry?" Seth gave a huff. "That'll be the day."

"Well, apparently it's to be tomorrow," Nancy said sarcastically. "If not, then he's promised to kill members of my family and see them blamed for supplying the Indians with guns. And he'll see me dead, as well."

"He'll have a hard time doing that—or getting married—from prison." He squeezed her hands, determination flooding through him. "I'm sorry you had to go through that, Nancy. Enough is enough. I'll speak to my superior tonight. He's just arrived in town. We're supposed to meet in the morning, but I don't think this can wait."

He glanced toward the door, where Clementine and Bedelia both stood with shocked expressions.

"I have to ask that neither of you ladies says anything about this to anyone."

Bedelia gazed soberly at him. "Of course not. I wouldn't do anything to risk Nancy's life."

Clementine nodded. "Nor would I. Do you think you can protect her from Mr. Berkshire? I mean, what if he drags her off again like he did tonight and forces her to marry him?"

"I'm going to see what can be done. The best for all persons concerned would be if Berkshire was arrested, but I'm not sure they'll see it the same way I do. Nevertheless, stay inside and keep the house locked tight. Don't answer the door for anyone but me. Understand?" He looked at each woman and finally settled on Nancy.

She nodded. "We'll do as you say, but you'll have to get answers very soon. He intends to be here at ten. Otherwise he's made very clear threats of what he'll do."

"Don't worry. I won't let it go that far."

CHAPTER 24

L ook, just arrest him, and we'll deal with the rest later,"
Seth told the army major. He'd gone to the hotel where
his superior Elijah Brady was staying, but Brady was
out for the evening and still hadn't returned. Since the army
was already involved, Seth had decided to call on Major Wells.
"We know Berkshire's involved in just about every detail, but
now he's making death threats, and I want him put away. At
least for a while so that I can better protect the people involved."

Major Wells lit his cigar. "But if we arrest him, it may scare
off the others, and we won't be able to catch the people at the
top."

Seth had already considered this. "If we make it appear that
we think Berkshire is the top man, then the others will believe
themselves safe. We have enough evidence to tie him to the
arrangement with the guns and liquor. We can plant stories in
the newspaper that say we believe him to be solely to blame.
Meanwhile, we can talk to Berkshire and offer him a deal if
he'll give up the names of the people at the top."

The major shook his head. "I can see the possibilities in using

Berkshire that way, but I really can't do anything until your man from Washington reports in. My superiors have made it clear that the Bureau of Indian Affairs is in charge."

"What if Berkshire just gets himself into a brawl?"

"That would be a local matter. You know that very well. I can't advise you to go start a fight with him."

Seth nodded. "I suppose it's grasping at straws, but I feel desperate to see him detained. I want to protect Nancy."

Wells smiled. "It sounds like she's become very important to you."

"She has. I suppose in many ways she always was. We've been friends since childhood."

"I'm guessing it's more than that now." The major took a draw on his cigar. "When will your man from Washington be available?"

"He's already in town, but I haven't been able to see him yet. I'm going back to the hotel after I leave here. I mean to get him out of bed if necessary." Seth got to his feet and extended his hand. "Thank you for your help."

"I wish I could offer more."

Seth wished he could too. He didn't like the idea of Berkshire walking the streets, threatening whomever he chose. "I appreciate your time, Major."

Back at the hotel, Seth checked in with the front desk clerk. It was nearly twelve thirty. "I was here earlier to see Mr. Brady. Has he returned?"

"Yes, sir. Came in just about ten minutes ago. I gave him your message, and he said to send you up if you returned. He's in room two hundred twenty-four."

"Thank you."

Seth took the plush carpeted main stairway. He thought

over what he would say and prayed he could convince Brady
to act.

Room 224 was at the end of the long hallway. Seth knocked
softly on the door and was relieved when Brady opened it.

"Seth Carpenter, I was surprised to receive your message. I
didn't expect to see you this evening." He had already doffed
his coat and loosened his tie.

"I know, and I realize the lateness of the hour. I tried to see
you earlier, but you were out."

"Yes. I had a dinner to attend, and we got caught up talking."

"Again, I apologize for the hour, but I didn't feel like it could
wait. Could you spare me a few minutes?"

"Of course." Brady stepped back. "Come in."

Seth did as instructed and lost no time in explaining the
situation. After filling Brady in on every detail he could, including the threats Berkshire had made against Nancy, he
concluded, "I just want him behind bars before he can hurt
someone else."

"Do you honestly think that will stop him? He has hirelings.
You said so yourself."

Seth nodded. "He does, but perhaps he won't be so inclined
to use them if he's behind bars."

Brady shook his head. "I think it's too risky to our case.
Berkshire isn't sure yet that we think him involved with the reservation uprising. We were careful to confiscate the wagon before it reached his house. If we arrest him now, his superiors—
the men we really want—will run. They'll have nothing more
to do with Berkshire, and the entire operation will fall apart,
only to re-form elsewhere, and we'll have to start all over again.
No, we can't risk it."

Seth's anger erupted. "But he'll kill her or force her to marry him. She needs us to help her. Berkshire even threatened her family members, so it's not like she can just go home."

"I understand your concern, Seth. I do. I just can't approve of doing something that will put us back at the beginning of our investigation. We've come too far. You've done good work. You got us Berkshire's connection and confirmation of Mrs. Pritchard's innocence. I don't have an answer for you regarding her safety and situation, but sometimes we are forced to put innocent lives at risk. You know that. All of this was discussed when you took on the job."

"Yes, but I didn't know the woman I plan to marry would be in the middle of all of this." An idea came to him. "Look, I know Berkshire is greedy. What if we don't arrest him but rather quietly bring him in and offer him a deal? We could show him the evidence against him and tell him he can either help us or we'll imprison him. I realize it's a risk, but honestly, Mr. Brady, I really think he'll take the bait. He has no loyalty to anyone but himself."

"And you feel confident that if we approach him with the promise of his freedom and . . . what, money?"

"Yes, or even land. Maybe even a government position, although given his deviousness, I wouldn't trust him. Putting him in such a position would only result in that office and its other employees being corrupted. Land or money ought to do the trick. Berkshire is a coward. He won't risk jail if he knows there's something else to be had."

Elijah Brady nodded. "It might save us a great deal of time in the long run. If Berkshire cooperates with us and agrees to expose those at the very top, it could be to our benefit. But are you certain that will be enough to get him to stop threatening your young lady?"

Seth hadn't considered that. He just hoped that by keeping Berkshire busy, he'd be too caught up in saving his own neck to care about Nancy. "I don't know, but while he's busy figuring out if he wants to deal with you, I intend to marry her."

Nancy had a restless night. She kept hearing the windows rattle or the house creak. Noises that never used to bother her now felt like alarms being sounded. She didn't know what to do about any of it. She had considered just going home to the farm and telling her mother everything that had happened. Perhaps her father would be back by now, and he could offer counsel as well. But Seth had said to stay put, and she had promised she'd do exactly that. Besides, going home might only bring Gerome or his men to the farm to find her. If they harmed her family, she'd never forgive herself.

By five she was up and dressed, having had no more than a few hours of sleep at the most. She knew that even if she remained in bed, however, that she would only toss and turn. Gerome had promised to be there at ten o'clock, but hopefully Seth would be there even earlier.

She went about her routine, building up the fire in the kitchen stove and laying out food for breakfast. Once the stove was adequately hot, she selected a cast-iron skillet and began to fry up sausage links. While those cooked, Nancy got out her mixing bowl and began to measure out the ingredients for biscuits.

She couldn't help but worry about what was going to happen. She had prayed and knew that God was able to manage it all, but would He? What if this was one of those times when His will went in another direction? Nancy couldn't bear the thought of her family members being harmed, nor could she accept that her aunt and uncle were working to stir up violence with the Indians. No one who knew them could ever imagine such a thing to be true.

Rolling out the dough, Nancy shuddered at the image of Gerome Berkshire showing up early and forcing his way into the house. She didn't want any of her ladies to be harmed. There had to be a way to ensure that Gerome couldn't hurt any of them.

If only I had a gun.

And then what? Would I really shoot Gerome? Could I kill a man?

Yes, he had threatened her and her loved ones, but Nancy wasn't convinced she could look a man—even Gerome Berkshire—in the eye and kill him.

A tapping sounded on the back door, and Nancy froze in place. Had Gerome come early? She didn't know what to do. She inched toward the back door. Maybe it was Seth. There was only one way to tell.

She didn't bother to bring a lamp. There was enough light to identify her visitor, and if it turned out to be Gerome, she'd just refuse to let him in. She'd tell him the ladies were in various stages of dress and it would be inappropriate for him to enter. Hopefully that would at least stall him for a few moments until she could come up with a better plan.

"Who is it?" she called, slipping to the side of the door.

"It's me. Seth."

She let out a sigh of relief and opened the door. "I was just getting breakfast." She hurried back to the sausages just in time to turn them before they started burning.

"It smells good."

Nancy felt suddenly awkward. She and Seth hadn't talked

about the issues between them. He had betrayed her with his secrecy and investigation. She sighed. Gerome had threatened her life if she didn't marry him. She had no choice but to forgive Seth and trust him. She was desperate for an ally.

She started cutting out the biscuits, trying to figure out how to bring up the subject, but found she didn't have to.

"Look, I know we haven't talked everything out, but I really am sorry about keeping the truth from you." Seth paused, and even without turning to look at him, Nancy could hear the regret in his voice. "It was never my intention to deceive you."

She finished cutting the dough into discs and nodded. "I was just thinking of our situation."

Seth came to her and turned her into his arms. She lifted her face to find him smiling. "Please forgive me. I love you, and I can't imagine my life without you. I think you feel the same for me."

Nancy saw no more purpose in denying it. "I do, but—"

He put his finger to her lips. "No buts, They won't do any good here. I love you and you love me. I want you to be my wife. After all, Berkshire can hardly marry you if you're already married to me."

"No, I suppose not," she said, shaking her head, "but I don't want that to be the reason I say yes."

He bent and kissed her. It was a gentle, loving kiss that seemed to promise much more. Nancy wrapped her arms around his neck.

"Berkshire isn't the reason I want to marry you," Seth whispered against her ear. "I want to marry you because I can't imagine my life without you at my side. I want to marry you because no one in the world is dearer to me."

Nancy smiled and laid her cheek on his shoulder. "I love you, and I want to marry you too. I suppose I understand why you weren't honest with me."

He hugged her close for several moments. Neither of them spoke, and Nancy relished the morning silence while in Seth's arms. Here she felt that nothing and no one could hurt her. She never wanted to leave his embrace, but she heard movement from the rooms upstairs and knew her ladies would soon arrive downstairs looking for breakfast.

Nancy pulled away and once again looked into Seth's eyes. "I hope you know what you're doing. I'm still rebellious and stubborn."

He grinned. "I know. It's part of your charm."

She laughed. "I never looked at it that way, and I'm pretty sure no one else has either."

"There's always a first time for everything." He kissed her nose. "I'm sure there are things about me that you won't applaud. But rest assured that deception does not come naturally to me, and I am truly sorry I ever hurt you with my lack of honesty."

"I understand you were doing a job and didn't yet know whom you could trust. But marriage requires trust *and* honesty." She lowered her head. "Albert was full of deceit and never really loved me. I can't go through that again. I need you to pledge that you will be honest and trustworthy."

Seth lifted her chin with his index finger, and she raised her gaze to his. "I promise I will be both, Nancy Armistead Pritchard. For so long as I draw breath. Even when it's difficult, I'll tell you the truth. I will trust you with my heart and with my life. I give you this as a pledge of my undying love."

She stretched up on her tiptoes, not waiting for him to kiss her. "That's good enough for me." She pressed her lips to his.

The grandfather clock struck ten, and Nancy's breath quickened. Seth had remained at her side while Clementine and Mimi went to the school to attend meetings for the fall term. Bedelia and Cornelia had gone to the Methodist church to help with the clothing collection, although Nancy could see the worry in Bedelia's expression. The spinster hadn't even said anything when Seth told her that he would remain with Nancy to ensure her safety. It was clear that everyone was fearful of what would happen, but apparently Seth was no longer a concern.

"You're going to pull the arms right off that rocker if you keep gripping them that way," Seth said.

Nancy looked down and saw that the blood had drained from her hands, leaving her knuckles white. She relaxed her grip but still found it hard to draw a deep breath.

They waited in silence until the clock struck the quarter hour.

"I don't think he's coming," Seth declared with a smile. "For whatever reason. Hopefully because my superior decided my plan would work."

"It's too soon to tell. He might just be running late."

Nancy stood and went to the window. She pulled back the drapes and looked outside. There was no sign of Gerome's carriage, but Bedelia and Cornelia Clifton were all but running toward the house.

"Goodness!"

"What? Is it Berkshire?" Seth was at her side in two steps.

"No, it's the Clifton sisters."

The spinsters reached the porch and hurried up the stairs.

Nancy opened the front door just as Bedelia was inserting her key in the lock. "What's happened?"

"We were downtown." Bedelia gasped for breath. "We saw Mr. Berkshire on one of the side streets, just a block from the church." She panted, trying to regain control of her breathing.

Cornelia couldn't remain silent. "Some soldiers were taking him away."

"Soldiers?" Seth asked.

"Yes." Bedelia nodded. "I have no idea what it was about. It was all done very quickly and without any fanfare. I don't know if they were arresting him or simply escorting him. Two men joined him in a carriage, and they left for parts unknown." She paused again, then seemed less breathless. "Since you feared he'd be here at ten, I told Cornelia we had to return and let you know what happened."

"Thank you," Nancy said. Her knees felt weak, and she thought she might well collapse.

"Come sit," Seth said, taking her arm for support. "You're as pale as a sheet."

Nancy nodded but said nothing. She hoped Gerome had been arrested. She looked at Seth. "I thought you said the army could do nothing."

"The major said he could do nothing until he heard from Mr. Brady. Perhaps something changed to allow them to arrest Berkshire." Seth shook his head. He looked just as puzzled as the ladies. "Or perhaps they figured out a way to offer him a deal. Either way, hopefully he's no longer a threat."

"I must say, this is quite a surprise, gentlemen," Gerome Berkshire said, leaning back in the leather chair he'd been offered.

Two men sat opposite him, one in a major's uniform and

the other in a finely cut suit. He didn't know either one, but when he'd been approached by the major that morning, along with several uniformed soldiers, Gerome had been afraid of their purpose. He had fully expected handcuffs and a jail cell, but instead they'd brought him to this nicely furnished office and offered him coffee.

A uniformed private came in with a tray. He poured coffee for each man, then asked about cream and sugar. The trio agreed on black, and the private handed out the cups and saucers, then left the room.

Gerome sipped the brew and glanced over the rim at each man. He was still on his guard. There was no telling what this was about, especially since he'd just threatened Nancy. Had she somehow managed to plead her case to these men? Were they there to threaten him? If so, why offer coffee?

"Mr. Berkshire, we are well aware that you are one of many citizens in Portland who does not care for the Indians. You are quite vocal on this matter."

"Indeed I am. I have little tolerance for their animalistic behavior and murderous intent."

The major nodded. "Nor do I. I have fought in far too many battles against the red savage and have little desire to continue fighting them."

Gerome smiled. "Well, perhaps if the army were more aggressive in their duties, we would have fewer Indians to deal with."

"The army has certain laws by which they must perform their duties," the major replied.

"Yes," the man who'd introduced himself as Mr. Brady interjected. "The laws of this country are important to uphold.

I work with the Bureau of Indian Affairs, and we often find ourselves constrained by legal limitations."

Gerome frowned. "And what do I have to do with any of this?"

"Well, the fact of the matter is that we know there are certain men here in Oregon who feel just as you do . . . and as we do. We are wondering what might be accomplished if we were to throw in with such men."

Gerome couldn't help the smile that spread across his face. "If I did know such men, I think it might be quite interesting."

Mr. Brady raised his coffee cup. "To interesting men and the alliances that might be made."

CHAPTER 25

And what did Mr. Brady say to you?" John Lincoln asked Seth.

"He told me that after a lengthy discussion with Major Wells, they were convinced they could entice Berkshire without letting him know they already had evidence against him. They were prepared to tell him if he refused, but he didn't. Just as I figured, he was excited about the prospect of being in the middle of this conspiracy. His thirty pieces of silver, however, is more like a pot of gold. He negotiated a deal for himself that included land and money. The funny thing is, he didn't insist on a clause that gave him immunity from his role in all of this. But then, he doesn't believe they know about his illegal activities. He's foolish enough to think he's smarter than everyone else and able to keep his role hidden."

"Of course he would think that." John shook his head. "Besides, I've never known that man to own up to anything he did. My question is, will it be enough to keep him from bothering Nancy?"

"Yes, I believe so. Brady convinced Berkshire that they are on his side, that they want to do whatever they can to see the

Indians defeated. They took the entire matter in a direction I never considered. Brady sent Berkshire to Sacramento on a fool's errand. He's to collect some information there. After that, he's to travel to Salem, where he's to meet with a group of men who are in on the ruse. Or will be. Mr. Brady is making his way there as we speak."

"And what about your role?"

"Berkshire is far too suspicious of me, so for the time being I'm off the investigation. I'll focus on my work here and my new job."

"New job?" John frowned. "Don't I keep you busy enough? What new job are you taking on?"

"Husband." Seth grinned. "I proposed, and Nancy said yes. We're going to be married in a few days at her parents' farm outside Oregon City."

"How marvelous." John gave him a smile as he extended his arm. They clasped hands. "I'm thrilled for you both. Nancy is a good woman, and I'm sure you'll be happy together."

"I shall endeavor to be worthy of her." Seth stepped back. "But that does bring me to another point. I would like a week's leave. That will give us a few days for the wedding and a little time alone afterward."

"Of course. You have it with my blessing. Consider it a gift," John replied. "When will you two head to Oregon City?"

"Tomorrow. I just came in to put my office in order and let you know what was going on. I felt fairly confident you wouldn't begrudge me the time."

"And if I had?" John asked.

Seth shrugged and gave a sly grin. "Then I suppose I would have resigned. After all, jobs are plentiful. Good women, not so much."

Nancy waited until they were nearly finished with supper to address the ladies about her plans. She could scarcely believe that she had agreed to marry Seth and to do so in a matter of days.

"I hope you will all bear with me a moment. I have something I'd like to say." Everyone looked at her, and Nancy smiled. "It won't take long."

Clementine sat smiling. She already knew about the engagement and no doubt guessed what Nancy was going to say.

"I have agreed to marry Seth Carpenter."

Mimi gave a little clap, and Mrs. Weaver bobbed her head in approval. Cornelia Clifton looked to her sister to figure out what her response should be. Bedelia smiled, so Cornelia did as well.

"I had anticipated this happening," Bedelia declared. "Congratulations. When is the happy day?"

"The second of August—this Saturday at my parents' farm. You are all welcome to join us, but I know the long trip is hardly sensible. Even so, I want you all to know that you are welcome."

Clementine pushed back her chair. "I'll be attending, and perhaps we can host a reception here after you wed. That would let us all celebrate together."

"I like that idea," Mrs. Weaver said, smiling. "Will you be away long?"

"No." Nancy dabbed the napkin to her lips, then placed it beside her plate. "We'll be back by Thursday at the latest."

"We?" Bedelia asked. "Do you mean Mr. Carpenter means to live here?"

Nancy nodded. "He will be my husband, after all."

"Yes, but this is a boardinghouse for ladies. It's hardly appropriate for him to live here."

Everything had happened so quickly, Nancy hadn't stopped to consider that this might be a problem. "But this is my home, and I have no intention of leaving it." In truth, she and Seth hadn't spoken about where they would live once they were married. But since she owned this house free and clear, it seemed like the natural solution.

"I don't mind living here with him as part of the household," Mimi said. "After all, our bedrooms are upstairs and yours is down here."

"But the bathroom is also upstairs," Bedelia pointed out.

"I hadn't thought of that, but I have enough money that I can have another bathroom built on the first floor." Nancy thought surely that would be an acceptable solution.

"That sounds fine," Mrs. Weaver declared, getting to her feet. She had a plate of food in her hands. "If you don't mind, I'd like to finish eating in my room."

Nancy was used to this and nodded. "Have a good evening, Mrs. Weaver."

"Good night, Mrs. Weaver," Clementine said, and the others joined in. Once the old woman had departed, Clementine looked at Nancy. "Of course I have no issue with Seth living here. Maybe until you can have the first-floor bathroom built, we can arrange a schedule for him."

"I'm sorry, but that won't be good enough. Sister and I believe in living above reproach." Bedelia looked sad. "Accept this as our notice. I will immediately begin to search for another place to live."

"I understand, but would you consider managing the place

for me while we're gone? I'll pay you, of course, and perhaps that will further assist you in your move."

Bedelia nodded. Nancy could see that she wasn't doing this out of spite, and truly admired her for sticking to her convictions. A part of her would even regret the loss of the Misses Clifton.

"Come, sister, we should start to pack. I will look through the newspaper and see what postings are available for our needs." Bedelia nodded to everyone at the table. "Good night."

"Good night," the ladies replied in unison.

Cornelia gave a little nod of her head and quickly followed Bedelia as she headed for the stairs.

Nancy began to gather the plates closest to her. "I didn't anticipate that. It's too bad she feels compelled to go." She lowered her voice. "I never thought I'd say this, but I will miss them."

Clementine smiled. "I will too. But while I will miss them, I want to know one thing."

Nancy looked at her future sister-in-law. "What?"

"Will you still add another bath?" Clementine put a hand to her mouth to suppress a laugh.

Nancy couldn't help laughing too. "Yes, I think that's the only wise thing to do. That way Seth will have no reason to be upstairs, and it will maintain integrity for all of us." She smiled. "Besides, one bathroom is vexing to all of us now. A second one is definitely called for."

"Or we could put in an outhouse," Mimi said, giggling. "Just imagine that."

"I think we can all imagine that, and I, for one, am happier with the indoor plumbing." Nancy got to her feet. "Now, if you'll excuse me, I want to get everything cleaned up so that I can pack for tomorrow."

"You go ahead, Nancy," Clementine said, taking the stack of plates from her. "I'll take care of this."

"I'll help too," Mimi declared. "Consider it a gift from us."

Nancy was touched that they were so eager to help. "Thank you. It's much appreciated. I feel like I have a great many details to take care of before I'll be ready to leave in the morning."

"It's the least we can do," Clementine declared. "Now scoot."

Nancy wasn't about to argue. She needed the extra time. Seth's proposal had been a pleasant surprise, but when he declared they should marry within days, Nancy had been shocked. He made a good argument for the haste, however. Gerome would only be away for a short time. It would be better for him to return and learn that their marriage had already taken place. There were also only a few short weeks before the school term would start and Clementine wouldn't be able to attend the wedding. Added to this was the fact that he didn't want to wait. He wanted them to marry as soon as possible because he was desperately in love.

She had to admit she felt the same way. She hated giving her folks so little time to ready the farm for a wedding, but she wasn't having a big affair. Just family, and most everyone she wanted in attendance either lived at the farm or in Oregon City.

Once in her room, Nancy looked around. Seth would soon share this space, so first things first—she needed to make room for him. They would need a second wardrobe cupboard. She frowned. That could be purchased and delivered while she was gone. She could leave a draft for Bedelia and instructions for the purchase. She felt certain the spinster would be honored that Nancy trusted her to manage the affair.

Thankfully the room wasn't overly feminine. The original

draperies were dark green and the wallpaper a gold-and-cream-colored stripe. The rugs were also green and gold and the furniture a dark mahogany. If Seth didn't care for it, they could always replace it.

She sat down on the edge of the bed and ran her hand over the quilt she'd made many years earlier. She'd never used it on her bed until after Albert's death, so she didn't feel it would be strange to have it on her marriage bed with Seth.

The thought of being married again made her smile. Seth was so attentive and sweet, as well as passionate. Albert had been none of those things. He had tried in the beginning to show her kindness with lavish gifts. Those gifts continued to come on special occasions like her birthday and Christmas, but the emotions were long absent. Poor Albert. He was so out of place in marriage. No doubt he would have been happier on the river.

"But he's gone now, and I won't think of him anymore," Nancy said, getting to her feet. "I'm going to start a new life." She smiled. She had been reborn spiritually, and now in a way she would have an emotional rebirth as well.

"Thank you, Father, for helping me through. I know I've been a less than perfect daughter, and I've had so many doubts and unkind thoughts about you. Thank you for your forgiveness. I am so sorry that I couldn't see the truth of your love through the pain." She thought of little Douglas and smiled again. "Thank you for the time we had with him, and Father . . . please give him a hug from me. He's such a dear boy, but no doubt you know that."

She drew a deep breath and let it out. "And, Father, please bless this marriage. Help me be a good wife and love my husband as I should. Let there be no deception, no lies, no reason to lose trust. Let me feel free to tell him all the secrets of my heart, and for him to share his with me. Amen."

"You couldn't have asked for a more perfect day," Aunt Hope said as she greeted the newly married couple. Uncle Lance was at her side and, if possible, his grin was even bigger than hers.

"Thank you both." Nancy looked at Seth and smiled. "We were just saying the same thing. It's not too warm or cool, and there's no rain. It's perfect."

"May you both be happy and blessed throughout your marriage," Lance said, leaning forward to kiss Nancy's cheek.

"Thank you." Seth put his arm around Nancy's waist. "I have no doubt we will be."

"But there are bound to be times when you disagree," Aunt Hope warned, her expression serious.

"Yes, we had one of those moments just this morning," Seth replied. "But I brought her around to my way of thinking."

Nancy rolled her eyes. "This time. He knows better than to imagine he'll always get his way."

Hope and Lance exchanged a glance, then burst into laughter as Nancy's mother and father approached.

Her father gave Nancy a curious glance. "What's so funny?"

Hope shook her head. "Your daughter is so much like her mother."

"Don't I know it," Father replied.

"What's that supposed to mean?" Mother asked.

"I think we've said enough," Lance declared. "Come along, wife. I'm hungry." He put his arm around Hope and pulled her toward the long food tables.

"Thank you again for hosting the wedding," Seth said, extending his hand to Nancy's father.

Instead, Alex Armistead pulled Seth away from Nancy and gave him a hug. "You're family now. None of that handshaking stuff. And you are very welcome. I'd do just about anything to see my daughter happy."

Seth stepped back and nodded. "As would I."

Grace gave him a hug as well, then put her arm around her husband. "We're glad to have you in the family, Seth. You always were a favorite of ours."

"As I recall, you were always a bit peeved with him for eating us out of house and home." Nancy couldn't help but share the memory. Seth and Gabe had eaten anything left out in the open. Her mother had taken to hiding things that she intended to serve for supper or needed later. "I think we all remember your angry tirade when you learned he and Gabe had eaten the coconut cake."

"Nancy, you don't need to tell him that." Grace shook her head and looked at Seth. "Pay her no attention."

"He'd better pay me attention," Nancy countered. "I don't mean to be ignored again."

"That will never happen." Seth put his arm around her again. "I'm going to pay you so much attention that you'll beg me to leave you alone."

Nancy smiled and gazed up into his eyes. "I don't think that will ever happen."

That evening, after the festivities of the day were over, Nancy took a stroll out to the cemetery. All day long she had thought about how blessed she was to be marrying Seth and to be so very loved by her family. Now she just needed a little time to herself, and the quiet of the small family cemetery gave her just that.

Meg had been out to tend the graves again, because they were all neatly cleared of grass and debris, and small bouquets of wildflowers lay atop each stone. Nancy gazed down on her little brother's grave and thought back to the days before he'd gotten sick. They had played in the fields and had even gone down to the creek to wade, but the water had been too cold.

Nancy had watched over him like a mother hen. She had loved him more than anyone else in the world, and losing him was like losing a piece of herself.

"I miss you, Doug. I often wonder who you would have grown up to be. Would you have gone into the lumber business like Gabe or wanted to preach like James?" She smiled. "I think you would have been more like Papa. You loved to explore and wander the property. I'll bet you would have wanted to go with him on his trips to visit Sam Two Moons in Canada. You probably would have learned to hunt and trap just like our father."

It pleased her to imagine such things, even if they would never come true. The thing that pleased her the most, however, was that she no longer felt the terrible anger she had once known. She still felt sorrow at the loss, but it was easier now. Not because so much time had passed or because it was no longer important, but because now she had God to help her through. What terrible pain she had put upon herself by avoiding the One who loved her most. The only One who could take her miseries and turn them into joy.

"Your mother thought you'd be out here," Seth said, coming to join her.

Nancy turned and nodded. "I just wanted a few minutes of quiet, and this seemed like the best place to come." She turned back to her brother's grave. "I feel I can finally lay him to rest."

Seth wrapped his arms around her from behind and pulled

her back against his chest. "I'm glad—for your sake. God never intends for us to carry such burdens."

He kissed her just behind the ear, and Nancy sighed. "I loved him so much. Do you think if God blesses us with a son, we might call him Douglas?"

"I'd like that. It seems more than fitting. Douglas Carpenter."

"Of course, there's a good chance I can't have children. We've never really talked about that, but in all my eight years of marriage, I was never with child. Not even once."

Seth kissed her neck again, then turned her to face him. "It doesn't matter. Either we'll have children or we won't. What is most important is that we have each other. That makes everything else pale in comparison. Not that children aren't important, just that our relationship and love for each other is a priority. After all, we can hardly be good parents if it's not."

"I know, but I want to have children. Your children."

Seth kissed her. "I want that too, and you know what? I believe we will. Don't ask me how I know—I just feel certain of it."

Nancy wrapped her arms around him and placed her head on his shoulder. "I love you, Seth. I love you more than I thought possible. I thought all the love in me had died."

"No, it was just hidden away. Hidden until it was time to be revealed."

Nancy stroked the hair at the nape of his neck and sighed. "Just waiting for you to find it and draw it out from the shadows and into the light."

Tracie Peterson is the bestselling, award-winning author of more than one hundred novels. Tracie also teaches writing workshops at a variety of conferences on subjects such as inspirational romance and historical research. She and her family live in Montana. Learn more at www.traciepeterson.com.

Sign Up for Tracie's Newsletter!

Keep up to date with Tracie's news on book releases and events by signing up for her email list at traciepeterson.com.

More from Tracie Peterson

From Montana to London, this series follows an all-women traveling Wild West show, with trick riders and sharpshooters who are on a mission to solve a perplexing mystery and find freedom in a world run by men. Will they all be able to overcome their pasts and trust God to guide their futures?

BROOKSTONE BRIDES: *When You Are Near, Wherever You Go, What Comes My Way*

BETHANYHOUSE

 Stay up to date on your favorite books and authors with our free e-newsletters. Sign up today at bethanyhouse.com.

 facebook.com/bethanyhousepublishers   @bethanyhousefiction

 OB   Free exclusive resources for your book group at bethanyhouseopenbook.com

You May Also Like . . .

When her grandfather's health begins to decline, Havyn is determined to keep her family together. But everyone has secrets—including John, the hired stranger who recently arrived on their farm. To help out, Havyn starts singing at a local roadhouse—but dangerous eyes grow jealous as she and John grow closer. Will they realize the peril before it is too late?

Forever Hidden by Tracie Peterson and Kimberley Woodhouse
THE TREASURES OF NOME #1
traciepeterson.com; kimberleywoodhouse.com

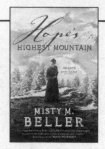

On her way to deliver vaccines to a mining town in the Montana Territory, Ingrid Chastain never anticipated a terrible accident would leave her alone and badly injured in the wilderness. When rescue comes in the form of a mysterious mountain man, she's hesitant to trust him, but the journey ahead will change their lives more than they could have known.

Hope's Highest Mountain by Misty M. Beller
HEARTS OF MONTANA #1
mistymbeller.com

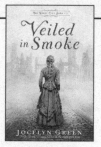

As Chicago's Great Fire steals away their bookshop, Meg and Sylvie Townsend make a harrowing escape from the flames with the help of reporter Nate Pierce. But the trouble doesn't end there—their father is committed to an asylum after being accused of murder, and they must prove his innocence before the asylum truly drives him mad.

Veiled in Smoke by Jocelyn Green
THE WINDY CITY SAGA #1
jocelyngreen.com

BETHANYHOUSE